Ben-Ami Lilandu

SNOWFLAKE RIVER

Ben-Ami Eliahu
SNOWFLAKE RIVER

SNOWFLAKE RIVER / Ben-Ami Eliahu

Translated by Rechavia Berman

Edited by Dave Eisenstark

All rights reserved. No portion of this book, except for brief
review, may be reproduced, stored in a retrieval system,
or transmitted in any form or by any means – electronic,
mechanical, photocopying, recording, or otherwise – without written
permission of the publisher.

Copyright © - All rights reserved to the author

*That was the strange mine of souls
As secret ores of silver they passed
like veins through its darkness.*

R.M. Rilke.

PART ONE

Chapter 1

The Minister of Health Hadassa Samter strolled out of the inner office, briefcase in hand, and said "good evening" to her staff, struggling to keep her voice casual. Her heels clicked as she walked down the stone steps of the ministry building, a remnant of four hundred years of Ottoman rule, and onto Yaffo Street, Jerusalem. A modest sedan waited just as they told her it would —*"under no circumstances should you take the official Minister of Health vehicle."* Hadassa climbed into the back seat of the car, absorbed in thought. *I couldn't have, anyway. You didn't tell me where I'm going.*

The Prime Minister's call came early that morning. The international investigative team, a confidential body made by a rare cooperation of more than a dozen state intelligence agencies, concluded its report about the BCP—the Body Cooling Phenomenon. They gave a copy of the report to each of the member states. The Prime Minister requested her to study the report for the coming BCP meeting of the Inner Cabinet.

This was likely the last governmental job to the sixty-five year old administrator Hadassa. Had she been a retrospective person, she would have had a mostly happy life to look back on. The BCP outbreak would be her last major project, a tragic conclusion to a distinguished career in a dozen different government departments, agencies and bureaus.

But my first time as a spy. A nervous chuckle followed her thoughts in an attempt to take the edge off her tension. The driver—a young, slightly disheveled man of twenty-five—gave her a questioning look.

He reminds me of Ari when he was young, like all the men do now. Hadassa twisted a simple silver ring on one of her fingers.

A mile away, on a nondescript street, at an address that remains classified to this day, stood another remnant, a building from British colonial days. The office on its third floor was also a throwback to another era, a generic suite, its door decorated with just a number— 302. Inside, a reception desk stood in front of a secured area containing all the modern paraphernalia of an airline boarding gate.

They checked, photographed and took Hadassa's identification documents, along with her purse, phone, briefcase, laptop, belt and jewelry—including the ring—all placed in a box and secured with a numbered evidence tag. Then, they instructed her to stand in the full-body scanner while a female technician analyzed her image on a nearby screen.

The room itself, comfortable and large, with enough space for an entire committee, surprised her. Hadassa descended into the single leather chair at a long table. The rules were simple and strict: "No pencils, pens or paper. No copying of documents, no taking notes, no photography or voice-recording. Communication with others outside the room is prohibited. You may touch only the items you are given. No destruction, mutilation, tearing of pages, or other alteration of any kind is allowed. The door will remain locked at all times. Should you need to leave the room for any reason, press the buzzer next to the door. An attendant will respond. Water, coffee and vending-machine snacks are available down the hall, along with toilet facilities. Under no circumstances are food or drink allowed in this room. While on this floor, an authorized attendant will accompany you at all times. Do you understand?"

Hadassa's voice quivered. "Yes."

The attendant left, leaving her alone inside the reading room. It was oddly reminiscent of old school, spy-craft era, with no computers, no internet, no files to leak across cyberspace— information under complete control, lock and key.

The attendant returned with a thick, loose-leaf notebook she placed on the table in front of Hadassa.

Body Cooling Phenomenon, the cover said, a simple title written in black marker. The attendant exited the room, and the door closed with a final clunk.

Hadassa stared at the notebook. Body Cooling Phenomenon. *Such a name for such a deadly disease... sounds like taking a swim in a nice pool on a hot day.*

Her movements slow, yet deliberate, Hadassa dared to open the book. Official stamps, signatures and the words "TOP SECRET" adorned the page.

Concentrate, she ordered herself. She put on her reading glasses, the single item they allowed her to bring into the room, after they inspected them for hidden cameras and transmitters. She read:

Summary:
Symptoms:
1. General decline in body temperature. Occurs over a long period of time. 2-5 degrees C. over weeks, months, years. See charts p. 1163.
2. Cold attacks. Intense, brief episodes lasting 1-3 seconds. Body temperature drops by 1-2 degrees C. Usually occurs during sleep, accompanied by severe hallucinations. See Hallucinations p. 883-1014.
3. Affected population. Age. Majority of the afflicted are children and young people (87%). See Demographic Breakdown p. 392. Reason: unknown. Geography: The spread of BCP is not equal throughout the world. Targets financially powerful countries, and the richer parts of the developing countries.

Finally pays to be poor. Hadassa turned the page:
4. Causes: still unknown.
Virus, bacteria, fungi, prions: excluded.
Toxins, gasses, food components: excluded.
Water contamination: excluded.
Atmospheric, including ozone contamination: excluded.

Nervous system, electrical changes, chemical changes in victims themselves: excluded.

"How can that be?! How can nothing be found for so long?" Hadassa had asked a hundred times in a hundred meetings.

"It may be that we are not looking in the right direction yet," the scientists had said. "Maybe the causes are right in front of us but we aren't seeing them."

They'd wanted more money, of course. *They always want more money.* For research. To find a cure. And because of the hysteria, the young age of the victims and the economic power of the parents, for the most part they got it.

Money poured into a black hole of ignorance. Medieval. Like the Black Plague.

Rats all around us.

Chapter 2

A black-iron stake-fence with red tops surrounded the school, running around an open playing field and a botanical garden. The gray concrete building, shaped like a huge rectangle with one of the short sides missing, sat in the middle, broad and brooding. It looked out on the expansive fields on the outskirts of Gat, Israel, a small town about twenty kilometers southeast of Rehovot. The buildings housed the State Comprehensive High School A and State Middle School #1.

Omer Lemm, a tenth-grader, sat on a simple chair in the principal's office, waiting in silence while the principal examined the papers she was holding. He wore his school uniform: pale shirt and shorts, sandals on his feet. Every now and then, he shifted and stretched in his seat, trying to appear upright and confident— only to slump back. He pressed his fingernail on the edge of the principal's desk.

His thoughts whirled back to the dream he had that morning. A nightmare. He'd been having more and more of them lately, always accompanied by a sudden chill. He recalled fear, and a sense of paralysis spreading through his body. Terrible, yellow, elongated eyes, a black dot in the middle of each one, approached him. And the scream he tried to let out, a cry for help stuck in his throat—

He snapped out of the memory, preferring to face the principal. The incessant, rapid foot-motion between the chair's legs betrayed him. So did the way he passed a flitting hand over his buzz-cut head, tickled by the tiny follicles.

Omer was a normal boy—a bit short for his age, dark-haired, thin but not terribly so, with a round face. When he'd smile, a dimple would appear in his left cheek. When he laughed, another would appear in the other, and his teeth would flash. Pretty teeth. At that time, though, a smile did not tug at his lips.

His eyes caught the gaze of the principal, and he looked away. They glinted with the first signs of tears forming in them. Omer fixed his eyes on the blinding blue sky beyond the glass surface of the office's window.

What a bright sun. I wish I could glide like that bird, up there. Like an eagle. It sees ahead for miles and miles, detecting motion, then folds its wings, dropping like a rock, and bam! They say the rabbit dies from the impact alone. Actually, it's amazing how—

Pages rustled. The principal laid them on the table.

"Is passing exams the only thing you're here for, Omer?"

Omer sensed a trap. "No...?"

"Good, because you aren't even managing to do that!"

"Yeah..."

"I fear you're missing very important lessons in this school," she said. "And failing your exams."

Omer knew when to stay silent.

The principal pressed her hand on the desk as though about to charge.

The principal's voice echoed through the office. "Aspire! You should aspire to be the best! To succeed! To excel..." She fell silent. It seemed as though she wanted to continue, but something made her change her mind and jot something down in her notebook.

When she spoke again, her voice was cool. "You're actually a clever boy. But you know, this path you're following won't take you very far. I'm not even sure it will allow you to continue with us here at Comprehensive A." She extended her hand, giving him a note. "Here. Have one of your parents contact me."

Omer rose from his seat, took the note and turned to leave. At the sound of the principal's voice, he stopped.

"You know the difference between clever and smart, right?"

Omer did not respond.

"With maturity, some of the clever turn smart. The rest just become smart alecks."

* * *

Joel Kramer sat on the surface of his desk near the blackboard, his short legs swinging from side to side. A bemused gaze floated from his milky-pale face framed by a short goatee. It caught sight of Omer, who had just entered the classroom. Joel chose to ignore his late entrance and motioned for him to take his seat. He hopped off his desk and approached the board. "Who's on the next team? Omer, what's your subject?"

Omer's tongue was stunned in surprise. For a moment, he couldn't figure out what his teacher meant by that. His mind was still in the principal's room.

Your subject...? The vacation assignment! How could I forget? I need to come up with a subject!

He scanned the list of subjects on the board, the one across from a list of pupil names.

"Uh... the Body Cooling Phenomenon." In an instant, he regretted his choice. *Why did you pick that, they'll want to know. Something you want to tell us?*

"OK, an important subject," Joel said. "And who's on your team?"

Who's on my team? Omer's mind raced to answer this question, troubled by the fact that he had forgotten the assignment altogether. Joel was one of the few teachers he actually liked, and regarding the teammate... Well, there weren't too many pupils who'd agree to do an assignment with him.

A furious flush blossomed on his face.

"I'd prefer to do it alone," he said.

Joel's hand traced lazy circles over his goatee. He shot a quick glance at the board. "But I prefer teamwork. What do we do now... Ah! Good, I see there's a trio ahead of you." His finger skipped over the names. The classroom buzzed.

"Noa, you win!"

A mocking voice rejoiced from the back row. "Whoopee! What a team, baldy and the robot!"

Noa's pale face flushed with anger. She stood up, her chair slamming backwards. "That's not fair!"

Noa's hair was red—not the soft brown-red type but the hard, fiery kind—resting on her neck, gathered with a simple rubber band. A metal brace hugged her left leg, from knee to ankle. The device rattled against the legs of the desk.

"You said we could pick the subject and teammates ourselves!"

"Yes, that's true," Joel said, "but you have to agree that his subject is also—"

"I don't care!"

She adjusted the glasses on her nose with the tip of her thin pinky finger. Joel reached forward in a conciliatory gesture.

"OK, let's not lose our tempers. In fact, no tempers at all, please," he said. "Let's keep an open mind, shall we? We'll write down that, in principle, you're joining Omer's team, but all three of us will sit and discuss it during recess, OK?"

Omer took a notebook out of his bag and placed it on the desk.

Aargh. There goes another recess.

As soon as the bell rang, Joel led the two to the lab. Omer breathed the biology lab air in, enjoying its smell. Sunlight reflected on a stainless steel surface, blinding him. He narrowed his eyes, his lips drawing into a smile. The glare of the sun, the teacher, the lab, they all caused a gentle, homey feeling to course through him.

A photograph of a tall black stone tablet hung on the lab's wall. As Omer passed by it, he paused for a moment. A large circle was engraved at the center of the tablet. Spiral lines dissected the circle. Beginning at its outer rim, they flowed in a whirlpool toward the center. Illegible symbols stood between the lines and outside the circle.

Where have I seen this weird symbol before?

Joel sat down and slammed the desk an open hand, his voice booming with authority.

"OK, we have gathered here to solve the dispute raised by Noa—"

"Me?! You're the one who decided I have to do the assignment with him!"

"Yes, but you're the one who refused!"

Noa stood speechless for a moment, then recovered. "What does that have to do with anything? Listen, it's not that I don't want to do the assignment with him specifically, but after I've already picked a subject—"

Joel cut her off, filled with new enthusiasm. "And your subject is fascinating! But you have to agree that BCP is also interesting. And you know that I prefer teamwork..."

Noa knocked her metal leg-brace against a counter, annoyed. "OK, OK, like I have a choice."

"Great! Noted for the record: The Noa-Omer team, the Body Cooling Phenomenon."

An expression of indifference adorned Omer's face, but within his chest, a thrill of excitement ran rampant. This was the first year Noa and him studied together. She came from another school. Until now, they hardly even spoke, as if they belonged to separate worlds. Noa was an outstanding student, confident, brilliant, and he... He preferred to disappear, dive into his thoughts, drift on the wings of his imagination.

Omer found it difficult to look Noa in the eye, so instead he kept his gaze locked at the teacher, sparing only glances from the corner of his eye towards her.

As they turned to leave the lab, Omer's step lightened. He paused once more in front of the photo of the stone tablet. Noa and Joel stopped beside him. Underneath the photo, there was a print of the symbol engraved in the tablet. Omer pointed.

"What is this symbol? I've seen it someplace before."

Joel's brows lifted in surprise. "Really? I find that hard to believe."

Omer's response was filled with flat confidence. "A million percent, but I don't remember exactly where. Maybe on my brother's computer or in some magazine."

"I received this photo from a former professor of mine," Joel said. "Professor Peretz. These spiral lines, if I remember correctly, represent arteries through which some kind of cycle runs. This is from the digs conducted by Professor Peretz in Mexico, in an area where an ancient civilization once flourished."

Omer moved closer to the photo. Despite having seen it before, to him it was as though he was viewing it for the first time. Noa pointed to a small sticker at the bottom of the print. "Synchronized 360+ Infra-red."

"What's that?"

"Photography method. Apparently some of these markings on the stone tablet were too eroded," Joel said. "So they photograph the artifact from every angle, and every angle of lighting creates a different shadow where something was etched. A computer processes all these shadows into a unified picture. Here they also added infra-red photography, and all of it together created this print—clear and legible."

Wonder crept into Omer's voice. "Amazing! Look at the difference between the photo and the print."

"Yes, but here is something way more amazing..." Joel's words resembled the narration from the mystery movies. He reached out, his finger tracing the symbols on the perimeter of the circle. "The letters... and these symbols... no one could understand how they could appear here together. Look—a letter in Sanskrit, and next to it, Assyrian script. A Native American sign alongside a Hebrew letter. An Egyptian Hieroglyph, a Greek letter, a Chinese character—all here! And there are dozens of other markings from different languages, you see?! On a stone slab thousands of years old from an isolated continent! How did they get here? Whoever engraved them had to know the various cultures, or at least the various languages, or at least know what the letters looked like. So how did they amass all this knowledge?"

Joel fell silent for a moment, straightened his back, and shook his head. "Impossible. Period. That's why this whole business just doesn't make sense. It's inconceivable. "

Chapter 3

Hadassa hit the buzzer. The attendant arrived to open the door and escort her to the coffee room. A number of doors lined the hallway walls, leading to the other rooms, but none of them were open.

Probably where they watch me read.

The coffee, water and vending machines, and a small office refrigerator sat in the tiny area down the hall. An upholstered chair was left in the corner but Hadassa couldn't bring herself to sit in it and stare at the machines, with the attendant staring at her. She had been sitting for hours anyway.

No windows. Are there any on the entire floor? She turned her attention towards the landscape paintings that adorned every wall, half of them realistic, the other half impressionistic, the kind of prints hospitals display to create the illusion of outdoors.

Ari's hospital had them, didn't they?

Hadassa was tired of the sickness, tired of BCP, sick of the sick. The Health Minister? *What was I thinking? Find out why, that's what.*

It started with a routine surgery—the removal of a benign intestinal polyp, too large for colonoscopy—and ended with Ari in bed all day watching his stupid sports: football, basketball, golf, cycling, track and field. *Even cricket for God's sake. What did Ari care about cricket?*

The doctors said Ari was too old for BCP, but they couldn't tell her what age had to do with the illness. They blamed it on his lifestyle: like his wife, Ari worked too hard, with too many long hours, too few vacations and not enough sleep. They told him to rest, read, watch TV, and sleep.

Thanks for nothing. Hadassa's mood shifted to a bitterness that matched the coffee that crossed her lips. With new urgency, she downed the cup, poured another half-cup, drank that, too, and marched back to the room, the attendant in tow.

Find out why.

* * *

The World Sales Corporation's executive jet idled on the tarmac at Biggin Hill Airport, southeast of London. A thin, incessant rain painted the skies gray and darkened the whiteness of the wings. Inside the plane, in a gray leather chair, sat the corporation's vice-president, Ernest Cole-Angel. In one hand he held a multi-page legal document, and in the other, one-third of an unlit cigar. At the sound of muffled speech from the front of the plane, he turned his head. Michael W. Lampston, Jr, President of World Sales, approached with a brisk pace, his thin lips pursed in the hint of a smile.

"I smelled you from the terminal," he said "I thought you'd kicked the habit."

Cole-Angel mumbled, squeezing the offered hand. "It's not lit."

"I can smell intent, as well."

Michael Lampston was of average height and slim build. His hair was thick, black, and luxuriously curled. His full eyebrows and strong chin created a youthful frame for brown, alert, intelligent eyes.

Lampston sat at his "jet desk", an exact, three-quarters replica of the one at his headquarters in suburban Washington, DC. The rest of the plane was also set up more like an office than a luxury jet, with only the seat-belts at each chair to give it away. Lampston pulled a simple, light-colored wooden box from one of the drawers, walked over to Cole-Angel and opened it before him.

"Well, do they look alike or what? Two euros for the four."

"Wow!" Cole-Angel said. "They really do look the same!"

The box held four rectangular, polished, semi-translucent milky stones, each about half the size of a matchbox. Cole-Angel inspected one in his hand, appraising it. "It feels a bit different than the original."

Lampston returned to his desk. "I thought of using them as paper-weights, but I think they're a little too small."

"Today's offices don't have much paper."

Lampston's chest shook with laughter. "Well, I wasn't thinking of marketing them."

"Prepare for take-off," the captain's voice came on over the intercom. "Please be seated and fasten your safety-belts."

Cole-Angel walked over to Lampston's desk. His large palm cradled the stone and shook it like a die. The jet jolted just as he was about to place it on the desk. It fell from his hand and hit one of the desk's metal legs.

"Oh, sorry!"

Cole-Angel sighed, annoyed. He picked the stone up and examined it, noticing a slight crack. His fingernail caught the corner as he handled the stone. "Sorry, it got nicked."

Michael Lampston chuckled, dismissing the matter with a flick of his hand. He put the stone in the box alongside the others. "You owe me a half a euro."

Cole-Angel sat down and buckled up. The jet began to move.

"Wait," he said, "isn't Gerryowen coming?"

"Up front," Lampston said, indicating another cabin toward the cockpit.

"He's not flying the thing, is he?"

"Let's hope not," Lampston said. "Let's hope not."

Chapter 4

As Noa rode her bicycle under the dark foliage of the margosa tree, the sunlight in her hair dimmed for a moment, then shone again, fire gleaming in the unruly ends waving in the wind. She moved from the paved road to a driveway, her hair bouncing along with her.

Noa slowed, rolling towards the steps at the entrance to a house. She propped her bicycle on the kickstand and stepped in front of the door. With a confident finger and a shadow of a smile, she pressed the doorbell.

Omer's mother opened the door. "Hi, you must be Noa. Right on time!" she said. "Come in. Help me move things along."

The TV in the living room blared a commercial. Omer's mother frowned with annoyance and turned the set off.

"Omer, you have a visitor!"

"Coming!"

Omer's mother took Noa to the kitchen. "He was actually getting ready for your arrival at nine, but then he got stuck in front of the TV, as usual." She placed a pitcher of lemonade and a plate of cookies on the counter. "I understand you're doing an assignment on the Body Cooling Phenomenon."

Noa nodded, and straightened the glasses on her nose with a pinky finger.

"Today we'll start looking for data on the Internet, and tomorrow or the day after we'll meet a friend of my mother's at the hospital. He's an expert on the subject."

"Oh, I do hope they find a cure."

"Yes."

"Maybe you and Omer..."

A hint of a blush shadowed Noa's cheeks. "Oh, I don't think..."

"Don't sell yourselves short. Stranger things have happened. Omer tells me you want to be a doctor like your mother."

Noa nodded, embarrassment stinging her cheeks further. She reached for an almond cookie, and changed the subject as she munched.

"You have a lovely house."

"Thank you. We moved in several years ago."

A yellowing parchment hanging on one of the walls aroused Noa's curiosity. The top part was covered by Chinese characters in black. Underneath these floated a dragon in shades of blue, long and twisted, above village homes. The dragon's legs seemed folded beneath it. Its talons were long, and on both sides of its mouth it sported short whiskers. There was a point in each of its narrow eyes.

Omer's mother noticed her curious gaze. "Pretty, isn't it?"

"Very. Very unique."

"I remember this painting since I was a little girl. It came from China many years ago." She fell silent for a moment. "It used to hang in my mother's house. Omer's grandmother. But she passed away three months ago..." Omer's mother turned her head at the sound of footsteps approaching quickly. "Here he comes."

Omer arrived to see his mother and Noa sipping lemonade, the best of friends all of a sudden, waiting for him. A mocking look flashed in Noa's eyes, which made him hesitate and blush.

Noa placed the glass on the counter.

"Shall we begin?"

Omer nodded.

But soon they discovered they couldn't begin; at the center of Omer's computer screen stood a bold error message.

Omer fumed. "He crashed my computer again!"

"Who?"

"My brother, the little moron! He does it all the time."

Noa laughed. "Why? Just to annoy you?"

"No, he thinks he's some kind of computer whiz and keeps installing his trashy software."

Omer stood, angry and embarrassed, frustrated and at a loss for words. And once again, he found it difficult to look Noa in the eye.

"We can start working at my place," she said. She stood right next to him, taller than him by half a head.

Omer heard a hint of a smile in her voice. He shrugged. "OK. But on the way, we're going to stop at that abandoned warehouse in the woods."

"What for?"

"To give my brother a piece of my mind! That's where they hang out."

"For real?" Noa said. "Let's go! Come on, we're going spying!"

The two teenagers pedaled away from Omer's house at break-neck speed. Long moments later, sweaty and less exuberant, they reached the dirt path leading to the large wood. They rode up the winding path towards the top of the hill.

Before the summit, they turned into a well-kept gravel road which separated the woods from large plots of deserted orange orchards—short, brown, skeletal trees surrounded by a dense thicket of dry, thorny weeds. Omer stopped, propping his foot on a large rock.

"From here we need to start being careful." Omer panted. He passed his fingers over his dripping scalp. "The heat is killing me."

Noa's cheeks were flushed. "Me too."

They sat for a moment, breathing hard, on the raised edge of the gravel road. Noa turned her gaze away from the sun. Omer noticed a eucalyptus leaf caught in her hair. The urge to reach out and pick it off tickled his mind. He refrained from doing so.

Noa held her hand to the ground, letting its warmth find its way to her skin. Tiny grains of dirt clung to the moisture of her sweat. When she wiped her hands, the dirt left a soft stain. She smiled.

"Look, I got a tan like yours," she said, bringing her arm next to his.

Omer's hand lay as motionless as a log, his gut twisted in awkwardness. His heart crashed against his ribcage.

"Huh, what a large hand you have!" Noa said, placing her hand on his. "Out of all proportion with your height."

His cheeks flushed. He wanted to disappear there and then, yet at the same time, for some reason, wanted the moment to last for hours.

But Noa sprang to her feet, and slapped her pants to dust them off. She wiped the lenses of her glasses with the edge of her T-shirt, got on her bike and began to ride. Omer mounted his bike and followed, glancing at his knuckles on the handlebar.

Large? Confusion and embarrassment pooled in his gut. *But it will even out when I get taller.* Edo, his dog, was the same way. *You can tell by a puppy's paws how big it'll be.*

Ahead, Noa pedaled with rapid movements. The brace on her leg showed through the sleeve of her pants, tilting with each move.

How can it not bother her when she rides?

Omer accelerated to catch up. The tightly packed gravel rustled under the tires. The road turned into a downward slope. They coasted side-by-side with effortless speed.

"Who needs such a good path to an abandoned warehouse?" Noa said.

"People come by here every few days."

"Really? Why? Have you seen them?"

"No, but I heard my brother talk about it. They come up to the warehouse and take something from there."

"Strange, no?"

Omer shrugged.

"A mystery, right?" Noa said.

"Yes, a mystery."

At the bottom of the road, the path was blocked by a tall gate, locked with a chain. A clearly visible sign warned: *"Private Property. No Entrance."* A tall fence stretched on both sides of the gate, topped with a tight roll of barbed wire.

Omer and Noa stopped a few feet from the gate.

"So how do we go on?" she said.

Omer turned towards the trees and pulled a thorny branch aside. He gestured with his chin at a narrow trail in the tall weeds.

He kept his voice quiet. "This is where the secret path begins."

Noa's lips curled into a smile. She entered first, leading her bike by hand. Omer followed, covering the path behind. Nearby, they saw four bicycles tossed on the ground.

"We have to hide ours," Omer said.

They hid their bikes in the thorns and then turned to a narrow, winding trail of trampled weeds, which passed through the trees and led to a little gap at the bottom of the fence. Noa squeezed through first. Omer followed. The trail continued beyond the fence, stretching through the same dry landscape of short dead trees and yellowing weeds.

In the middle of a clearing, between tall wild growth and thorns, there stood an old, large, dilapidated warehouse. The roof was made of corrugated asbestos, the plaster on its walls was cracked and peeling. Its windows, long and narrow, were shuttered by crooked, rough wooden blinds. A tall fence topped with barbed wire surrounded the building.

One of the walls was ruptured—a narrow, elongated crack revealing nothing but darkness. An arm and a leg showed through it, and a chubby youth leapt out, stood with his back to the wall and stretched.

"That's Oren," Omer said. "They're coming out. They'll pass by here soon."

Noa and Omer retreated a few steps off the beaten trail, and hid at a new vantage point. From there, they watched three other young boys skip out through the crack in the wall and walk around the corner of the warehouse.

"There's a gap under the wire there," Omer said.

Within a few moments, the group of boys reappeared, this time on the outer side of the fence. They advanced in single file to the first row of trees and passed one by one, crouching as they did. They kept going and disappeared from view in the thicket.

When their voices were far enough, Noa rose from where she crouched and went back to the trail.

"That's it, we can go on."

"Go on where?"

Noa turned to Omer. "The warehouse! That's what we came for, isn't it?"

"We came to spy on them."

"We're still spying, just without the spied-ers," Noa said. "Come on, what do you care? We're already here."

She bent down and passed under the branches of the last row of trees, then stood up straight, patiently removing a lock of hair that got tangled in the shoots. She quickly pulled a branch aside, making way for Omer.

"It's not a good idea," Omer said. "You don't know what might be in there."

"What can possibly be there? They just came out of there, didn't they?"

When they reached the gap underneath the barbed wire fence, Noa held the wire between the steel spikes and pulled upwards.

"Hold it." Noa wiggled and crawled under the wire. She dusted her pants off, reached out and held the fence for him. "Come on, it's easy as pie."

Bad idea. Private property! Didn't she see the sign? Of course she did, but who cares, right? Well, I care!

Yet he found himself following her in silence—his nervousness mixed with curiosity—directly to the old warehouse.

They peered into the darkness through the crack in the wall. Uninviting gloom. Dusty strips of light floated within the warehouse, projected through holes in the ceiling, forming little rings of light on the floor.

Noa entered first. Omer followed, taking his first tentative steps in the darkness of the warehouse.

Careful. Be careful not to step on something. Or fall into anything. Pupils dilate. More light gets through. Like the shutter of a camera. Cats' eyes do it, too, but a lot more.

Not far from him, Noa extended her arm, placing the palm of her hand in the middle of one of the light strips. It radiated white light on her face. She stepped forward and stood right under the light. Her hair shone. *What a beautiful sight.*

The darkness brightened with every passing moment. Omer advanced across the dusty concrete floor, following Noa, trying not to skid on puddles of pigeon droppings. He touched a tall stack of old loading pallets, looked at the elongated, rusty, skewed light-bulb sockets, and passed by a row of blue plastic containers.

"This was a packing warehouse," Noa said. Her eyes followed a long conveyor, a row of metal cylinders set along a track. Her hand moved the metal tubes and they rolled around their axles, rustling, slowing down.

A slight burning sensation grew in Omer's nose, forcing him to squint and seek a source of light.

"Achoo!"

Noa laughed. "Bless you thrice! You must be allergic to something."

Omer soaked his shirt-sleeve in his tears. "Probably to dust."

"A packing warehouse for oranges," Noa said. "Would have been interesting to see it work, wouldn't it? Lots of machines, lots of people, oranges everywhere." Her gaze took in the interior of the warehouse. "I wonder when they stopped."

"My dad told me that some investment firm bought the whole orchard," Omer said, "but they lost millions because they wanted to build houses but couldn't get building permits."

Noa nodded. She stood at the entrance to a huge cold-storage room that gave off a musty smell. She couldn't see what it held—too dark inside. She touched the door—thick metal, wide and high. It was stuck open, its bottom hinge twisted. Noa tried but couldn't get it to budge, not even a little.

Omer's foot stepped on something soft and springy—a bird's nest: a jumbled heap of twigs and dry grass, and remains of black-and-white droppings and feathers. He picked up the nest.

Huh, a dove's nest. Peace dove. White and chubby. They have a crop in their throats. They secrete and feed the chicks. And that stupid look in their eyes. And they're full of lice, and carry disease. This whole building is probably full of it. And this nest. Yuck! It's probably all over me!

Frightened, Omer threw the nest away in disgust.

No love, dove.

Noa's voice echoed at him from the end of the warehouse:

"Do you think we can open these doors?" She stood in front of the large wooden doors of the main entrance, with her back to him. "I want to open these. Then there will be lots of light here."

One of the doors was anchored to the floor by an iron bolt. Noa pulled at it, twisting it left and right. The bolt came loose. She pushed the doors hard, but couldn't open them.

"It's probably locked from the outside," Omer said.

"OK, so wait here," she said, and instantly darted through the crack in the wall.

Noa cut a new path in the tall weeds through the thorns, trampling left and right. Her hands rose like the wings of a waterfowl trying to take flight. Her fingers pulled aside thorns that threatened her face. She disappeared around the corner of the warehouse, and a moment later the rattle of a bolt echoed between the walls. A blinding rectangle of light appeared in oily silence. A small figure stood in the center of it.

"It looks different in the light," she said.

By the light of the sun the neglect became apparent. The floor was strewn with many packages of wrapping paper and empty cardboard boxes carrying the legendary "Lowland Citrus." All around were bookkeeping folders, trampled boxes full of stamps and pens, pieces of wood, and machinery parts.

Omer rummaged through the various boxes with new-found enthusiasm, turning things over, examining them, throwing them away. Clouds of dust rose and enveloped him. Noa moved away and sat on a narrow concrete ledge next to the cold-storage room. She began counting his sneezes out loud.

Laughter rose from her lungs. "Eleven!" She pushed a stack of packing paper aside, making room for him to sit beside her. Omer drew close. His eyes were closed, trying to hold back a sneeze.

"This place is killing me," he said. Another forceful sneeze followed. A plume of dust rose from the ledge, revealing something underneath. Omer's eyes grew wide with amazement. His heart skipped a beat.

He reached out and touched it; roughness, letters, familiar yet not. He blew, raising another plume of dust.

"Look!"

Noa was stunned with his discovery just as much as he was. She looked at the drawing engraved in the concrete surface.

"That's the symbol..."

Together, their fingers traced the circle and the letters surrounding it, running along the spiral lines.

Omer's voice was reduced to a whisper. "I told you I've seen it before."

"So you've been here before?"

"No, never. My brother must have taken a picture and uploaded it to the computer. But that's exactly it, right? We have to tell Joel."

Noa nodded, drew her cell phone from her pocket and took a picture.

"Nope, can't see anything," she said, and immediately pointed to the side. "Get a pencil from there."

She smoothed a torn sheet of packing paper on the concrete ledge, and with rapid, fluttering motions rubbed the pencil over the page. Omer stood beside her and looked at the letters and the symbols that appeared. Noa lifted the paper and held the drawing in front of them.

"Now we can show him."

Chapter 5

"The Birmingham meeting went well," Michael Lampston said when the jet reached cruising altitude over the North Sea. "They're finally making good progress."

Cole-Angel opened his laptop and looked at the screen.

"Yes, I got a detailed email from them this morning." His eyes left the screen. "I understand that the problem in China has been solved," he said, his eyes turning this a question.

"Yes, Gerryowen worked his magic on them," Lampston said.

"Ah, magic."

Michael Lampston's lips curled into a smile. "Sometimes I get the feeling you just can't bring yourself to like the man."

Ernest Cole-Angel fell silent for a moment. When he spoke again, it was in a cool, low tone. "It's not a matter of liking. There's something... scary about him."

"So let's be happy he's on our side," Lampston said.

Cole-Angel returned his gaze to the screen.

Amusement reflected in Lampston's eyes. Everything had gone according to plan. In fact, the entire endeavor had exceeded Lampston's wildest dreams. From a lowly public-sector research project to a private startup to multi-millionaire status for all of them in less than five years—who could ask for more? And now, with this new, second facility opening, the whole thing was on the verge of a spectacular breakthrough, all the growing pains behind them. But Cole-Angel, always the one to worry, insisted on seeing danger at every turn.

Did the man ever relax?

"Can't see the forest for the grisly bears," Lampston's mother had said once about Lampston's father, another worrier, whose failings in business were legendary, a result of misplaced kindheartedness, Lampston firmly believed.

"You ready to hear Dr. Pok's resignation letter now?" Cole-Angel asked.

Lampston sighed. "No, but go ahead."

"'After long and fascinating years, I have decided for personal and health reasons to tender my resignation as head of the Human Resources Department of the World Sales Corporation.'" Sensing Lampston's disinterest, Cole-Angel skipped down the document, his lips moving, reading the words silently, then louder. "'Furthermore, lately I have been feeling a physical and mental fatigue which makes it difficult for me to carry out my duties.'"

"He's just tired," Lampston said, feeling tired himself.

"Still," Cole-Angel said, "that 'mental fatigue' doesn't sound too good. Not for him or for us."

"Have you met with him?"

Cole-Angel reclined in his seat. "Yes, I met him a few days ago and he looked... agonized."

For emphasis, a slight tremor went through the fuselage of the plane. Lampston grasped the armrest and checked his seatbelt again.

"Agonized...?" Lampston said. *He's exaggerating again.*

"Pulling his Hamlet routine," Cole-Angel said. "Why does he live there, anyway?" Cole-Angel said. He was referring to Dr. Pok's estate in Denmark.

"Says it's 'civilized,'" Lampston said.

"Yeah, well, give me the jungle."

Lampston stifled another chuckle at the false bravado.

Security Chief Dan Gerryowen appeared at the front of the cabin. He was a man of about sixty, with a kind, grandfatherly face, adorned by a trimmed mustache and thin-framed glasses. He was of average height, but his tendency to corpulence made him look shorter. All in all, not the look of the "go-to" guy in the company, their hard-nosed enforcer. He took his bear steps towards them on the stiff rug and shook their hands.

"We were just talking about you," Michael Lampston said, a half-smile on his face.

Gerryowen's tone brought his disinterest in plain sight. "Really?" He walked to the coffee stand, poured himself a cup, and replaced the glass pot in its secure place. "The captain says we might be in for a bumpy ride."

Ernest Cole-Angel got out of his leather armchair, slipped to the back of the plane and buckled up again. "Great, just what I need."

On Lampston's signal, Gerryowen sat next to him. Lampston reduced his voice to a whisper.

"You see the email from Dr. Pok?"

Gerryowen nodded.

"Check him out," Lampston said. "I don't like his wording."

"I'll check," Gerryowen said, "and I'll raise the monitoring on him to constant surveillance level."

Lampston nodded. "Good idea."

Chapter 6

From his car, Joel scanned the apartment building numbers in a middle-class neighborhood of Rehovot, a twenty-minute drive from Gat.

"OK, there," he said, "third floor, see? The balcony with the birdcages."

Joel parked. He turned to Noa and Omer.

"By the way, you should know there's a chance that Professor Peretz won't remember anything about the symbol."

Omer nodded with sympathy. "He's senile."

"No, he's not senile at all!" Joel said. "But a few years ago, during a secret research project, he had some sort of nervous breakdown. After that he was hospitalized for a few months…"

"He was in a loony bin?" Omer said. "Was he in one of those suits with the hands tied behind the back? Is he aggressive?"

Astonishment rose in Joel's tone. "Aggressive? No way! Are you nuts? He's the nicest, most pleasant man in the world. It's just that he doesn't remember a lot of things from those years. It's like entire periods have been erased from his mind."

The modest foyer of the building was open, and had no intercom system. Well-worn stairs led to the top floors. They stopped at the third floor. Joel pressed the doorbell. An electronic bird-chirp sounded.

A hurried voice came from within. "One minute, coming!"

The door to the apartment opened wide and Professor Peretz appeared at the entrance. A meter and sixth-tenths of chubby energy, he was dressed in shorts and a T-shirt, and his head was almost completely bald, save for gray hair at the temples.

"Joel, hello!" Professor Peretz said, shaking their hands. "Pleased to meet you. Come, come in, what are you standing in the doorway for?"

With quick steps, he led them to a coffee table at the center of the living room. He left and returned a moment later carrying a plate of fruit.

"Well, until the kettle boils, why don't you tell me what you found that is so interesting?"

"Here, this is what I told you about on the phone," Joel said, excitement evident in his voice. He placed two pages on the table. "You see? Exactly the same."

Professor Peretz examined the pages at length, shifting his gaze from one to the other, bringing them closer to his eyes and then further away.

"Indeed, they are identical. And you say you received this one from me... and this," he turned to Noa, "you copied this from a warehouse not far from here?"

"Uh huh. An orange packing warehouse."

"Hmm, yes," Professor Peretz said. "Synchronized photos." He laid the drawings on the table. "There is an interesting combination here of letters and symbols in different languages from different periods."

The three drew closer to the table and followed his stubby finger gliding over the various letters.

"What does it say?" Omer said.

"Hmm, I don't really know," Professor Peretz said. "They would need to be deciphered. But the mere combination of them together, in an artifact thousands of years old... I would say this is, uh, not so logical, yes?" He lifted his eyes to look at Joel. "Are you sure you got this from me?"

"Yes. It's from digs you conducted in Mexico."

Professor Peretz fell silent for a long moment. Joel's words had instantly stirred a tightly controlled tension within him. He took a deep breath.

"Sometimes I don't know if the loss of memory was a curse or a blessing," he said at last, his voice heavy. And with the same heaviness he rose, stepped away from the others and stood in front of the wall, by a framed photograph of a smiling woman. His voice softened. "Until the day Marta died, I did not stop trying to remember. I really fought to recollect. But since she passed..."

Professor Peretz inhaled, his moist eyes glittering. "That was a difficult time. People carry memories like cargo, and I carried forgetfulness. I carried it like a burden that tried to crush me into the ground. It was beyond the power of my meager shoulders to lift." He sniffled and lowered his gaze to the floor. "So when Marta passed away I decided to stop trying to remember. I was too tired. I preferred to leave it all behind me."

It was as though Professor Peretz froze into the moment. A sheer curtain fluttered on a soft breeze over the window beside him. Joel pulled at the end of his goatee, his lowered eyes revealing he was upset with himself. His jaw tightened.

"I'm sorry," Joel said, at last. "We had no intention to cause you... I just thought you might find it interesting and perhaps..."

Professor Peretz snapped out of his reverie. He walked over and placed a hand on Joel's shoulder, who flushed and fell silent.

"What is done with good intent causes no harm, in the end," the professor said with a smile. "I'm glad you came. Truly. You know, sometimes I feel as though my entire memory is hidden underneath a huge blue tarp. Like my memory is a covered excavation site, and once in a while one of the edges is lifted and I see something, recall something. It's an amazing feeling."

He indicated the drawings spread on the table.

"Maybe these are here as a hint that I should just grab the edge of the tarp and lift, reveal the edge of a memory and then find the rest of it."

The electronic bird-chirping startled all four of them. Professor Peretz approached the door with his hurried gait. In the doorway was a smiling, elderly woman with silver hair.

"I hope I'm not interrupting. I just wanted to know if we're going as we planned."

Professor Peretz glanced at his wrist-watch. "Varda, you are right. Somehow I didn't notice. Of course we're going. I'll be ready in a few moments."

After she left, Professor Peretz's hand remained on the doorknob. His eyes studied the door with great intensity.

"Door... an iron door... " His brow furrowed as he turned towards Noa and Omer. "Green. Was there a green door there? A green iron door?"

"There's an iron door there!" Noa said. "A cold-storage room door. But it's gray."

"Right, a big one. We found the symbol right next to it!" Omer said.

"No..." The look in Professor Peretz's eyes grew hazy. "Not big... about this size." His hand hung at the height of his forehead.

Noa bit her lower lip, trying to remember. Omer shook his head in the negative.

"Hmm, never mind. I thought I remembered something." Professor Peretz shrugged. "A big help I've been to you, huh? Now you know even less than when you came! Ha! Research with a man with no memory: one step forward, two diagonally."

He then turned towards Joel with a firm voice. "I want to make it clear that I really am glad you came. Really. When you called I was a bit frightened, but now I feel that my fear of remembering is beginning to crack, as though some weight has been lifted... "

His voice died down. "Weight...cargo," he said, drawling the word, dissecting it into syllables. "Cargo. You put the cargo on... on... how was it called? *Sumai tangiee*...? Hmm? Yes, *sumai tangiee*."

The kettle in the kitchen screamed like a banshee. The professor hurried off, leaving his audience in suspense.

Joel stood. Noa and Omer did the same.

"I'm afraid I didn't time things well," Professor Peretz said once he returned.

"It's okay—"

"But I remembered something!" the professor said. "A *sumai tangiee* is like a narrow table, a sort of stone slab placed on two tall stones. It used to serve the farmers in India for rest."

"A stone bed?" Joel said.

"No, not a bed. In the past the farmers used to carry heavy loads on their heads over long distances, loads they could not lift on their own. So at the beginning of the journey there was someone who would help them, but in order for them to rest from time to time, they built these tall tables alongside the roads. They'd transfer the load from their head to the tall table, so later they only had to bend a bit and grab it from there. You can still see these tables along the roads in the south. Sumai means cargo and tangiee is carrier. Or vice versa. It's in one of the languages they speak in southern India. In Tamil. And now ask me why I told you this."

"Why did you tell us this?"

"I have no idea! I haven't the faintest idea. It just surfaced in my memory."

Chapter 7

Hadassa returned to the reading room and took her seat again. The book remained open to where she last left it. *Had it moved at all?* She wasn't sure. *Would they do that? Look to see what she read and what she didn't read? Certainly,* Hadassa decided. The security services were thorough that way. The massive length of the volume before her was a testament to that.

Why they'd even begun to investigate the Body Cooling Phenomenon was still a mystery to Hadassa. *Wasn't it a job for the medical establishment? For scientists?*

Deciding she'd never make it through from start to finish, at least not in one session, Hadassa decided to take a look at the thing as a whole and get a sense of where she should seek more detail. She turned pages, noting the tabbed sections along the edge of the huge manuscript: Origins, Demographics, Hypotheses, Treatment and Control... *Hallucinations.*

Hadassa swallowed hard. Ari's hallucinations had been severe, getting worse towards the end, to the point it was never clear whether he was awake or dreaming. The researchers had requested that Hadassa draws Ari out, so she listened to his farfetched ravings and tried to write them down, which seemed to calm Ari considerably, but other than that, Hadassa couldn't see any reason to record them.

Maybe those are here, Hadassa nearly gasped. *Those things I wrote down.* She had no idea how many patients were asked about their dreams. *Just me? All of them? How widespread was that research?*

With courage borne on curiosity, Hadassa took a deep breath and turned to the middle of the book.

Chapter 8

Joel dropped Noa and Omer off at the school parking lot and drove away. The two teens sat on the sidewalk in the narrow shade-strip of a concrete wall, most of their bodies sheltered from the sun. Omer picked a gray pebble up and began drawing on the sidewalk. He drew a circle and marked spiral lines through it, from the perimeter to the center. Around the circle he began drawing letters and symbols, but soon gave it up and substituted them with little x's.

Their heads rested back against the wall, facing each other. Noa's cheeks were slightly flushed from the heat, and tiny drops of sweat beaded on her upper lip. She released her hair from the simple rubber band and lifted it from her shoulders, letting the air cool her neck, and then arranged her hair against the wall as a comfortable pillow. With a ginger strand of hair she tickled her chin, passing it back and forth along the skin like a feather.

Her face was pretty—smooth and fair, gently sculpted in straight lines rising from the chin and curving at the top of the cheeks. The sides of her nose were strewn with little freckles. A face of restrained serenity—the hint of a smile hiding behind sealed lips, clear, thinking, silent eyes behind thin glass lenses.

But now, due to the glare of the sun, those eyes had narrowed into twin slits, and the look in them changed, as if she was angry. Omer returned his gaze to the sidewalk and kept drawing. Out of the corner of his eye he saw her wipe the dust off the metal strips and leather straps of her awkward leg-brace.

Robot. That person called her a robot. Because of that thing, but she didn't care about him. Didn't care about anyone. On the contrary. Everyone seeks her attention. But she has no boyfriend. Smartest kid in class, that's for sure. Maybe in the whole age group.

"It's interesting that we didn't see that door," she said.

A green iron door.

Noa gathered her legs, pressed her knees to her chest and laid her chin atop them.

"Well, there are still a few places to look there," she said.

"There's also a chance he's imagining things," Omer said.

Noa did not reply. She bent forward, balanced herself, and rose on her feet, without using her hands. Without hurry, she re-gathered her hair in the rubber band. The red hair sparkled in the sun. Omer stood beside her, shorter by half a head, and unwittingly stared at her. Something about her posture didn't match her skinny build. She was strong, which showed in her movements as well.

Noa caught his gaze and her expression changed. A smile lifted her lips. "What?"

Omer stirred as though just awakening. He touched his face, flustered. "No, nothing. You're right, we didn't look everywhere."

His fingers left dusty streaks on his brown cheek. Noa moistened a finger with saliva and wiped the dust off his face. Omer stepped back, blushing. Noa's chest shook with laughter.

"So, four o'clock? To the woods?" she said.

"But Mr. Kramer said not to," Omer said. "We told him we wouldn't."

"You do everything your teachers tell you to do?"

"He said it might be dangerous!"

Noa gave Omer a look that broke down all resistance and won him over without a single word. "Okay, four o'clock."

At five-thirty, after exploring every nook and cranny of the large warehouse, every niche and alcove, the two sat down on the dirty warehouse floor, despondent, leaning with their backs against the cold-storage room door. Their clothes, arms and hair were stained with a mixture of dust, machine oil, pigeon droppings and spider webs.

Omer held a black flashlight in one hand. The other hand drummed on the floor with a broken stick. Noa hugged her knees and rested her chin on them.

"I thought we'd find the door," she said, disappointed. "I guess he really doesn't remember anything. My mother said that maybe he was traumatized, to lose his memory like that."

Omer's brows rose with astonishment. "Your mother? You told your mom about all this?"

"Uh huh. I tell her almost everything."

"And she let you come back here?"

"Oh, I didn't tell her that," Noa said. "I said I tell her almost everything."

Omer's mouth rose into a wide smile, and he threw the stick up in the air. It hit one of the ceiling beams, scattering the pigeons perched there, igniting a distressed hum of chatter among them. Noa raised her chin from her knees and tilted her head backwards. Omer began to turn the flashlight on and off.

"OK, we need to get going," he said. "It will be getting dark soon."

"There's plenty of time till it gets dark," Noa said. "Besides, it's a lot more fun being here than writing a paper."

Omer turned the flashlight on, illuminating Noa's face for a moment, and turned it off right away.

"I thought you liked to study."

Noa shrugged. "I don't really need to study. Definitely not for tests. But for papers you need to sit down and work a little."

"Lucky you." Omer's voice was gloomy, a little angry even. He didn't tell her that sometimes he really crammed for a test, for a month. *But I always flunk. Always. And sometimes I lose all hope.*

"Guys in class say you're lazy," Noa said, as though reading Omer's thoughts.

The words hurt him. His hand moved sideways. Sudden fatigue burdened him.

"They can say anything they want," he said, mustering the strength to appear indifferent.

"It's actually pretty interesting," Noa said, "because you do know and remember lots of things."

"I remember things that nobody needs. Things that have nothing to do with school."

"That's not 'things nobody needs.' It's things you like. Anyway, I'm not sure that making grades is more important than knowing things."

"The teachers think it's more important."

Omer buried his gaze in the floor and took a deep breath, holding the air in his lungs for a few moments. He rose and slapped the back of his pants.

"I want to see the machine from the top," he said, pointing at a tall packing machine.

"OK," Noa said, "I'll close the doors in the meantime."

* * *

A white van cruised along the gravel road at about forty kilometers an hour, raising a pale dust-cloud behind it. Small gravel pebbles flew from the wheels of the vehicle and hit the chassis with clicking sounds.

As it approached the perimeter fence of the packing house, the vehicle slowed, finally coming to a halt in front of the entrance gate. A man in a gray uniform leapt out, the word "SECURITY" emblazoned on the back of his shirt. His belt held a flashlight, a two-way radio and a pistol in a holster.

He turned to the gate, his hand touching his gun. He opened the lock and let the van through.

* * *

After closing the large entrance doors, Noa waited by the crack in the wall and counted sneezes.

"Four, five, six. Omer, I don't think you want to stay there."

His head appeared from the tall metal container, adorned with cobweb strings. His face was illuminated from below by the beam of the flashlight he held. He leaned backwards and sneezed again, raising a new dust plume to his face.

Noa burst into a rolling laughter. "You look like a demon!"

But then she fell silent, listening. The whir of the wheels reached her ears, rubber on gravel. She peeked out and saw the dust trail.

"Omer, quick!" She leapt towards him. "People are coming!"

In an instant, Omer turned hysterical. "What? Where?" he said. "Who?"

He scrambled out of the container and began feeling around for the iron ladder with his feet. Noa saw the back of the van stop in front of the entrance. She ran to Omer, guiding him. "On your left! Hurry!"

His feet found the ladder. He began descending—too fast—his foot slipped and he hugged and held onto the ladder with both hands. The flashlight slipped out of his hands and crashed to the concrete floor.

Noa reduced her voice to a whisper and extended her hands towards him. "Be careful! Come on. Here."

The clack of the bolt on the front door echoed through the warehouse like a gunshot. Both Omer and Noa's hearts leapt in their chests. Omer let out a frightened gasp and jumped off the ladder. His leg hit the corner of one of the wooden crates.

"Hurry!" Noa said.

Evening light entered through the opening door. With swift movement, Noa kicked the broken flashlight, sending it under one of the crates. She pulled Omer toward her, behind the packing machine, and squeezed in beside him.

The security guard entered the warehouse first, scanning the room. After him came a short, stocky, impatient man carrying an empty carrier—a wood and steel sled—on his back like a backpack. He also held a small, sealed metal box in his hands.

The security guard let out a juicy curse and spat in an arc.

"The little punks were in here again, huh?" he said. "This time they made a mess. Why are we leaving the place open for them anyway?"

The shorter man ignored his words and stepped to the wide-open cold-storage room door. He knelt by the door and stuck his finger into a small hole at the bottom. The security guard raised his hand and stuck his finger into a hole at the top of the door.

"Ready?" the short man said. "Three, two, one, push!"

The two men pushed hidden buttons in the holes. A click sounded. The short man stood up straight and pulled the door. It detached from the wall behind it with ease, and there, to the astounded eyes of Noa and Omer, a short, narrow, green iron door appeared.

"Go get the cable," the short man said. "I'm going in."

After ascertaining that the security guard had moved off and was no longer in sight, the short man pressed a secret code on a panel.

"Six-three-seven-two-eight-hash," Noa said. "Six-three-seven-two-eight."

A red bulb lit up underneath the control panel. The short man pressed his thumb to a small identification surface. A beep sounded and the bulb turned green. The short man pushed the door and it opened inwards, into a dark space. He did not enter, first he turned to the large cold-storage door and pulled it behind him, until it hid him and the little door once more.

The security guard returned to the warehouse, dragging a long electric cable behind him, which he plugged into a socket in the corner of the cold-storage room. He backed away, taking a pack of cigarettes out of his shirt-pocket.

"No, no!" Omer said. "Don't let him smoke!"

The security guard lit the cigarette and rose from his crouching position. He inhaled deeply and released the smoke like a long jet stream.

Omer let out a repressed, inward sneeze. "I think I'm allergic to—"

"Shut up!"

"Achoo!"

Startled, the security guard turned his head and looked all around him. He took a step, pulled out his gun and cocked it. He drew the flashlight from his belt and immediately began scanning the warehouse, taking small steps, pointing the light front, back, and up.

What a mess, what a mess! Fear sank its claws into Omer. He couldn't understand the situation he was in, let alone believe it. *We should never have come! He'll shoot? He won't shoot. I hope he doesn't shoot. How stupid. There are signs there. No entry. Just don't let him shoot.*

The security guard approached the packing machine. By the light of the flashlight he examined the wooden crates, the conveyor belt, the tall container. Something was ground under his shoe. Glass. He looked at the shards, moving them with the tip of his shoe. He tensed even further, cold sweat staining his collar.

Terrified, staying still as a pair of stones, Omer and Noa sat pressed together, their hearts pounding, shaking their entire bodies. A sharp beeping sound rose in Omer's ear, long and annoying.

Above the security guard, a pigeon hummed, followed by a gurgling sound, like a bubble released from a tube. Another gurgling sound followed and then a thin, delicate, gray-white stream landed straight on the tip of the burning cigarette at the corner of the security guard's mouth. Slow to understand, he raised his head and heard the bubble sound once again.

"Argh, filth!" he said, wiping white waste from his cheek. He bent in anger and picked up a piece of wood from the floor, throwing it at the bird.

A click sounded behind him, and the cold-storage room door moved, revealing the hidden crypt. The short man appeared at the entrance, both hands holding the carrier by its handles with considerable effort. The sealed metal box was attached to the carrier with rubber straps.

"Come and help me already!" he said. "Say, what are you doing?"

"Nothing, I'm coming," the security guard said, replacing his pistol in its holster and his flashlight on his belt. "Stinking pigeon almost got me."

Using both hands, the security guard helped the short man raise the full carrier and place it on the narrow concrete ledge beside the cold-storage room. The short man slammed the green door shut. Then, he pushed the cold-storage room door against the wall, hiding the smaller door once again. When he was done with the doors, he turned to load the carrier onto his back. He approached the concrete ledge, stepped back and slid his arms through the carrier straps. He bent backwards for leverage and then forwards, lifting the carrier from the ledge. Swaying slightly from the weight, he walked towards the entrance to the warehouse.

Omer, spying from his hiding spot with caution, stared at the concrete ledge. The fright that gripped him before was gone as though it had never been. Excitement filled him.

"That summery thing," he said. "The summery tangerine."

"What?" Noa said, confused. "What are you talking about?"

The security guard unplugged the extension cord and wrapped it around his arm. He left the warehouse, slammed the wooden door and bolted it with a metal clang that echoed through the enclosed space. The vehicle's engine roared and its wheels whirred on the gravel, receding rapidly.

Behind the packing machine, the two waited for a few more moments. Noa rose, feeling for objects she might hit above her head.

"Don't you remember?" Omer's voice grew impatient, and he hurried to the cold-storage room door. "A stone table! You know, that thing in India, summery something, that you place loads on and—"

"*Sumai!*" Noa said, astounded. "*Sumai tangiee!* How could I forget? A loading table."

"Yes!" Omer said. "Exactly on that *sumai* is where we found the symbol."

The symbol could no longer be seen in the gloom of the warehouse. They stood shoulder-to-shoulder and let their fingers trace the symbol.

He remembers everything.

"He doesn't remember anything," he said. "Yet he remembers everything."

PART TWO

Chapter 9

While the jet flew east into a rising sun, Michael Lampston worked the figures on his laptop. There was no doubt that with the new installation they could double the World Sales revenues in three years, just as they'd doubled them in the last three, starting with nothing only five years ago. That would be doing only what they'd been doing all along: marketing, sales, advertising, consumer profiling, blah blah blah.

Lampston chuckled. Small potatoes. *The kind of stuff my dad would do.* A wave of guilt showered him. *Dad did his best, just failed miserably.* The one thing Lampston was not prepared to do was fail. He'd started out in science—*"that's where the big strides are going to happen, son"*—and ended up in his father's profession after all: sales; except Lampston was now successful far beyond his father's wildest dreams.

He hadn't done it alone. The thought darkened his eyes, with a shiver that matched the sudden, turbulent shake of the jet plane, just then crossing the Arctic Circle on its polar route. Lampston gripped the armrest and looked down at ice and snow lit yellow in the sunrise.

Wouldn't last long down there even if we did land safely. I should call my wife, find out what the twins are up to—

Another sudden horror shot through his mind: *what if we're all lost—me, Gerryowen, Cole-Angel?*

Lampston turned to the back, to tell Cole-Angel that this was a mistake, that they should have taken separate transportation, that this was a foolhardy risk—the entire top echelon of the company riding the same missile through space—

The fear on Cole-Angel's face stopped Lampston cold and made him chuckle. There was no way Lampston would say anything to the man—he couldn't be that cruel. With a smile, Lampston turned back, catching Gerryowen's smile in return.

Is he thinking the same thing?

"Maybe we should travel in separate planes next time," Gerryowen said with a glint of fun in his eye.

The plane hit another air-pocket, tossing all their hearts into their throats, reminding them this was serious business.

"Definitely."

Five years ago, before the discoveries, before the incredible universe of possibilities opened up to him and revealed their secrets, Lampston would have thought it was coincidence that he and Gerryowen had the same fear at the same time.

That was then. Now you know better. Now you know you share the same space. Now you understand you're both puzzle-pieces in a larger universe. And soon... if the endeavor goes as planned...that universe will be yours to have and hold in the palms of your hands.

Lampston snickered, a hollow hint of a diabolical laugh.

"What?" Gerryowen said.

"Nothing," Lampston said. "A private joke."

Chapter 10

Professor Peretz watched Joel try to cram another bicycle into the trunk of his small, green car. The professor placed his hands flat on the roof and drew a deep breath. "My situation reminds me of a line in a poem: 'Memories dressed in kindly cobwebs.'"

Something in Professor Peretz's voice caused Joel to stop and raise his eyes.

"You're... you're afraid to go there, aren't you?" he said.

"I don't know exactly what I feel," professor Peretz said. "One moment I'm afraid of the past, and another I'm excited about the future. I want to remember, but am afraid of the possibility of remembering."

Joel hesitated for a moment. "Maybe we should go without you. We can tell you what we saw, and then you can decide—"

"Are you mad? Without me?" Professor's mood turned ebullient. "I can't wait to get there!" He walked over to Joel and helped him tie a reflective triangle to the bicycle wheel. "They actually told you that they saw the green door, eh?"

"Yes, and the *sumai tangiee* too."

"Wonderful! Wonderful," Professor Peretz said. "Let's go! What are we waiting for?"

* * *

They hid the four bicycles in the weeds and Omer covered them with tree branches. From there, they advanced along the trampled path to the last row of trees. Noa and Omer navigated with confidence, helping Joel extract a thorny branch from his curly hair, then helping Professor Peretz slip under the barbed wire fence.

Noa was the first to stand by the narrow crack in the warehouse wall, and the first to wiggle into the darkness beyond it. Omer and Joel then helped Professor Peretz get inside.

They let their eyes adjust to the darkness. Professor Peretz looked all around—at the packing machine, the long conveyor belt, the piles of trash, and the crumbling cardboard pieces.

"I remember a warehouse, a warehouse like this..." he said.

Omer, Noa and Joel waited, hesitating to speak. Professor Peretz pointed at the packing machine.

"I don't remember this," he said, "and I don't remember the rest of the things here. I remember an empty warehouse." He took another few steps towards the center of the warehouse. "Where...?"

Omer crossed the room, skipping over piles of dusty packing paper. "Here's the loading table, the *sumai*," he pointed, "and behind this cold-storage room door is the green door."

Professor Peretz approached the concrete table with slow, deliberate steps, and stood next to it. He reached out, his hand trembling, and touched the symbol stamped upon it. His fingers passed over the spiral lines, the strange letters.

"The veins!" Professor Peretz said. A strange look filled his eyes: excited, frightened, joyful. "The vein!"

He allowed himself a few moments to calm down. "I have like a quarter of a memory, an eighth of a memory, of the moment we stamped the symbol in the concrete. And somewhere here is the door..."

Noa stood by the cold-storage room door and pointed at the holes at the top and the bottom.

"Inside these holes there's something that needs to be pushed simultaneously," she explained, "and then it comes loose from the wall and behind it is the green door."

Joel approached and raised his hand, stretching. He inserted his finger into the top hole.

"Gee," he said. "there's a button here."

"Just like we told you," Omer said, kneeling by the lower hole. "There's one here too."

"So I'll count to three and we'll push together, OK?" Noa said, her voice brisk. "Three, two⎵"

"It could be dangerous," the professor said.

Omer withdrew his finger from the hole.

"Do you remember danger?" Joel said.

"Hmm, actually, no," Professor Peretz said. He approached and rapped gently a few times on the cold-storage room door. "Actually, I don't." A spark lit in his eyes. "On the contrary, I remember excitement, work, enthusiasm. I remember..." He fell silent for a moment, and when he spoke again his voice was slightly different: "Marta, my wife, spoke a lot about danger. She spoke about evil. Bad feelings and bad people." He frowned. "At that time I was still recovering from the nervous breakdown. I think she was trying to warn me before she passed away. Warn me without understanding herself what to be careful of."

He reached for the symbol, caressing it. "I'm sorry that I'm..." He fell silent, but after a moment or two, a smile broadened on his face. "So, what do you say? Shall we try?"

"I think we can start the count," Noa said, her voice reflecting barely suppressed excitement.

Start the count? Omer hardly believed his ears. *After what he just said about these dangers and bad feelings? Let's talk about it at least. Bad feelings. I have them too. Bad people. That guy had a gun. We mustn't go in. It's not ours either. She doesn't care about anything. I have to stop this—*

"Omer, what do you think?" Noa said.

"Uh, yeah," he said, gloom creeping into his voice. "We should start the count."

Joel stretched again and inserted a finger into the top hole. "I'm ready!" he announced, the excitement clear in his voice.

Omer inserted his finger into the bottom hole. His heart thundered against his chest. He felt his pulse in the tip of the finger touching the button.

"Me too," he said.

"So, we're starting," Noa said. "Three, two, one, push!"

A metallic clicking sound came from the cold-storage door. The door swung from the wall in a smooth motion and revealed the green door behind it, to the amazement of Joel and Professor Peretz.

"This!" Professor Peretz said. "This is the door."

The professor drew nearer. With his fingertips, he touched the number pad. His thumb pressed the ID scanner lens.

"Nine-seven-two-eight-four-hash," Professor Peretz said, elated.

"Six-three-seven-two-eight-hash," Noa said.

Professor Peretz's thumb pushed again on the lens.

"They must have updated this too," he said, regret apparent in his voice.

"Might as well check," Noa said. "Shall we try it?"

"No use," Omer said, somewhat relieved. "It'll never work. These things never fail."

"But since we're already here..." Joel said.

"Exactly," said Noa, and she immediately began punching the code in. "Six-three-seven-two-eight." She stopped for a moment, hesitating, and then pressed the hash mark.

A red bulb lit underneath the keypad.

Their eyes turned toward Professor Peretz. He brought his thumb to the ID scanner.

Will it open? Omer's mixed feelings shook his entire body. *I hope it opens...*

Professor Peretz pressed his thumb to the scanner lens. The red light turned green. The green door made a soft clicking sound and opened.

Up close, the dark tunnel looked narrow and threatening. Joel put a headlamp on his forehead and turned it on. A powerful, purple-bluish beam of light cut into the interior of the tunnel.

"Wow, how deep," he said, astounded.

"Cool!" Noa said, adding the light of her small flashlight. "Shall we go in? I'm first!"

With the words barely out of her mouth, she skipped in, over the raised threshold of the iron door, and in an instant she stumbled and disappeared from sight, collapsing into the tunnel.

"Noa!"

Joel was the first to recover from the shock.

"Noa? Noa, are you all right?" he said and rushed inside, hurried yet cautious.

"I'm fine, I'm fine," Noa's said from the dark. "Watch out for the first step—it's really deep."

Joel sighed in relief. Noa climbed towards him, motioning to him with her light.

"Are you sure you're OK?" Joel said.

"I'm totally fine." Her voice betrayed none of the pain in her leg.

When Professor Peretz saw Noa smiling, he relaxed a little.

"Lucky her hair is so shiny," Joel said. "I saw her from afar."

"Hmm, like the sea sparkles," Professor Peretz said. "*Noctiluca scintillans*. Those tiny organisms that live in the sea in large groups. There's something fascinating about the cooperation between them because when they feel the presence of a predator near them they glow, and then it's easier for the predator to hunt them, but then the predator's stomach glows, and its enemies see that and eat him, thereby saving the rest of the sparkles."

Noa listened to the explanation as she peeked from the entrance.

"Nice..." she said, "but I'd rather not glow and stay outside the predator."

"Most of us, probably," Joel said, "that's why we don't glow in the dark. Shall we continue?"

Professor Peretz followed Noa into the tunnel, with Omer right behind him. Joel entered last.

"Wait, what about the doors?" Omer said.

"True, you're right," said Noa. "That man closed both doors behind him."

"The little door opens from the inside, I actually remember it!" Professor Peretz said instantly, with a burst of joy.

Joel skipped out of the tunnel, and for a moment or two examined the little door, then the cold-storage door.

"This one opens from the inside as well," he said.

Joel re-entered the tunnel, pulling the cold-storage door behind him. His headlamp focused for a moment on a simple electric switch near the wall of the tunnel. He raised his head and noticed a small light-bulb hanging from the ceiling.

"Hey, did you guys notice there's a light switch here?" Joel said, and immediately reached out to press the switch. The bulb didn't turn on. "No power," he said, disappointed.

Omer turned to Noa. "You remember? That must be why he attached the cord from the car."

"Hey, that's right," Noa said. "That guy didn't have a flashlight."

When you're in a cave you can tell if it's day or night outside by the light of a candle. That's what they say. If it's day outside the flame will be yellow and if it's night it'll be white. Or vice-versa. But that doesn't sound right. I mean, what's one got to do with the other? In here it'd be pitch black dark if we turned the flashlights off. Gee, it's hot. My neck is as sticky as duct-tape.

"Careful, deep step!" Noa said. "There's another right-hand turn here."

And I hope there's enough oxygen here. Actually that short guy was here so there must be enough. Wow, what a dig. So deep. Look how she charges in front all the time. Has to be first. Okay, that's totally fine with me.

The tunnel had a regular pattern going forward—a steep decline and then a turn to the right, another decline and another right turn. The ceiling was sometimes high and sometimes low, but never so low that they had to walk bent over. At some places wooden planks mounted on metal scaffolds protected them from loose stones overhead. At other points small wooden bridges spanned the rocks.

"What's that?" Omer said, turning their attention to a thick, continuous metal strip attached to the bottom of the tunnel wall.

"That's a conveyor track," Professor Peretz said "They use it to raise heavy loads from the depths of the tunnel. The electricity from the car was used for that as well."

"Ah, I did wonder how he carried that weight all the way uphill," said Noa.

"Right," Omer said, "because he could barely get it from the ledge to the car afterwards."

"A collector!" Professor Peretz said, stopping. A delighted look shone on his face again. "It was a collector. He was carrying a full collector."

"Collector," Noa played with the word in her mouth. "What does it collect?"

Professor Peretz began walking again, frowning.

"I don't remember," he said after long thought. "We would collect something in it and bring it to the lab."

"What's it look like?" Omer said.

The professor shook his head again.

"There's a fork here," Noa said.

She lit the way forward with her flashlight. The tunnel split in two, and at that point the conveyor's metal strip came to an end. The entrances to both tunnels were similar, with the left one a bit higher. Noa illuminated the two entrances alternately, finally choosing the left one.

"No!" Professor Peretz said. "We have to go the other way."

Joel squeezed between the three of them from behind, stretching his head into the lit interior.

"Are you sure?" he said, pointing his headlamp at the left tunnel. "This looks like the main route."

"You ask if I'm sure?" Professor Peretz said. "Not the right person to ask. Sometimes I barely remember my own name. But I feel it, and for some reason I also feel that we're close."

"Close to what?" Joel said.

"Hmm, I don't know," the professor said. "Close to something."

They turned into the right-hand tunnel, and after a few steps realized that they were indeed close—to a small, empty room at the end of the tunnel. It was circular, its walls solid rock. The floor was made of concrete.

"End of the road," said Joel, disappointed.

"We need to check the other tunnel," Noa said.

Professor Peretz's face lit up with excitement. He touched the rock wall with both hands.

"Nothing has changed," he said.

"Because there's nothing here," Omer said.

Professor Peretz nodded as though in agreement, but the look on his face said otherwise.

"We need to check the other tunnel," Noa said.

"Right," Omer said.

"Shall we?"

"Who?

"You and me," Noa said, standing at the entrance to the room.

Oh, c'mon, why me? "Uh, maybe we shouldn't split up?"

"Let's go. It's probably short like this one," Noa said. "Come on already. We'll be back here in a minute."

"But don't go too far, OK?" Joel said. "If it's long we'll check it out together."

At first, the second tunnel was comfortable to walk through. But soon it became low, narrow, and rough. Further on, the two were walking on fallen dirt and rock gravel. It kept winding left and right with no discernible order, as though dug by a mole. Its walls kept closing in. Omer and Noa's hands and clothes were filled with dirt, their nostrils stuffed with suffocating dust.

Aargh, so stupid. Pointless risk. Would have been better to all go together. This looks like a dangerous cave. It could collapse at any moment. Trap us forever. Probably full of ticks. We could get cave fever. And bats? We should turn back. Just going deeper. She's never careful. We could fall into a deep hole. The way she fell before. And her leg with that iron thing.

They were forced to advance on their hands and knees. Omer stopped before the end of the tunnel. Noa advanced into a small niche.

"Man, this is so depressing!" she said, her voice filled with frustration, "there's nothing here either. So where did he bring this freaking collector from?"

Relief washed over Omer. He wasted no time turning back.

When they returned to the small room they found Joel and Professor Peretz crouched on their knees, closely examining the rock wall.

"What are you doing?" Noa said.

Joel pointed at a thin, almost invisible slit that cut across the rock.

"There seems to be something here," he said. "See, here underneath it is another one, and to the sides as well."

The lines created two laptop-sized squares in the wall. Noa and Omer knelt beside them as well.

"But what are we looking for?" Omer said.

Joel shrugged. "If we knew, we'd find it."

But Professor Peretz's excitement only grew. He backed away from the wall and approached it again. He backed away again, stood in the center of the room and looked all around, turning right back to the hidden squares. He began tapping them with the butt of a pen. His excitement infected the others. Omer and Joel re-examined one of the slits. When they reached the bottom corner of one of the squares Omer suddenly stopped. Something caught his attention: a thin, deep perforation in the rock.

"Wait, look," he said.

Joel illuminated the point Omer indicated. The other three heads crowded next to Omer's.

"Maybe we need to stick something in there," Noa said.

"Maybe the cartridge of the pen," Omer said.

Professor Peretz offered the pen. Joel took it apart and gave Omer the cartridge. Omer's hand, slightly shaking, inserted it all the way in. Only the metal tip remained outside the wall. Omer nudged it in with a fingernail.

At first nothing happened, but after a moment the squares began sliding out of the wall before their astonished eyes. Professor Peretz was beside himself. He walked around the room agitated, his palms entwined on his bald head.

"There it is, there, there," he said, and instantly froze where he stood and watched, fascinated.

At the center of the space that was revealed they saw a flat black device about four inches wide. The device stood on short metal legs. Delicate, purple-white light illuminated it. Dozens of fine wires were attached to the sides of the device. On the device, behind a plate of protective glass, was a cylinder of gleaming metal.

"The collector!" Professor Peretz said. He tapped the protective glass lightly with his fingernail. "Apparently this shouldn't be touched."

"Can you get an electric shock from it?" Noa said.

"No, I don't suppose so," Professor Peretz said. "There must be another reason." Suddenly, he stood up. "But the collector isn't the important thing here," he said in a troubled voice. "Hmm, no. I remember that there's something else, far more important here."

Professor Peretz backed away from the cubbyhole and began to pace the room, scanning the other walls with his flashlight. Noa and Joel were quick to join him.

Omer remained in front of the cubbyhole, staring with fascination at the device, the wires, the collector. He reached out and touched the protective glass, pulling it a little. The plate opened with a smooth slide.

I wonder if it's hot. Things that get charged get hot. Like a cell-phone battery. But that doesn't actually look hot. He put his finger close, trying to gauge the temperature. No heat radiated from the collector. *Doesn't look dangerous. A collector. I wonder why you shouldn't touch it.* He said it doesn't electrocute.

Omer tapped the collector with the tip of his fingernail. Then, he left only the nail touching it. After that, with the tip of his slow and cautious finger, he touched the collector.

In an instant, he lost all ability to move. A mild pain hit his fingertip, sharp and swift like an electrical spark, shocking him like a needle prick. He couldn't make a sound. A feeling like cold liquid flowed into his hand through the finger—like chilled quicksilver. The sensation flowed under the skin to the elbow, and from there to the shoulder and neck, seeping into his spinal cord, falling and thumping from vertebra to vertebra, flooding his abdominal cavity and chest.

Terrified, Omer felt his insides turn to stone, his body paralyzed, frozen, ending.

A slight pat on his head and shoulder detached him from the cubbyhole and knocked him on his side, motionless.

"Ouch, sorry," Noa said. She lowered her flashlight toward him and looked at him, amused. "Say, did you fall asleep or what?"

He had not regained his voice yet. *What was that?* His body felt as stiff and heavy as a stone. *It almost swallowed me.* "Uh, no. I just sat down."

Professor Peretz stopped his ambiguous search He drew near the cubbyhole. *Don't touch that,* Omer wanted to scream. But the professor just looked inside and backed away again. "We won't find it," he said with soft serenity. "We should get going."

"But what is it, anyway?" Joel said.

Professor Peretz pointed at the cubbyhole. "I have no idea, but it's deep inside there."

Chapter 11

Hadassa slammed the book shut with a sound resembling a gunshot. She jumped, half-expecting the attendants to rush in, Uzis drawn. But she only heard the echo of the sound fading in the wood-paneled reading room, mocking her reaction.

Hadassa had been shocked how Ari changed in his final days, claiming he'd visited the afterlife, telling her about an alternate, parallel universe. She and Ari were practical people, devoted to each other, their children and their families, and public service. Ari was a research scientist, after all, an oceanographer, who demanded proof in all things. They'd never been religious people, and it hurt Hadassa deeply to hear him speak of other worlds he claimed to have visited in his dreams near the end.

She couldn't explain this pain. She'd always been tolerant of others' beliefs, but this change in Ari seemed like a personal affront.

"Jerusalem Syndrome," Ari's doctor explained. "We live in the epicenter of the three great monotheistic religions. Sometimes people go a little... overboard."

Not my Ari, Hadassa wanted to reply.

But here they were, the same dreams, the same characters in the dreams, the same landscapes, a shared hallucination or delusion, whatever they want to call it.

And not just in Israel but all over the world, in all sorts of cultures. No matter where in the world, BCP patients reported the same otherworldly images and experiences.

The biologists, the doctors and the psychologists had all weighed in at the end, along with the anthropologists.

"It's in our genes, our DNA, the very makeup of the human being," they claimed, without providing much in the way of proof. "If only we had more funding..."

The clerics, priests, rabbis, ministers, swamis and imams had been kept out of the loop, fearing religious strife over the subject, but that hadn't kept the undercurrents from flowing, Hadassa knew, and great efforts had been made across the globe to underplay this aspect of the disease.

With the sleeve of her blouse (the attendants took her handkerchief), Hadassa dried her tears. The Body Cooling Phenomenon had been hard on everyone, not just the patients. She hoped Ari's delusions had been a comfort to him at the end, even as they caused her such grief. The pages indicated BCP victims were, in fact, exuberant about these dreamlike experiences, and anxious to relate them to others. Eventually, the illness spread and its sufferers seemed to prefer those other worlds, until they dropped into comas... *and then...*

Hadassa forced herself to think of something else.

"What about the other symptoms?" she said aloud, hoping her attendants weren't watching.

Hadassa dug back into the book. There it was.

Compulsions.

Chapter 12

Michael Lampston gripped his seat as the World Sales executive jet landed at a small airport in the Vladimirskaya Region, Russia, two hundred kilometers east of Moscow. Lampston looked out on green, rolling landscape as the jet circled slowly, then taxied back on the runway and finally came to a halt within a marked asphalt area.

A small helicopter, engines running, awaited them. From the front of the jet, the co-pilot appeared, opened the cabin door and folded out the staircase. A Russian security guard in a tailored suit appeared at the door and looked around. After approving the passengers, he waved at his colleague standing under the helicopter.

"Let's go, gentlemen," Gerryowen said, leading CEO Michael Lampston and his deputy, Ernest Cole-Angel, off the plane.

At the top of the stairs, Lampston surveyed the entourage awaiting them on the ground. Drug operation was all he could think of, with the security, the vehicles, and the chopper. *And warmer than expected.* Lampston smiled. *This is just Russia, not Siberia. Beautiful, actually.* Someday, he would bring the twins here.

Sergei Barilov, Manager of Site 2, stepped up, shook hands and led the visitors to the chopper. Again, an uneasiness settled in Lampston's gut about all of them aboard the same aircraft, but he also knew it would be an insult to his hosts to imply the helicopter was somehow unsafe.

"This is where I leave you," Dan Gerryowen said at the last moment, nodding toward an awaiting limousine instead of getting on the chopper.

Both Lampston and Cole-Angel were taken aback by this sudden change of plans.

"You're not coming?" Cole-Angel said.

"The science mumbo-jumbo's not my thing, I'm afraid," Gerryowen said. "Bores me to tears, and I have some business to attend to."

If Gerryowen had rigged the helicopter to crash or explode, he sure was being cool about it. Wow, I'm paranoid today.

"Right," Lampston said. "We'll catch you later."

The hatch closed with a deadly finality. Lampston checked his seatbelt and tried to steady his breath.

After twenty uneventful minutes in the air, the pilot lowered the craft, and at Barilov's request circled three barren rocky hilltops. A narrow dirt path could be seen snaking up one of the hills. Two-thirds of the way up the hill stood a few parked cars and mining trucks. Sunlight flitted in reflection off the windows of the stationary vehicles. On the adjacent hilltop, a man in day-glo overalls motioned with both hands, conveying landing instructions. A car approached the landing spot.

Sergei Barilov, carrying a slim, metal briefcase, accompanied by an armed guard, descended the chopper first. Michael Lampston and Ernest Cole-Angel followed. Upon noticing the approaching car, Cole-Angel removed an unlit cigar from his mouth:

"How about we walk? I feel like stretching my legs."

"Not a bad idea," Lampston said.

"Nu, then I'll join you," Barilov said.

The group started to walk. Cole-Angel lagged behind to light his cigar.

The hill they climbed was surrounded by rolls of barbed wire. A smiling, unarmed guard stood beside a small hut at the foot of the site. He saluted and opened the gate.

"This guard is just to keep the curious outside, of course," Barilov said. "Up ahead there are armed guards."

A young man wearing a yellow protective helmet descended towards them.

"Our geo-technical engineer," Barilov said. "He is in charge of all our digging and drilling here."

The engineer shook their hands and apologized. "We can't go in yet. We're about to have a little detonation."

Chapter 13

Omer was different that evening—quieter, withdrawn. He answered his parents' questions with brief sentences, and went up to his room early. He sat on the edge of the bed and recalled his finger lifting the glass cover and touching the collector. He recounted the painful flash and the frozen liquid sensation that seeped into him. The fear still infected his limbs, giving him chills. When he finally went to bed he lay for a long while on his back with his eyes open. He tried not to fall asleep, and once he did, his sleep was fitful. He tossed and turned, moving from side to side, muttering meaningless word fragments.

Early in the morning, he had a bad cooling attack. He shook all over between waking and hallucination, feeling the paralysis spread through his limbs, weakening them, preventing him from getting up or calling for help. Like an insect paralyzed by poison, he lay frozen, staring at the ceiling in terror. There they were, a pair of long, yellow eyes, a black dot in the center of each. They approached him, surrounding him, threatening. They came so close that Omer stopped breathing from fright, and only a powerful internal scream saved him, woke him up, left him panting rapidly, appalled.

He wouldn't think about it. It couldn't be. Not BCP, the disease that had ravaged so many. He was imagining this. *A touch of hysteria. It will go away.* He was always thinking he was sick when he wasn't. *Isn't that what Mom always says?* Breathing back to normal, muscles sore but functioning, Omer went back to sleep.

He got up early, dressed and prepared himself. It had been agreed that Joel would pick him and Noa up at seven-thirty. At precisely that time, the old car stopped by the curb. Omer climbed into the back seat, said hello and good morning and fell silent, thinking only of the cooling attack and the terrible nightmare.

He looked out the window at the bright sun, which caused a glow to spread throughout his being—he always preferred heat to cold.

Hot day, cold night, that's all it is.

Noa's hair in the front seat blew in the wind from the open window. Her fingers kept gathering it. Omer looked at the thin fingers and mused about the pinky motion straightening the glasses on her nose. He thought about her freckles and pretty teeth. He remembered how she laughed the day before when they rode their bicycles. He was no longer afraid to look at her. A quick rush of joy ran through his chest.

* * *

Professor Peretz opened the door to his home and welcomed them. "Hello, hello, good morning. Please ignore the mess."

The living-room floor was strewn with dozens of books, notebooks, photo albums and documents. Professor Peretz led them, stepping carefully, to the couch and chairs.

"Our little expedition yesterday left me wired," he said. "I looked for material about that period. All night long I've been rummaging through these papers, but I couldn't find anything. Not about the collectors or about the tunnel. Not even about the symbol. At the time, they kept anything that had to do with the breakdown away from me, to make it easier for me."

"There must be a way to find out where the material is," Joel said. "You'll have to talk to whoever treated you."

Professor Peretz leaned back in his armchair and folded his arms over his chest, his face suddenly serious.

"I'm not sure it will be so simple," he said. "It was this one doctor who saved me, who managed to shed light on the darkness I was trapped in. An amazing man. And at one point he suggested that anything that had to do with the research be kept away from me. Eventually, Marta and I decided to take his advice, and that was the smartest thing we did. Only then did my recovery begin."

He fell silent for a moment. "All I know is that this physician came especially from abroad to treat me. And that he was brought by a student of mine who made a great effort to care for me. And yet look how my mind reacted—I don't remember a single detail about any of them. As though all the data was deleted."

Professor Peretz rose, picked up an old photo album from the table, and leafed through it. "Sometimes I'm positive that Marta left me clues. Here, this for instance." He placed his finger on an old photo, showing himself, much younger, beside a young woman and a child playing a wooden recorder. Written on the photo were the short lines of a poem in a stiff, square hand.

Professor Peretz suddenly got up, walked to a nearby cabinet, rummaged in its drawers for a moment, and returned with the same old wooden recorder as in the photo. He pointed his finger at the words of the poem and began to read aloud.

"The sound of the wailing wood is muffled
but its mind is clearly heard
along with a tune it holds
one and another word.
Can we go back?
Word by word, part by part
from the ending bravely
back to the start."

"A clue," Joel admitted, "if that's what it is."

Professor Peretz shrugged. His lips curled into a smile when Joel examined the inside of the recorder against the light.

"Nothing," Joel said.

"'Wailing wood,'" Noa said, "what a great name for a recorder."

Omer, who had kept quiet until then, searched his alert mind. *Wailing wood. No, it is not a recorder...* A vague memory kept eluding him. His thoughts accelerated. An old book surfaced in his memory, and a mischievous boy. He now tried to simultaneously remember a name and a musical instrument. It took him another millisecond or two:

"The wailing wood is a violin," he said. "It's from a book about a boy, Pete Bell. That's how he used to call his violin, mocking it."

"A violin," said Professor Peretz. "Hmm, that makes sense..."

"Great!" Joel said. "I see progress. Where is it?"

"Where's what?" the professor said.

"The violin, of course."

Professor Peretz shrugged. "We never had a violin."

"Wait, so why, then..."

"Too bad. There goes the clue..." Professor Peretz said, his gaze stuck on the joint between the wall and the ceiling. He scratched his head. "A violin... Hmm, I think Willy, Marta's brother, had a violin..."

* * *

Willy, a pleasant man of average build, in his early seventies, living only a few kilometers from Professor Peretz, handed the musical instrument to Noa, then stood on his tiptoes, stretched up, and removed the bow from two nails sticking out of the wall.

Noa blew at the dusty violin, took the bow and passed it over the four strings, producing a dramatic sound.

"Och, it sounds terrible," Willy said. "Totally out of tune."

"Sounds more like furniture being dragged," Joel said.

Each of them examined the violin in turn—shaking it, tapping on it, trying to peek through the slits in the sound box.

"Why are we looking for a note in the violin, actually?" Noa said.

"'Along with tune it holds one and another word,'" Joel said, recalling the poem.

"I know, but maybe it's something else."

"Hmm, we're looking for something, not necessarily a note in a violin," Professor Peretz said.

"'Along with a tune it holds...'" Joel said, "'one and another word.'"

"A music book..." Noa said. "A music sheet has tunes and words as well."

"That's right," Joel said. "A music sheet. Where does that lead us?"

"It leads us to the attic," Willy said. "Hold on a moment. I'll go look."

Upon his return, he brought a rigid and dusty violin case. The interior was covered with blue velvet. Inside, the empty space lay a disintegrating music book. Underneath it was a large yellow-brown envelope.

"Here," Willy said to Professor Peretz, "I think this belongs to you."

★ ★ ★

"Sinking into the Great Spirit,
A diamond to the bottom of the sea shall be gathered.
What is a life?
A man's soul, dew drop on a leaf's tip
What is death?
A gust of wind."

Professor Peretz paused for a moment before continuing to read from the paper he held.

"What is knowledge?
A man's soul, thick as blood, falls away.

What is eternity?
It hits the lake, pales, fades, stays
Forever."

He fell silent and kept gazing at the sheaf of pages—plain lined pages, packed with rounded, pretty letters. He raised his eyes, and for a long moment remained with his gaze fixed on an indeterminate point in space.

"After death," Professor Peretz said, "the soul of a human being sinks and connects with the Great Spirit, the common soul of all people."

They were seated in the tiny garden of Willy's home around a metal and glass table, where the brown envelope, now empty, laid. A strange object shaped like an octopus laid next to it; a box-like center from which extended seven short rubber arms with suction cups for hands.

"I should probably see what else Marta stuck up there I don't know about," Willy said, coming out of the house with another one of the strange, aquatic-looking gizmos. He placed it on the table alongside the first one and then produced a thick notebook with a worn, hard cover which read: "Travel book—Mexico." Professor Peretz took the book in hand with a wide, joyful smile spread across his lips.

"For each journey I prepared a book like this," he said. His hand passed over the cardboard cover, caressing it. He leafed through the first pages and exhaled with amusement.

"Preparation stage: schedules, coordination, climate data, gear preparation, final consultation. Pulling strings for the permits."

"What kind of expedition was it anyway?" Omer said.

"Hmm, completely half-baked and amateurish," professor Peretz said. "Two years prior we dug in the same area and found the remains of a settlement. That's why we decided to go back there. We were just a few people: my friend Shimesa, who's a physicist and a dabbler in archaeology, his brother, a photographer, myself, and a couple of local escorts."

Professor Peretz brought the book to his nose, closed his eyes, and took a deep breath.

"It's amazing," he said. "I don't need to read. It's enough for me to smell these pages and I remember. The smell is like the wind, the wind blowing the tarp off my hidden memory."

He opened his eyes and turned a page, and another.

"'Finally we're on the plane. Landed in Mexico. Bad start. Shimesa broke a leg going down the plane ramp, and insists we go on without him. Then bad luck struck again. His brother Hiroshi was bitten by a stray dog.'" Peretz looked up from the book, memories flooding back. "Which meant that now I was stuck, with all the equipment, neither here nor there. At first I thought to return home, but I went on. I got to the site and began to dig, and then everything changed."

"You found the symbol?" Joel said.

"The symbol was the first thing we found, engraved on a stone slab. After that, I found more slabs. Nineteen slabs." Professor Peretz tilted the notebook towards the others, his finger marking one of the pages.

It showed a partial drawing of the symbol—spiral lines surrounded by strange letters.

"It totally amazed me," Professor Peretz went on. "Here, look what I wrote about the symbol. 'Something here doesn't make sense, either the stone or myself. Letters in ancient Arabic, Chinese, ancient Hebrew, Sanskrit, hieroglyphics. Totally unlikely.'"

"Amazing," Joel said.

"But it's not just the single letters found in the symbol," Professor Peretz, his excitement growing. "We could somehow regard them as a miraculous coincidence. But when the slabs were dug up, the situation turned crazy: there were entire lines on them, entire sentences composed of letters in different languages! On stone slabs thousands of years old. There could be no logical explanation for it."

"Unless they weren't a thousand years old," Joel said.

A flash of anger passed over Professor Peretz's face. "A hoax?"

"It makes sense—"

"Impossible!"

Joel said nothing. Neither did Omer, though he had some ideas of his own. He'd read about the possibility of aliens visiting the Earth through the ages, building the pyramids in Egypt, settling in North and South America—

Keep your mouth shut. She'll think you're crazy.

"I'm sorry," Professor Peretz said, then fell silent, sweating. "It bubbles up and floods my mind. I recall how amazed I was."

A slight breeze ruffled the pages. Joel laid his hand on them, drew them nearer and read the lines once again.

"Sinking into the Great Spirit,
A diamond to the bottom of the sea shall be gathered.
What is a life?
A man's soul, dew drop on a leaf's tip
What is death?
A gust of wind.
What is knowledge?
A man's soul, thick as blood, falls away.
What is eternity?
It hits the lake, pales, fades, stays
Forever."

Willy finally broke his silence. "You can actually see the diamond sink, glittering like that all the way to the bottom."

Professor Peretz nodded. "The sinking of souls into the Great Spirit is described in other parts of the slabs as well. Sometimes as a sinking through veins in the ground. Some kind of flow in which the human soul merges with the Great Spirit. Becomes part of it. What is eternity? The drop hits the lake, dissolves and becomes part of it. The soul of the dead person joins the pan-human spirit."

The idea of the flow, the Great Spirit, astounded Omer. He envisioned transparent bodies, devoid of specific shape, passing at dizzying speed through crevices in the ground, landing inside a large subterranean space, vanishing in it. But something didn't seem right.

"But wait," he said, "if the soul dissolves into this general spirit, then it doesn't survive for itself, right? I mean it doesn't exist anymore. So when someone dies, his spirit won't... be there forever? It will, I don't know, just melt into this humungous human spirit and...that's all? Nothing stays?"

"Does that disappoint you?" Professor Peretz said.

Omer thought about the matter.

"I find it odd that nothing remains. As though something exists, and a moment later it suddenly doesn't. Just like that."

Professor Peretz laid a hand on the notebook. "And not just something, but the most important thing of all... our soul, our thoughts, feelings, awareness... Life is the source of the Spirit's existence. That's how they saw it. Life is the source of the Spirit's energy. When one ceases to be, the other must also end. And they also believed that a human's spirit is not contained within the body but rather engulfing it, radiating outside of the body, creating a sort of aura around it. Our thoughts and emotions, they believed, look like beams of light bursting through holes. And these beams go on and pass through other auras, meeting thoughts and emotions of other people, combining with them to create something large and shared that we are not aware of. And to which we are always connected... the Great Spirit."

"Connected to the Great Spirit..." Omer said.

Noa wasn't convinced. "I'm trying to imagine my thoughts bursting out of me, but... my thoughts are inside me, aren't they? Inside my head?"

Joel pulled at his goatee, dubious of his own words. "Maybe it's like an electro-magnetic field around an electric engine. We can't see it but we know it's there."

"If the Great Spirit is the intersection of the thoughts and feelings of all people, then it actually contains all human knowledge, doesn't it?" professor Peretz said.

"Huh?"

"Say you encounter a problem you can't solve," the professor said, "and when you 'sleep on it' as they say, the mind solves it on its own. You'll wake up and have the answer. So maybe during that time we get ideas from the Great Spirit?"

Joel didn't look convinced. He looked at Noa and Omer, who weren't taking sides.

"That's in fact what the Indian shamans do, isn't it?" Professor Peretz said, to all of them now. "They take hallucinogenic drugs and go into a trance, and imagine that they're floating in the sky like an eagle. And they see things that are far away and understand things that others don't. They manage to enter into this Great Spirit, the shared unconscious."

"Well," Joel said. "That is in fact how they explain the experience. As floating in the Great Spirit."

"Exactly," Peretz said.

"I have to think about it some more," Joel said.

"I'm not sure thinking is going to help you much here," Professor Peretz said, a wry smile spreading on his face.

"Yes, I suppose so," Joel said. "Some faith is required here too. It's a completely different concept of reality."

"The line between reality and imagination sometime derives from the culture you live in," Professor Peretz said.

Joel smiled. "The old Indian shamans probably would regard our reality as pretty flat."

They fell into deep silence, eventually disturbed by a short and charged sentence. "There was something else buried there too."

Curious eyes hung on Professor Peretz. His gaze sharpened as he looked at them, bravery reflecting in his eyes. "Archaeological theft is a despicable thing. You need to be cynical, and arrogant, unbearably so in order to..." for a moment he fell silent. "Underneath the last slab we dug up I found a small stone box. No one was around me when I found it. In it were four rectangular stones. Nearly translucent. Milky. I couldn't resist them."

Professor Peretz fell silent again. He took the travel book in two hands and leafed to the end. Then he laid it back and shrugged. "From here on, I truly have no idea what happened.

My memory only extends to the last pages of this book. Then the blue tarp covers my memories again."

The silence lengthened. The thoughts seemed to condense and swell. It was Willy who finally broke it. "Finally we learn the origin of the stones," he said with checked excitement.

Professor Peretz looked at him, astonished. "You saw them? You saw the stones?"

Willy nodded. "I only saw one, and only once." His gaze met Professor Peretz's eyes. "The Stone of Three Transparencies, that's what you called it. The Stone of Three Transparencies."

"Three Transparencies..." the professor said.

Willy narrowed his eyes, and a shiver shook him. He extended his hands for them to see. "Look at this! I have goosebumps just from the memory!"

"What was it?" professor Peretz asked, horrified. "Was it so terrible?"

"It wasn't terrible," Willy said. "It was strange, wonderful. And this feeling that the stone... It was so weird that it's hard for me to remember exactly what happened. And entirely impossible to forget." He looked at Professor Peretz with a fond smile. "After that, you no longer asked me to join you at research sites."

"Apparently, I suddenly had something to hide," said Professor Peretz, embarrassed. "Do you remember what the research subject was?"

Willy shrugged. "I have no idea. But I do remember that on that day we went down the tunnel that I helped you clear and reinforce. You, me, and two other students of yours went down with some sort of a radiation detecting device. It was about two years after the trip to Mexico. Anyway, that device drove you all crazy that day. It kept beeping occasionally for no reason. We took it to the end of the burrow, came back up, went down again, but nothing changed. Once in a while, it would make a rumbling sound, or a beep, for no apparent reason."

Willy fell silent for a moment. The gleam in his eyes revealed his excitement. "At a certain point, you said that maybe there's a vein in the rock. You took the Transparencies Stone from your pocket and said you wanted to try something ridiculous. I remember those words clearly—'to try something ridiculous.' There was a large crack in the wall. You asked us to turn the flashlights off, and put the Transparencies Stone in the crack. And then it happened. There was a sensation like a shock wave, and a noise. Now, this will sound crazy but listen carefully—when you put the stone in the crack it glowed, but it glowed with an invisible light!"

Chapter 14

Dr. Lester Pok, the resigning World Sales Corporation executive, sat motionless at his desk in the den that he called his house. His eyes were closed, his hands covering his face. Eventually, he opened his eyes and looked at the yellow folder before him.

Dr. Pok closed his eyes again. A short and strange sound escaped his throat, a gasp of rage and pain. He rose from his chair, his body heavy with gloom. His well-groomed, athletic build did not show his seventy years of age, but now his gait was hunched. He staggered to the window and looked out at the darkness of the lake on a gently lit night in this wealthy suburb north of Copenhagen.

Restless, he turned his back on the window and fixed his gaze at the framed MD diploma. He walked away from the wall to the file cabinet and searched, his fingers moving in a frantic hunt for something. Suddenly, he stopped, forcing himself to calm down. Once he regained control, he found the folder almost instantly.

Dozens of letters of thanks and appreciation were inside. The doctor began reading them, then slammed the folder closed. He returned it to its place in revulsion, turned back to the desk and sat down. He put his face in his hands again and closed his eyes for a long while.

The creaking of the wooden stairs caused him to sit up straight and put on a calm expression. He hid the yellow folder under a blank piece of paper. His lips curved at the sight of his wife's worried face. Her eyes met his for a long moment. Her voice was warm and sympathetic.

"What's wrong, Lester?" she said with soft directness. "You've been suffering from something for a long time now. Tell me. Maybe I can help."

His hand moved in a dismissive way. "I'm not suffering from anything,"

"No, please, tell me," she said. "Do you regret quitting the job? You know they'll be glad—"

"I don't regret anything!"

They fell into a long silence; their eyes argued. The mask of calm evaporated from the doctor's face. Wet honesty rose slowly in his eyes. His voice turned hoarse. "A few years ago... I made... a huge mistake. A terrible mistake. Unbelievable. Now I'm trying to cope..."

He fell silent and lowered his gaze. A warm hand laid on the back of his head stroked his neck. He raised his eyes to look at his wife's face. He read the surprise in her eyes, and the question.

"I'll finish... a few things here and come down, OK?" he said.

The doctor's wife turned, left the room and closed the door behind her, reluctance reflecting in her movements.

Alone again, Dr. Pok sunk back into murky thoughts. He forced himself out of the chair. He retrieved the yellow folder, turned to the shredding machine and stood next to it, weak and empty. He opened the folder and took out the first page.

"Patient name: (Prof.) Y. Peretz."

Dr. Pok's hand shook as he lowered the page to the waiting shredder. The machine awoke to life, recognizing its prey. The decisive hand lowered. Dr. Pok's fingers felt the thrust of the blades at the edge of the paper.

"I wish you could forgive me, Professor Peretz," he said in a quiet, shaken voice.

The page caught, pulled into the shredder with surprising force. Frightened and confused, Dr. Pok tried to hold on to it, but had to let go. He looked at the page being swallowed in absolute wonder. Sharp pulses of pain echoed in his head. He took another page from the folder. His hand released the page, and it was caught, sucked in with a revolting noise of finality.

A large tear stained the third page.

Chapter 15

At his apartment, Professor Peretz put the black rubber apparatus on his head, trembling with excitement.

"It looks like you're wearing an octopus," Omer said.

A joyful smile rounded Professor Peretz's eyes, like the eyes of a child at the sight of a present. "No, not an octopus—a floater. We called these things floaters. You attach it to your head." His finger felt the buttons at the bottom of the rubber bands. He pushed and attached one to his forehead. "It sticks with a special gel."

"What's it for?" Noa said.

"Actually nothing, as it turned out," Professor Peretz said, "but they were supposed to enable one to float in the Great Spirit."

"What? Like the Indian shamans?" Omer said, astonished. He took the other floater from the table. "No way! I gotta try it!"

Joel dampened his enthusiasm. "I don't think you'll be taking off so fast."

"But what does it mean?" Noa said. "What is 'floating?'"

Professor Peretz removed the multi-pronged device from his head. "Mental flotation in the Great Spirit. But Joel is right. I don't remember us ever succeeding at it."

"Well, how's it supposed to work?" Omer said.

"When you bring the Three Transparencies Stone close to the vein, it glows in an invisible light," Professor Peretz said "In the stone tablets this light was called 'The Radiance of the Spirits.' It said that with the help of this light it is possible to float in the Great Spirit."

"We gotta check it out!" Omer said. his excitement growing.

Noa shrugged. "How exactly? We don't have the Three Transparencies Stone."

Professor Peretz's eyes took on a mysterious expression. The hint of a smile rose to his lips. "It's true we don't have them here, but I'm pretty sure I know where one of them is."

His words electrified the room. Noa, Omer and Joel leaned closer.

"In the tunnel, near the collector!" Noa said. "That's what you were looking for!"

Professor Peretz nodded. "There's a vein that goes through there, and they must have placed a Three Transparencies Stone nearby."

"To radiate the 'Radiance of the Spirits,'" Joel said, skepticism strong in his voice.

"To be collected in the collector?" Omer said.

"Which nobody can see," Joel said.

"That's the idea," Professor Peretz said, ignoring Joel's tone of voice.

"OK... and where do the floaters kick in?" Joel said.

Professor Peretz was careful with his words. "A floater can supposedly use the unseen shine, the invisible radiance, to enable one to float. And if I remember correctly, the connections for all the devices are identical."

"Then we can try to connect the floater and float!" Noa said.

"We'll need contact gel—"

"Can you get that?" Noa said, turning to Joel.

Joel nodded. "It'll take me a half-hour—"

"Then we move at five o'clock!" Noa said.

★ ★ ★

"Three, two, one, press!"

The cold-storage door detached from the wall. The four of them operated with the efficiency of a medical team—the secret code for the green door was punched in, the finger was placed for identification, the warning for the first deep step was whispered. Noa, Professor Peretz and Omer skipped inside, turning their flashlights on. Joel closed the doors behind them.

"Last man reporting," he said.

"Ready to move," Omer said

"So move," Noa said, laughing as she descended.

Moments later, Omer's mind filled with worry.

I wonder if there are toxic gasses here. People die in mines because of that. They used to keep birds. Canaries. Their heartbeat is fast so the gas reaches the brain quickly. They pass out before it hits people. Poor birds, actually. Today they have equipment to monitor.

"The fork!" Noa said from up ahead. Without hesitation, she turned into the right-hand tunnel.

Professor Peretz stopped for a moment in front of the left-hand tunnel, shining a light into it, then turned to follow Noa.

Forks are dangerous too. Confusion in caves. You hear of cases. Although, here it's not so complicated. Right, down, right, down. Like circling a square column. And there are no animals here. Maybe scorpions, at most. Maybe rats, too. Although, then you can have snakes as well. And then weasels. Smart animals. Can be dangerous under certain circumstances. Rabies? Teeth as sharp as knives...

"Aouuuuuuuuu!"

The horrible howl came from the depths of the tunnel, cruel and bloodcurdling. It felt like sharp fingernails stuck into Omer's body, heart and spine. He froze where he stood but did not shout. Even if he'd wanted to, he couldn't.

"Are you out of your mind?" Joel said to Noa, and resumed walking.

"I once read that wolf howls don't have an echo," Noa said, and released another wicked howl.

"A myth!" Joel said from the back.

"We're here!" Noa said.

They located the opening slit by the light of Professor Peretz's flashlight. Omer inserted a pen refill into it and pushed with the tip of a fingernail, careful not to touch anything else. The hidden aperture opened, exposing the square device upon which the collector was mounted.

Four heads squeezed into the small opening.

"Where do you think they stuck the Transparencies Stone?" Joel said.

"Deeper inside the rock," Professor Peretz said. "It's far too important to leave in such an accessible place."

"Accessible?" Noa said. "We passed two secret doors to get to it."

Professor Peretz smiled. "But we got here nonetheless, didn't we? And quite easily at that. They left the collector outside so it would be easy for them to get to, but the Three Transparencies Stone they set within the rock, as close as possible to the vein. And between them they set connecting pipes."

He bent over and pointed at the bottom of the device bearing the collector.

"You see? Connected through the bottom?"

"Yes, three pipes," Joel said. "Two thick ones and a thin one."

"The thin one is ours, I think," Professor Peretz said. "Detach it from the collector gently, and then carefully pull it out. And be very careful not to touch the collector. It could be dangerous."

I'll say! Omer remembered his recent paralysis.

Joel placed his cheek on the edge of the cubbyhole and slipped his fingers underneath the collector. "OK, should I detach it?"

"Go ahead."

"Done."

★ ★ ★

In the control room of Site 1, an orange warning flashed on a computer screen, accompanied by a warning beep. The message on the monitor said "faulty reception." The technician on call in the control room clicked the "event response" button, his reaction swift. The protocol window displayed possible causes—detached contacts, loose contacts, malfunction of the sensors, contact of a foreign object with the diamond.

The technician spoke into her intercom. "Diamond Merchant, this is Switchboard."

"Switchboard, this is Diamond Merchant."

"Switchboard here, I have a warning that occurred twenty-two seconds ago."

"Color?"

"Orange. Probably a loose contact."

"OK. I'll be there immediately. Have two wait for me at the entrance."

* * *

In the fingers of one hand Professor Peretz held the end of a pipe, while the other held a floater, the complex octopus-like apparatus. He meant to connect the pipe with the floater, but hesitated for a moment.

"Oof, I'm a little excited," he said.

Noa chuckled, her voice turning into a whisper. "We can tell."

Professor Peretz turned decisively—he brought the pipe to the center of the floater, to the small box where the arms came out. With a quick motion he stuck the end of the pipe into a matching aperture in the box.

"Hey, did you see? It moved!" Omer said.

"What moved?"

"The ends of the arms, the moment you put the pipe in," Joel said. "Didn't you see?"

"Hmm, I didn't notice," Professor Peretz said. "That's probably because of the organic matter inside the pipe. It was found back then that only organic matter is able to conduct the invisible light."

It's reacting! God help us. Organic. Half alive. Crazy scientists. Willing to take such risks. If it reacts, who knows? It could get angry, lock onto your head like a vice. But he says he's already done it. Maybe that's what caused his—

"All ready!"

Professor Peretz sat on the floor with his back against the wall. He placed the floater on his head. One by one, he attached the buttons with the contact gel.

Beams of anxiety floated through Omer. "Are you feeling anything yet?"

"Maybe you need to turn it on?" Noa said.

Professor Peretz closed his eyes. "No, now I just need to concentrate. Concentrate really well."

Heavy silence flooded the room. *Silence of the bowels of the earth.* The smile vanished from the professor's lips. His expression turned calm, his breathing a slow, heavy hiss.

The sharp pinky motion and then the clenching of his hand into a fist indicated the end of the professor's calm. His breathing came in great gasps. His closed eyelids, trembling.

Joel's panic was overwhelming. So was Noa and Omer's excitement.

"He's floating!" Omer said, trembling himself, his voice nothing more than a whisper.

"Shhhh!" Noa shushed, laying a quick hand on Omer's mouth.

The motion behind the eyelids of professor Peretz ceased, his breathing relaxed. The clenched fist gradually opened. A smile tugged at the professor's lips. He opened his eyes and whispered. "No, I didn't float yet, but the truth is—"

"Man, Omer!" Noa said. "You're such a doofus. You just interrupted him."

"No, no," Professor Peretz said, "the thing is—"

"What do you want?" Omer said. "How could I know he could hear me?"

"Wait! Hold on a second!" Professor Peretz said. "I just remembered that we can't float at all!"

"Hah!" Joel said.

"Can't float at all?" Omer said, surprised and disappointed.

Professor Peretz took the floater off his head, careful not to damage it. "I remembered that this was exactly the problem we ran into back then. All I can see are white flashes. As though almost... as though there's not enough energy to float."

One after another they sat next to Professor Peretz, backs against the rock wall.

"Too bad," Joel said, lament obvious in his tone.

"Couldn't we get more energy?" Omer said.

Professor Peretz shrugged. "At the time, I developed at least ten floaters to overcome this problem. These two are admittedly some of the older ones, but the other ones didn't work either. We reached the conclusion back then that the fault wasn't in the floater, but in the lack of energy. The Three Transparencies apparently don't glow enough here. Not enough to allow an adult to float."

"And if it isn't an adult?" Noa said.

"If it's not an adult..." Professor Peretz said. "Hmm, there might be a better chance—"

Excitement gleamed in Noa's eyes. "Then it's my turn now! I'm floating now!"

She grabbed the floater and raised it before her eyes. "Do I need to think of anything special in order to float?"

"Hmm, it's best not to think of anything, like in meditation," Professor Peretz said. "But I think, uh, it will be a bit of a problem for you, won't it?"

Noa's face grew serious, her voice sharp. "Why?"

"Because of all this redness," Professor Peretz pointed at her head.

Noa wished she could pretend she didn't understand, though she understood perfectly. She stomped on the concrete floor. "Oof, that's awful! Can't we do anything? Put loads of gel on so it'll pass through my hair?"

Joel's teasing voice pinched her nerves. "For you we'd need a whole bucket of gel!"

"Very funny. This is so annoying. And now he lucks out because of his stupid shaved head!"

"He" was busy looking at her up to that moment: at her ginger hair, her dusty hands, at the blue eyes that suddenly fastened on him without mercy. Omer grew terrified. *Me? What?! No way. No floater and no nothing. It moves! Organic. What am I, crazy? That's what drove him mad. Not for me thanks. They make me laugh. If she wants she can volunteer herself, but*

enough is enough. She can forget about it. She really makes me laugh.

"OK, come on."

Her voice enveloped him like a lead blanket. The battle was lost. His palm felt her warm fingers. She walked him over as though leading him to the gallows. Her hand pressed down on his shoulder.

Omer sat down, with his back to the wall, next to the floater.

* * *

The security vehicle thundered at full speed from the paved road to the dirt path, down to the dry riverbed where it slowed. Once it began climbing back up, it accelerated again. It crossed the rocky dirt road with ease, raising brown dust clouds on all sides. It turned onto the gravel road and kept going faster. Only a short distance from the gate did it begin to brake, stopping in a huge cloud of light-colored dust. Before coming to a full stop an armed security guard, dressed in gray, jumped out of the car. He rushed to the gate, key in hand, and opened it wide to let the car through, then caught up with the vehicle and jumped in without closing the gate. The security vehicle sped towards the warehouse.

* * *

"He reminds me of one of those poor lab monkeys from the animal cruelty ads," Noa said with relish. "With all these wires coming out of his head and the depressed look on his face."

The curve of Omer's lips was sour. Noa stuck on the last attachment button.

"You sure about this, Omer?" Joel said.

Omer nodded, his face wearing the heaviness of a condemned prisoner.

"Of course he is," Noa said. "Close your eyes and focus."

His hesitation grew, but so did Noa's impatience. "Come on, close your eyes already!"

With a heavy heart and great reluctance, Omer closed his eyes.

For a moment, he still noticed the glare of the flashlights through his eyelids, but then a slight dizziness overcame him, and he was wrapped in darkness. It was not a darkness of black, but one with tiny shards of color throughout it. A whisper reached his ears, and a suppressed cough. A body knelt next to him—close, and yet far away. And again he felt dizzy.

Am I still sitting on the floor? Feels like on a boat. What a strange darkness. Like when you rub your eyes. Lots of babbling. What are those knocking sounds? Like drops. Glass maybe. But quiet. Is he calling me? Sounds really far. This is so much fun. Not scary at all. But what... what's that down there? Amazing, looks like a sea. Yes, it's a sea. I'm high above the sea. An ocean. Ha! I can even see the glints of sunlight. I'm right above the sea. And there are no clouds. It goes on forever. Am I getting closer to it? Seems like it. Now she's calling me. Can I get close to the sea? Gotta check it out. Learn how to control it. He's calling me again. To open my eyes. Pity, it's so beautiful here. But they're worried about me, that's not nice. But, how, actually? How to open? Strange, but I feel so far away. My body is deep inside the earth and I'm so high above an ocean. In order to open my eyes I need to find them. Need to find my arms and legs. How do I go back? He's calling me again. Sounds worried. I hear it. I'm here and my ears are in the tunnel. How do I go back? Got to get away from the sea. Get away from the sea. Ha, I'm getting away. Just have to think about it, and it happens. Can hardly see the sea. Whose voice is that? Sounds close. yaam. Do I hear something? It's all black. Pitch darkness. Am I back? Am I underground? Open my eyes. But I can't feel. Ha, I feel them. Open! Ah, there's Noa. And Professor Peretz, holding my hand. I can't feel it yet. Joel's knees. Ha, smiling, laughing, clapping.

Chapter 16

With eager fascination, Hadassa worked her way through the findings in the "Compulsion" section of the huge BCP tome. The strangest symptom of the disease, mocked by late-night comedians and politicians alike, was the rampant consumerism of the victims. The need for "things," from juice-machines to luxury cars, seemed to overwhelm the poor unfortunates at the worst time, when they were forced to their beds and no longer able to make a living.

Ari had been the same way, ordering gizmos, knives, kitchen utensils and nifty inventions from the TV, until Hadassa took his credit card, and eventually the phone, from him. After he was gone, she'd taken the stuff to the local charity shop, only to be turned away—they were overwhelmed with the same things from others.

To Hadassa's shock, here was the list in cold black and white—brands, models and prices. The Body Cooling Phenomenon compulsion to buy was not as random as everyone believed.

* * *

The blasts shook the air and earth around Site 2. The mouth of a wide tunnel ahead of Lampston and the others emitted a thick cloud of dust.

"What are you blasting?" Michael Lampston said.

"A path for vehicles," the engineer said. "A horizontal tunnel."

"The service car will enter right up to the pedestrian tunnel," Barilov said. "Right up to the conveyor belt of the collector."

"Nice, great idea," Cole-Angel said. "How far to Moscow?"

"Ah, currently about three-and-a-half hours drive, but we're working on some problematic sections along the road, and I estimate we'll bring it down to two hours."

"Two hours is reasonable," Lampston said. "Not too close, not too far. And the teams are all ready?"

"Of course," Barilov said. "Three security teams and two diamond cutters. We trained the diamond cutters exactly as instructed. We have also begun setting up temporary production studios around the city. I estimate they will be operating in less than two months. Concurrently, we will begin constructing the permanent studios."

When the smoke cleared, they entered a pedestrian tunnel—a squared spiral downward—right, down again and right again—as though descending around a square chimney. The floor was free of dirt and paved in concrete. A few hallways branched off to the side, all blocked by warning tape.

They finally came to a halt in front of a semi-sheer plastic sheet, with a zipper closing it up the middle. Fuzzy, white-dressed figures could be seen through it on the other side. Barilov addressed the technicians through the plastic. One of the figures hurried and pulled the zipper down. The security guards remained outside while the rest stepped past the barrier.

Two women and a man, all clad in overalls, worked around a table. Barilov addressed one of them. "What is left to be done? How long will it take?"

"Ah, we still have four boards to mount," the technician said, "so that will take us two to three hours. Tomorrow, the collector will arrive. We will install it and test the entire system and... that's it, actually."

"Great. Thanks. Okay, everybody out now," Barilov said.

The technicians gave each other looks, then cleared the room.

Pausing, suddenly not so sure of himself, Barilov placed the metal case on the work-bench. Inside it, on a black velvet bed, lay a rectangular stone—milky, semi-transparent, half the size of a matchbox.

Chapter 17

Professor Peretz held Omer's forearm, close to the wrist, feeling the pulse with his fingers. "Hmm, up to sixty now."

Joel sighed with relief. "Better than forty."

"It's good we began to walk right away," the professor said.

"Why did his pulse drop so much?" Noa said.

"I don't know," Professor Peretz said. "I'm still in shock that he managed to float at all."

"He's lucky," Noa said. "Just because of his stupid skinhead."

Omer, with a winner's dignity, ignored the remark. Noa let out another grumble and kept leading the climb up the tunnel.

Professor Peretz turned to Omer. "You saw no flashes, huh? Not even one?"

"Not even half a flash," Omer said. "At first it was all black and then immediately that sea underneath."

"Amazing!" Professor Peretz said. "I only got those flashes. Like a faulty fluorescent light. Boom, boom—"

He didn't have time for another boom. Shocked into silence, he narrowed his eyes at the light filling the tunnel ahead of them.

"We're dead," Noa said.

"I told you we'd get caught," Omer said, his voice a wail.

Noa hurried to silence him. "Omer!"

"Very bad," Joel said. "Come on, quick, we'll hide in the other tunnel!"

"No, we mustn't," Omer said. "They'll find us there for sure. We have to give ourselves up right now."

"You can stay here alone and give up if you want to," Noa said.

"We must hide," Professor Peretz said. "They mustn't find the floaters."

They turned back. Joel became the point-man. At the fork they, turned into the left tunnel. At first they made quick progress, but soon they were forced to slow—the path became a low-hanging, rocky crevice, difficult to traverse. They squeezed through it, careful not to hit their heads on the jutting rock.

Professor Peretz stopped. He stood straight and looked up toward the wooden slats of one of the scaffolds.

"What happened?" Joel said.

"I think he saw something," Noa said.

"There should be... there should be..."

The distant sound of a metallic door being slammed shut caused them all to jump.

"Let's go!" Noa said. "We have to get away from here!"

Their panic grew. They scrambled on and on. Now they found it harder to be careful, scraping against the rock outcroppings. Towards the end of the tunnel they were forced to crawl through a narrow, low passage on hands and knees.

"Is there much more to go?" Joel said, choking on the tightly-packed dust.

"No, we're right at the end," Noa said. "You'll reach a small space."

The dead-end cubbyhole was just large enough to fit them all. They squeezed in and sat down, taking off their backpacks and placing them on their knees. Quickly, they turned off all their flashlights. Darkness engulfed them. Utter blackness. Joel muffled a persistent cough into his shirt.

"Stuffy in here, isn't it?" he whispered between coughs.

Not enough oxygen! That's why it's hard to breathe.

"Yes, lots of dust," Professor Peretz said.

"It's hot too, really hot," Noa said.

That's because there's no oxygen! How can they not understand that? But I won't say anything. No point in scaring them.

"Shhh. I hear something," Noa whispered.

A distant sound reached their ears: a man talking, muffled and broken. Another voice replied. Silence resumed, heavy and more threatening now.

"I think they're by the fork," Joel said.

"Wow, wow," Omer sighed. His voice dripped with despair. "Too bad we didn't turn ourselves in. We could have said we got here by mistake."

Noa turned to face him, flabbergasted."By mistake? What sort of mistake, exactly? We crashed our spaceship straight into the tunnel?"

Omer was too frightened to take offense. "What's better, that we tried to hide?"

"I think being caught here with the floaters and with me is really not a good idea. Very bad, actually," Professor Peretz said.

The rustle of pebbles sounded not far from them.

"Someone's coming," Noa said.

"Shhhh!" Joel said. "From now on we have to shut up."

"If he gets this far we'd better attack," Noa said.

"We're not attacking anyone!" Joel said.

"OK OK, it was just a suggestion."

A halo of light shone through the passage, and there was a sound of dragging feet and the labored breathing of a man approaching. The halo became a clear flashlight beam, sharp and focused. A security guard, on his hands and knees, came a yard closer, then another, and instinctively the four backed up into the cubbyhole's walls and floor, trying to sink into the dirt and meld with the rocks.

Thick, yellow dust floated in the tunnel air, as though moving through water. The security guard hit his head on the edge of a rock, then let out a sigh, followed by a long string of vitriolic words. He picked up a large rock and meant to throw it to the end of the tunnel, but hit the tunnel's ceiling. He chose a smaller one and threw it, this time more accurate.

The impact sound was strange, like the knocking of rock on wood. But it satisfied the security guard—he squeezed out and withdrew on hands and knees.

In the tiny space at the end of the tunnel, Joel rubbed his leg, his eyes tearing with pain. "He got my leg. Jerk. I'm lucky he didn't hit my head."

Only after a long while did they decide to go back out. They crawled on all fours in the silent darkness, taking as much care as possible until they could stand straight again. Staying quiet, they held their breaths and listened—utter silence. They dared to light one of the flashlights.

As they approached the main tunnel they stopped again, waited for a moment or two and resumed climbing. With every step their fears decreased and their mood improved.

"I assume," said Professor Peretz, "that our connection created a temporary reception problem for them. But we can solve that."

"It's strange that there's no alarm system in the warehouse, isn't it?" Noa said.

Joel limped in the rear. "That's just it! This place is wonderfully camouflaged. They let people sneak into the warehouse on purpose and look around, so that they'll tell everyone that there's nothing here!"

They approached the green door in total silence, pressed an ear to the cold steel and listened.

"I think there's no one there." Omer pulled the handle but the door wouldn't open. He tried again, harder, to no avail.

"Stuck?" Joel said. "Let me try."

He pulled the handle and pushed the door with his shoulder. It did not respond. He took a deep breath. "I think they locked it from the outside."

It was as if lightning struck Omer. His thoughts went into a deep freeze. He never knew how cold despair could be. *We're dead. Literally... dead...*

Joel leaned against the wall, his body betraying his emotions. He pressed his head against it, closed his eyes, clenched his jaws and took a deep breath.

"What a mess," he said. "How do we get out of this now?"

Omer's thoughts thawed in the face of Joel's plight. *They'll blame him for what happened to us.*

Joel collapsed, the pain in his leg too much for him. "I'm a teacher," he said. "At the least..."

I shouldn't get my students killed... Omer finished the thought.

Only Professor Peretz didn't seem worried. He walked a few steps away, absorbed in thought, hands held entwined behind his back.

Just another academic puzzle to him—

"There's another way out," Peretz announced.

Joel's eyes popped open.

The professor started walking. "Yes, someplace in the other tunnel."

They descended the entire way down, and at the fork they turned into the tunnel on the left. At one of the ceiling scaffolds, they stopped.

"Here." Professor Peretz pointed his flashlight upwards. Then he began moving and dismantling a wooden board. He was showered with dirt. "Willy built the scaffolding. We put them in places where the ceiling was unstable. Once he ran into this burrow and showed it to me. We later hid it because..." Peretz paused, trying to remember the reason. "Because we didn't know who to trust, I think..."

They dismantled another wooden board, and another.

"There!" Omer said, lighting a small aperture at the top of the tunnel.

"Give me a boost," Noa said to Joel. With his help, she climbed into the hole and disappeared. A moment or two later she showed her smiling face again, surrounded by dusty red hair. "This is a long tunnel!"

Professor Peretz climbed up after her using Joel's knee, shoulders and head for steps. Omer steadied both of them while Noa pulled from above. When he managed to grab on to the edges of the hole and disappear, Joel's black curls looked like a rug.

Once all of them were up in the burrow, Joel put the boards back in place. He sat back and took a deep breath. "I'm exhausted. I have the stamina of a slug."

"I can't wait to see the sun," Omer said. "I feel like we've been here for two days."

The burrow inclined upwards. Along its walls were small niches carved in the rock.

Previous dead victims, Omer decided. *Last signs of life.*

"Holes for candles," Professor Peretz said. "This is a very ancient tunnel. And amazingly, it ends parallel to the collector chamber. Three meters vertically. By its shape I realized that this isn't a coincidence. The two tunnels simply circle the same thing."

In many places the tunnel's ceiling had collapsed. The four of them advanced in silence, helping each other across piles of rock. The tunnel became steadily lower, forcing them to crawl. And when it seemed to be nearly blocked, Noa's whispering voice came from the front. "I can see the entrance. I see light!"

Infused with renewed strength, they advanced, forgetting their weak muscles and the painful dust in their eyes. Noa approached a small opening and pushed the thorns blocking it aside. Her dusty glasses reflected the sunlight. She turned back with a whisper directed at Professor Peretz. "Do you know where we come out?"

"No. We have to exit carefully."

The tunnel led into a tall thicket of thorns and weeds. One by one they emerged, blinded and blinking. At first they took care to remain hunched over, until they realized they were well-hidden. They had exited the tunnel into an ancient, wide, water cistern that had become mostly clogged by stones. After a short survey they stood up straight, taking deep breaths of evening sunlight. Their dirty faces, stained with dust and glistening with sweat, beamed with smiles.

Omer laughed, wiping his chin with his sleeve. "We look like orcs!"

"I feel like I have Brillo growing on my head," Joel said.

"Yeah?" Omer said, "well, get a load of her haystack!"

"My hair is lovely as usual, thank you," Noa said coquettishly. Then, feeling her hair for a moment, she conceded. "Wow, it's tough as cardboard."

Professor Peretz stretched and sighed with relief.

"Ah, that's good. I was beginning to feel like a gopher."

Chapter 18

Barilov pulled gloves on, picked up a pair of rubber-tipped tongs, and removed the stone from its box. With his other palm flat underneath, he walked the stone to the others, holding it in front of Michael Lampston and Ernest Cole-Angel like a wine-steward at a fine restaurant.

Lampston nodded in assent. With great delicacy, Barilov carried the stone to a small cubbyhole carved into the wall. He once again looked back, awaiting instructions.

Lampston signaled his approval. Barilov inserted the stone into the wall and released it.

An instantaneous, sudden weakness overcame the site manager, and forced him to hold on to the wall. Ernest Cole-Angel, standing next to him, responded differently—like a man dunked into an ice-bath. He took a sharp breath and held it in his chest.

Michael Lampston also inhaled, and tightened his jaws. He clenched his eyes shut and smiled. He opened them and looked at Cole-Angel, who looked back at him, astonished.

"I never imagined the sensation would be so powerful," Cole-Angel said.

"Neither did I," Lampston said. "This is a strong vein."

"Strong enough to float?"

"I hope so," Lampston said and turned to Barilov: "I think it can be removed."

The stone was removed, but Lampston continued to stand motionless, like a man searching his thoughts, listening for a sound after it had suddenly ceased. "We'll connect the floater today," he said, snapping out of his reverie. "I want to try it." His eyes met Barilov's surprised gaze.

Barilov hesitated. "That wasn't... The original plan was, uh..."

"Plans change," Michael Lampston said, as he approached the workbench and looked at the Three Transparencies stone on its velvet bed. "In a few hours they will finish installing the system and immediately afterwards, we'll connect the floater." Lampston did not smile, but his sharp eyes shone. "Finally, we reach this moment, after years... to float in the Great Spirit. This time it will happen, no flashes and no... This time it will happen. I know it. I can feel it."

PART THREE

Chapter 19

Worry pooled in the eyes of professor Peretz as he observed Joel, who leaned on the edge of the cubbyhole and manipulated the tubes beneath the collector.

It had taken Noa and the professor hours to convince Joel to return to the site. Omer, who had mixed feelings himself, didn't participate in the argument, though his strong urge to "float" again was overwhelming. Omer could see Joel's curiosity, as the science won over his responsibilities as a teacher and an adult.

"Hold on... that's it," Joel said, his voice strained. "The bypass is connected. Are you sure this will work? Won't they detect the disconnection again?"

"Hmm, I believe they won't," Professor Peretz said. "I hope not."

Joel frowned. "OK, I'm disconnecting the tube."

His eyes closed for a moment as his hands manipulated the connectors with delicacy.

"That's it. We have the tube," he finally announced with satisfaction. He straightened on his knees, pulling the tube he had detached from the collector out of the hole.

Omer sat next to him, leaning with his back against the rock wall. The floater rested on his head, with most of its tentacles connected. Noa finished connecting the last metal button. Professor Peretz leaned towards him.

"Don't forget to pay attention all the time, OK?" he reminded for the third time. "It's very important. When we ask you to come out, try to come out immediately, otherwise we'll get worried."

Omer nodded. His eyes moved from Professor Peretz's face to Joel's, and then to Noa's. His eyes met her blue ones for a moment, and then he closed them.

The darkness was not complete. It showed thin scratches and tiny color blots. The silence was flawed, flooded with infinite tiny lines of thin beeping sounds. It was obvious to Omer that the whir and the scratches were two faces of one thing—something passing through the dark quiet.

A large, clear, blue blot of light glared at him from below. He wasn't surprised; he had expected to see the blue.

The sea! Get closer to it. Want to get closer. Wow, this is such fun, I can control it! Get even closer. So fast. Huh. Sun glints. I wonder if I can swim.

"Yaam!"

The voice astounded him, struck at him. Sounded so close. He stopped.

Am I imagining it?

"Yaam, Rain Forest Woman."

He circled with rising panic, searching but finding no one.

"Yaam?"

Could it be talking to me?

Hesitating, Omer tried. "Ya... yaam?"

"And who are you? I'm Rain Forest. Rain Forest Woman."

And who am I? She's a forest. Forest woman. I'm a boy...no, I'm a man. Orchard man? No, I'm, I'm the man of...

"I'm Town Man," he said.

"Town Man," Rain Forest said. "Oh, there you are."

Town Man was astonished.

"You can see me?"

"Yes," Rain Forest said. "You can see too. You just have to want to."

"I want to see!" Town Man said.

Her laughter surrounded him from all sides.

"Ha! Not like that, really want, want from within."

Town Man looked around—wanted to see, tried to see, tried again.

"I can't do it!" he cried in frustration. "Do I need to close my eyes to concentrate?"

"Close your eyes?" Rain Forest sounded surprised. "You're floating in the Great Spirit, you don't see through your eyes here, you can't close your eyes here. In the Great Spirit you cannot not see." Rain Forest fell silent for a moment. "Can you even see yourself?"

Her question surprised him. He looked around, looked up and down, but all he could see was the blue stain of the sea far beneath him.

"I can't see myself!"

Rain Forest's voice sounded calm and relaxing, as if she were smiling. "That's why you didn't see me. You have to succeed in seeing yourself first. Try, want to see yourself."

Try, aargh, but how? That she didn't say. Enough of that. Concentrate. But what am I doing wrong? Don't despair. Want to see. From the inside.

Ha! Unbelievable!

"I can see myself!"

"Now see me."

He saw her: squat, elderly, with a round, dark face, clad in a sort of layer-dress made of coarse, gray-brown cloth. The smile she gave him was pleasant, warm and toothless.

Her thick hand reached towards him, adorned by thin gold bracelets. Town Man extended his hand. He saw their hands touch but did not feel the contact. She took him by the hand and led him. He noticed that they were moving high above the glittering sea. They glided until the horizon darkened vaguely ahead of them, opening into widespread greenery: a rain forest. They floated high above the forest above the puddles of fog stretched between the treetops.

Rain Forest Woman slowed. Her hand left his. She descended into the top of one of the giant trees. Town Man followed her down among the broad leaves. He stretched his palms forward, trying but failing to touch them. The leaves seemed close one moment, and far away, translucent and ever-changing the next. He stretched his hand again and followed the slow, heavy motion with wonder.

Rain Forest looked at him from a distance, hovering motionless above the ground, next to a wide fern-laden tree stump.

"Strange feelings," Town Man whispered. He descended towards her, trying once again to touch the leaves.

Rain Forest strode among the stumps. A thin trail of leaves and tiny flowers dropped in her wake with a gentle rustle, like sawdust falling on an attentive surface. She stopped next to the large leaf of an equatorial plant. She reached out and her hand passed though the leaf as though it was made of air, or projected on a screen of dust. She withdrew her hand and re-extended it, and this time her fingers grasped the edge of a leaf. She lifted it gently, exposing its silvery bottom.

"How do you...?" he said, then fell silent at her glance.

Want. I need to want.

Next to Town Man were thick, dangling air roots. He reached out to them and was astounded to be able feel them. He circled them with his fingers and shook them.

Rain Forest advanced among the trees, looking for something. With a gentle push, she moved the branches from her path. She knew this part of the forest well. Town Man, gliding behind her, toyed with leaves along his way. Some he pushed aside, some he passed through.

Rain Forest stopped, allowing Town Man to approach her. Her gaze was fixed on the lower part of a wide stump, where a blurry stain could be seen, the size of a palm. Town Man found it hard to look at the blurred area.

"It's spread all the way here," Rain Forest said.

"What is it?" Town Man said.

"Blurs. Blurs in the Great Spirit."

She withdrew from the stump, resuming her motion through the thicket, seeking. Finally she found it—a long, entwined shrub, with jagged leaves. Between gentle fingers, she rubbed a leaf.

"There's a gate between the Great Spirit and the little one. Thanks to it, I stay me. But this gate is also a barrier. The potion I make from these leaves helps me open the gate to the Great

Spirit just a bit." She looked at Town Man, her eyes beaming with curiosity. "And what's your potion?"

"The Three Transparencies," Town Man said, surprised he knew the answer. "My potion is the Three Transparencies."

"The Three Transparencies...?"

Rain Forest advanced to a small group of rocks. At the jagged edge of one of them Town Man noticed two colorful marks, one neon yellow and the other glaring orange. On the bottom of the rock he noticed another blur stain. He couldn't keep his focus on it; it caused dizziness to spread through him.

The color marks moved, and only then did Town Man notice that they were two thin, lithe lizards. Their eyes were closed, but their severe faces indicated attention.

Rain Forest glided toward Town Man and offered her hand.

"Come. To find the other components for the potion I don't need the Great Spirit's help."

The brilliant lizards scurried from the top of the rock, bypassing the blur. From there, they climbed the elongated trunk of the bush and stopped underneath the dark leaves. They peeked at Town Man with a grave expression. Rain Forest's lips revealed a smile. "They mark the spirit vine for me, both here and outside. With their help, I'll find it when I leave."

Town Man looked at Rain Forest's hand. This time he felt it: the rough skin, the knuckles, the warmth. When he looked away, he noticed that the forest was gone, and in its place, the immense glittering blue underneath could be seen once again.

Town Man spread both arms and twirled several times. Infinity engulfed him. He stopped spinning and turned to Rain Forest. "What is the Great Spirit?"

"The Great Spirit is you and me. It's the joint spirit of all people." Rain Forest descended toward the blue below, Town Man following. "The Great Spirit connects people," she added, "connects them on infinite levels."

As they descended toward the blue, the sense of aerial space changed, becoming more compact and less pleasant. The calm quiet was replaced by sudden gusts of strong winds. The glittering blue became gray, tempestuous and snarling, awesome.

"The river is where the spirits of all people flow to," Rain Forest said in a muffled voice.

They stopped descending. Her voice reached Town Man at once from all directions, as though drenched in spray and wind. He wished to keep moving down.

"You mustn't touch the river, it's frozen," she said.

The furious howling of the wind and the force of the river's proximity fascinated Town Man. He found it hard to gauge how close or far it was. The river pulled him with an uncertain force. Town Man continued his descent.

Rain Forest glided to him. Her voice was soft against the maelstrom below. "Come, let's move away."

Her hand touched his. The stuffy sensation vanished. The windy gusts grew lighter. The blue glittered once again far below.

The quiet after the storm. I wonder who came up with that. Probably floated too. The quiet before the storm, actually.

Rain Forest seemed very far away, but strangely, Town Man could see her in minute detail. More than that, he felt her—her presence. He felt the presence of another, and heard a voice. "Yaam, Frozen Tundra."

"Yaam, Rain Forest. Hello, Frozen Tundra."

"Hello, Rain Forest."

Town Man hesitated for a moment. "Yaam, Town Man."

"Town Man? Hello to you too. Can you see me?"

Town Man had no problem seeing Frozen Tundra—wrapped in a huge Inuit coat. Only his face showed, rosy-cheeked and angry, from the fur lining of his cowl.

"Frozen Tundra will tell you stories about snowflakes," Rain Forest said, her voice brimming with benevolent mockery.

Frozen Tundra frowned. "Stories?"

"Yaam," Rain Forest called out from afar, the sense of her presence vanishing.

Frozen Tundra bellowed. "Snowflake stories she calls it!"

Town Man noticed a glistening ice wilderness far below him—a giant white space stretching as far as the eye could see. A thin strip of river divided the expanse, blue and winding. Tiny glitters of light flashed from its surface. Town Man looked for Frozen Tundra. For a moment he couldn't see him against the white background. Eventually, he noticed a distant motion, and flew down towards it. Frozen Tundra was having difficulty letting go of his wrath.

"Stories she calls it."

"What are these snowflakes?" Town Man asked.

"Memories!" Frozen Tundra said.

"Memories?"

"The memories packed into the last moment of life," Frozen Tundra said. "That is what passes eventually from us to the Great Spirit. That's what the Great Spirit wants—our memories, our unique life experiences. At the last moment all the memories freeze into a tiny speck, and it goes down into the Great Spirit."

A diamond to the bottom of the sea.

"Memory creates thought, thought becomes memory," Frozen Tundra said. "Thought appears and vanishes, memory remains."

He arched his eyebrows at Town Man. "Have you ever seen your thoughts? Your memories?"

"You can see thoughts?"

"Of course! Look at yourself and desire to see."

Look at myself and see?

"How am I supposed to look at myself?" Town Man said. "It's not like I'm holding a mirror."

"Not like he's holding a mirror," Frozen Tundra mocked. "Then look at yourself through the palms of your hands!"

The words and tone angered Town Man, but then he raised his palms and looked at them, wanting to see. Dizziness overcame him, a sense of losing his visual focus. He felt as though he was rolling forward like a wheel. Everything around him became smooth, then whirled around, re-connecting.

Town Man's sight focused. He saw his own face, mouth agape, and he burst into laughter. He moved his hands to the side and realized, stunned, that he was seeing himself from two completely separate angles.

Like a chameleon!

He moved one of his palms further to the back.

"I can see the back of my neck!"

"Ah, the back of your neck," Frozen Tundra said. "I'm glad you can see the truly important things."

Town Man repositioned his palms in front.

See the thoughts.

The sight of his face began to fade, becoming more and more transparent. Soon, he couldn't make out the outline of a face. Instead, he saw an empty space. Fog surrounded him, dry and gray, a frenetic motion within: shards of fog connected and disconnected, created shapes, simple and complex, some almost geometrical.

Town Man was drawn towards the shards of fog. Somehow, he knew there was more to them than he managed to see. He wanted to see better, up close. Soon he felt himself drawing near, growing small, entering deeply into the fog. His environment became more gelatinous. He was an insect trapped in a thick liquid.

Total silence engulfed him. He glided between the fog shards, which were now as large as he was. They looked like giant, colorful shards of glass, slowly spinning. With no small effort, he reached out and touched a nearby shard—the sound of a drop of water falling. He bent and touched another one—the smell of a lemon peel. Town Man found it hard to move, but he touched more shards—the high note of a piano, an upside-down letter A, a bitter taste, a fluttering candle flame, a single red hair.

Moving through the gelatinous environment exhausted him, wore him down with suffocation. Town Man moved away from the memory shards until he saw them as shapes forming and breaking apart in the fog. Now, in addition to the shapes, he noticed some sort of purple blobs.

"I see the memories too!"

"You see your real self," Frozen Tundra said. "You are almost seeing your consciousness."

The gray fog dispersed. Town Man looked down and noticed that the ice wilderness had disappeared. He saw the blue, the tiny glints of light. A strong wind blew around him, whistling. He couldn't see Frozen Tundra, but heard his voice clear and close-by. "When the Great Spirit grows, people also grow."

The sense of Frozen Tundra's proximity disappeared. Town Man moved away from the blue. The wind died down.

Grows. It grows thanks to the memories. Packed into the last moment of life. Snowflakes. Then they go down into it. Through the veins. So that's what passes through the vein! That's what makes the transparencies glow.

He felt presences near him again.

"Yaam! Town Man," he said with a thrill.

"Yaam, Moonlight."

"Yaam, World Man."

He saw them—seated cross-legged on a small dirt mound, motionless. Their hands rested in their laps, their eyes fixed straight ahead. Town Man turned his eyes in the direction they were looking and noticed a small pool of water fed by a silent brook. He returned his gaze to the two of them. Moonlight's face was round and full, his head bald and his body covered by a gleaming silvery robe. World Man, thin and tall, wore a dusty safari suit and walking shoes.

World Man's eye motions indicated a tense curiosity. Moonlight, in contrast, was calm. With an expansive motion he threw two small pebbles into the pool. The pebbles hit the water at the same time. The sound of their impact, surprisingly loud, filled the air. They sank in the shallow pool.

Moonlight pointed at the growing ripple circles. When they touched one another he motioned with his chin. "That's where we'll meet, where the dreams connect."

As soon as the words were uttered he began to float-glide, with feathery slowness, towards World Man, until he stopped against him, shoulder to shoulder, elbow to elbow, knee to knee. For a moment nothing happened, but then sparks flew at the contact points, gentle, like on a birthday cake. Town Man soon noticed that these weren't sparks, but rather tiny dots of color.

They moved in a colorful tumult, like bees whose hive has been disturbed. The bodies of Moonlight and World Man dissolved into infinite tiny balls, until after a moment the two became a pair of buzzing commotions. They mixed and blended, and soon created a single action-packed block, or cloud. And with the same speed, they began to separate and take form: bodies, clothes, faces, expressions.

Moonlight remained calm, but at the sight of World Man's shocked face, Town Man burst out laughing. His mouth was agape and his eyes wide open, delirious.

Town Man's laughter seemed to wake World Man. "What?"

"Nothing. You should have seen yourself."

"I can imagine," World Man said. "That was totally screwy."

"But what was that? What were you doing?"

"Passing, through one another," World Man said. "That's so we can have a shared dream afterwards."

Moonlight, still sitting on the dirt mound, looked at Town Man, questions in his gaze. He extended a hand and spread its palm: It held another pair of pebbles. Town Man hesitated at first, but he sat next to Moonlight, legs crossed, and placed his hands in his lap. Moonlight threw the pebbles in a broad motion into the pool and followed them with his eyes till their ripples met. He placed his hands in his lap.

"Now don't think, or think of nothing."

Think of nothing?

Town Man felt Moonlight gliding-floating towards him, approaching him.

How can I think of nothing?

A familiar voice struck him.

"Omer?"

Her quiet call seemed to cross dozens of barriers. He felt as though it was whispered both within him and in the space surrounding him.

In the tunnel! They're waiting. How long? Too long. Worried! I need to get out. Need to want to.

But he didn't have the time. A shoulder touched his, elbow to elbow, knee to knee. A tingling, rustling sensation went through the contact point. Town Man was drawn into a vortex, a storm of loud noises and intermittent flashes. Sounds were twisted, sharpened into screeches. Pungent shards of scent surrounded him like a cloud of sulfur. Fragments of indeterminate sights swirled around him, like falling leaves caught in a sudden gust.

And all at once, everything stopped.

The fury was replaced by quiet and dissipating fog. A short burst of laughter reached Town Man.

"Now I understand what I looked like," World Man said. "Strange, isn't it? Strange to know who will appear in your future dream."

"In the Great Spirit, the past and the future are friends," said Moonlight.

"The past flows into the Great Spirit through the veins," World Man said, "and the future...?"

The past flows through the veins.

Something about that thought bothered Town Man. Worried him. He tried to recall, to think, but couldn't.

I need to see the thoughts. Want to see.

Fog thickened around him. Within the fog Town Man noticed a frenetic movement of shards: forms taking shape. Shards coalesced into thought structures, only to fall apart. Other structures were more stable. Town Man advanced towards them. He looked for a certain structure he knew would be there, and soon found it.

He approached the thought structure and entered it. His environment became gelatinous and difficult. Complete silence engulfed him. The fog shards were as big as he was. He floated among them, and with some effort reached out and touched one: an abrupt monkey shriek. Touched another: the suffocating smell of dust. His surroundings became more and more dense. His movement became more labored. He touched another shard: a short figure lugging a heavy suitcase.

Thought merged with memory, memory created thought. Now it was all clear to him. He withdrew quickly from the thought shards, left the fog.

"They're taking the snowflakes!" he said. "Stealing them from the veins!"

His eyes met with Moonlight's astonished gaze.

"With the Three Transparencies," Town Man said, "they collect it. I don't know exactly how it's happening but they're doing it."

World Man approached him, floating. His proximity suddenly sent a shuddering chill through Town Man. "Who is taking? And to what end?"

"They're using it for—"

"Omer!"

The call that rose from within him, around him, shook him.

I need to get out. They are worried. Need to want to get out.

"I need to get out," Town Man said. He tried to look straight into World Man's eyes. "They're using it for something... something wrong."

The look in World Man's eyes chilled him to the bone. "Who is 'they?' And how do you know all this?"

Who? Who indeed. They're worried about me. Get out now.

Town Man began to recede. Beneath him stretched the immense glittering blue. He still had time to hear Moonlight's voice. "How is this possible... that can't be. Must speak with Qualia urgently."

Chapter 20

One by one, Michael Lampston detached the arms of the floater in dense-thought slowness from his newly shaved head. He removed the apparatus and gathered it in his lap. Dreamy haze gathered behind his eyelids.

"Never, in all my life, have I had such a colorful, detached, and surreal experience," he said, a smile lighting his lips. "Surreal, and yet so... real."

Ernest Cole-Angel exhaled in relief. "I'm glad to hear you talking. I was worried for a moment there. You seemed really out of it."

"I'm still a little dizzy. It'll take me a while to process this psychotic trip." Lampston got up from his plastic chair, seemingly mistrusting his bearing, his movements restricted with caution. "I felt as though I emerged from some perforation, into a different world. Actually not a world, but..."

"A different dimension?" Cole-Angel said.

"Dimension... yes, perhaps. As if I exited into a different dimension. A completely different dimension." He paused for a moment. "And it's all so different there, like, like a bat sees the world through its sonar instead of its eyes."

"What did you see there?" Cole-Angel said.

Lampston's brow furrowed. His fingers clutched the floater's arms. His voice changed. "You know, these things, all this channeling and telepathy and spiritual stuff always seemed so idiotic to me, but now..." He fell silent, his eyes locking onto those of his deputy. Cole-Angel's astonished expression made

Lampston smile. "When you see something yourself, when the voices speak to you..."

"Too much spirituality at once, eh?" Lampston said. He turned to a metal case and placed the floater inside it, careful not to damage it.

"You're telling me you met other people in there?!" Cole-Angel said.

Michael Lampston let out a brief, joyful laugh. "Yes! And at first I was as shocked as you. But then so many strange things happened to me that—"

"And you just communicated with them? Just like that, you spoke and they answered?"

Lampston nodded, smiling. "Yes, precisely. Just like that."

Cole-Angel remained silent for a long moment. "You're right. I'm shocked."

"So imagine how I felt."

Lampston closed the floater case and stopped. His gaze sharpened at once. The smile on his lips vanished.

"Dr. Lester Pok..."

"What about him?"

"Have you been in touch with him since he quit?"

"Yes. I told you on the plane. We met a few days ago."

"That's right. 'Agonized.'"

"What about him?"

Lampston thought for a moment, but finally shook his head. "No, nothing."

Cole-Angel's eyes opened wide. "Don't tell me you met him there too?"

"No, I didn't meet him there," Lampston said, his tone cold. He tried to cover it with a dismissive hand gesture. "Nonsense, let's get going. Gerryowen's probably waiting for us at the hotel."

The noise of the helicopter prevented all talk, which Michael Lampston felt was a blessing. He laid his head against the vibrating bulkhead and closed his eyes. Every now and again he would open them, look through the round porthole at the view rushing below them, and return to the confines of his ruminations. After the short helicopter ride, an SUV drove them to the hotel. Chief Security Officer Dan Gerryowen met them in the lobby, exchanged a few words with Ernest Cole-Angel and Sergei Barilov, and turned to confer with Lampston, making no comment on his boss's new, shiny, bald head.

"Pok," Lampston said. "What's going on with him?"

"Under close surveillance," Gerryowen said.

"I've run into things only he could know."

"Recently?"

"Real recently."

Gerryowen clucked. "We'll tighten the watch around him," he said in a quiet, flat voice, his eyes locking with Lampston's, "tighten it real good."

"And Professor Peretz," Lampston said, his voice quivering. "See what he's up to..."

Chapter 21

"It can't be two and a half minutes!" Omer said. "Two minutes and twenty-four seconds to be precise," Noa said.

"Well that's even worse!" he fumed. "It's impossible that I was floating for only two minutes or so. Simply impossible!"

Noa sat in the front of the car next to Joel, her knees raised to the cracked plastic dashboard. She lowered them and turned back to Omer and Professor Peretz.

"You saw the stop-watch yourself," Noa said.

"That crummy stopper doesn't mean a thing," Omer said.

Professor Peretz drummed on his forehead with his chubby fingers. "Most strange, isn't it? Strange how the sense of time..." He fell silent, recalled something, and began reciting:

> "Time past and time future
> Allow but a little consciousness.
> To be conscious is not to be in time."

Joel turned the car at the corner and looked for the house numbers along the darkening street, and then glanced to the back seat. "Is that from the tablets?"

"No, nothing," Professor Peretz said. "It's from a poem. Eliot's Quartets. The sense of time is sometimes very strange."

"Right," Joel said, "like when dreaming."

"Yeah, only this wasn't a dream," Omer said, sour.

"Oh, so it was real," Noa said.

"I didn't say it was real, but it wasn't a dream."

"It could have been an indeterminate situation," Joel said, looking at Omer through the mirror. "A state of being between dream and reality, or perhaps a different state altogether."

"What other state?" Omer said.

Joel shrugged. "I don't know. Maybe hypnosis?"

"I wasn't under hypnosis."

"I didn't say you were. I just said that maybe you were in a different state, neither dream nor reality." He stopped the car, parked, undid his safety belt and turned to the back seat. "Maybe that's how it makes sense. Because it all only happened in thought, and in thought time—"

"But two and a half minutes?! I met like a hundred people there and all in two and a half minutes?"

"Looks like someone's exaggerating again," Noa said. She tried to open the car door but it was stuck. She used her leg, and the door opened with a jarring creak.

"I need to get that oiled sometime," Joel said.

Noa stood outside the car, straightened and stretched. "Maybe you can call it a conversation of thoughts."

"Right, like you were there."

Her chilly gaze rested on him for a moment.

Hava Edry was waiting for the four of them in the hallway outside her university office. When he saw her, Professor Peretz rushed forward.

"Hava, hello, hello!"

Hava hugged him. "Oh, Professor Peretz, I'm so glad to see you!"

Professor Peretz held on to her hand. "Thanks for seeing us on such a short notice. You know, I wasn't sure I'd remember what you look like, but a single instant was enough."

Moved and slightly embarrassed, Hava gestured, inviting them all into her small office, making room for them to sit on two chairs and a couch. She settled on the corner of her desk.

"I understood from Joel that you're looking into the spiritglow again," Hava said.

Professor Peretz froze. "Spiritglow?"

"The strange energy brought to the lab in the collectors," Hava said.

"Spiritglow..."

"The dark glow?" she said.

"Dark glow... yes... 'a darkness shining in brightness, which brightness could not comprehend,'"

Hava looked at him, puzzled.

"That's just a quote from... but I suppose that the name of spiritglow comes from the expression 'glow of the spirits. An expression that appears on the stone slabs in connection with the vein."

Hava slowly nodded, her lips curving into a smile. "It's strange to hear you speak so freely about the slabs and the vein. It's against the code of secrecy you set yourself."

"I think you can use somewhat harsher words," Professor Peretz said.

"Uh, don't get me wrong. It's not that I don't think that secrecy was warranted, but... how shall I put this...?" Hava turned to Joel and the two teens. "As time went by he became a little hysterical about it. No one except for Professor Peretz and Aaron was allowed to see the entire picture."

"Hysterical is a mild word to describe the way I behaved," Professor Peretz said. "I became suspicious, stopped trusting, separated teams to maintain secrecy. I created a monster of secrecy that bared its teeth at my amazing students..."

He fell silent, sad, rapt in thought.

"What did your research discover about the spiritglow?" Joel asked Hava. "Did you find any use for it?"

Her eyes thanked him for changing the subject. "We weren't anywhere near finding uses. The research revealed something completely different to us. I am purposely not using the word 'energy' to describe the spiritglow, because the spiritglow didn't have any wavelength or electric charge, nor was it observed by any electronic device, et cetera, et cetera. But still, whatever arrived in the collector made the stone glow."

Joel was confused. "The Three Transparencies Stone glowed in the laboratory as well?"

"Of course. Where else would it glow?"

"That's the result of over-secrecy," Professor Peretz said. "One Three Transparencies Stone was installed in the tunnel, near the vein. There it glowed, and the glow was collected in the collector. We brought the collector to the lab where we connected it to another Three Transparencies Stone. Which also glowed, probably through a process of discharging."

"Pretty amazing, isn't it?" Joel said. "And how long did it glow in the lab?"

"About one minute," Hava said.

"Only a minute to discharge?" Omer said, disappointed, "after two days of charging?"

Hava nodded. "At first, much less than that. And yet it was amazing. The invisible glow—"

"Wait, one second," Noa said. "Excuse me for interrupting, but how come everyone sees this invisible glow?"

Hava Edry bit her lower lip, holding it like that for a few seconds. Her eyes focused on Noa. Thoughtful, she remained silent for another moment. "You don't see the spiritglow. It doesn't give off light. But you feel it. I remember feeling like, like there was... something next to me. Something real. And it doesn't matter if your eyes are open or closed or if it's light or dark around you. You feel that... how can I explain? You feel that something changes. That the environment becomes more condensed." She smiled, as though waking from deep thoughts. "I didn't help you too much, did I?"

Noa laughed. "No, not too much."

"Well, no wonder. I don't think I could have explained it properly even to myself. It's an unexplainable experience, I guess." She shrugged and turned to Joel. "You asked if we found any use for the spiritglow."

"You said you weren't anywhere near."

"That's correct. And after Professor Peretz's incident the research was halted. But later I learned that in another research group they came up with ideas about how to use it."

"The Biology Department!" Professor Peretz said.

"Exactly," Hava said. "Your secrecy wasn't as tight as you thought."

"Lucky for us," Professor Peretz said. "And as a consequence, we're moving from 'divide and conquer' to 'share and share alike!'"

Hava laughed, relieved.

"Remember Tamara Stiebelman?" Hava said.

"Yes, I remember."

Hava scribbled a phone number on a piece of paper and handed it to Joel. "I'll let Tamara tell you herself."

Chapter 22

At the entrance to a well-kept apartment building, Joel's finger ran down the row of intercoms. A whisper crossed his lips, along with a brief push of a button. "Stiebelman."

Almost instantaneously, a series of hysterical barks rose from the building, as though fired from a machine gun. The voice of a young woman, thin and clear, came from the intercom between barking bursts.

"Joel? Hi, come on up, sixth floor. Boina, shut up for a second! First door on your left, OK? Oh please shut up for a moment."

When the door of the apartment cracked open, the angry mug of a chubby black dog reared itself. Delicate, straining fingers held on to the collar.

"Boina, please behave yourself, these are friends. F-R-I-E-N-D-S!"

The nervous wreck fell silent. Its skittish eyes moved from one guest to the other. A smiling face, framed by short black hair, appeared behind the opening door. At the sight of Professor Peretz, a blush passed over the face, like a shadow of a passing pink cloud.

Professor Peretz beamed with delight. "Tamara, hello!"

Tamara let go of the dog's collar and approached the professor, giving him a warm hug. "I was so glad to hear that you were coming. Hava said that you're here about the spiritglow."

"We think someone is using it," Professor Peretz said.

"Yes, she told me that. Interesting. Although all sorts of ideas were raised back then, they were so far-fetched that I find it hard to believe that anyone truly implemented them."

On the table around which they gathered, in the middle of a spacious and impeccably tidy living room, sat a gray, faded backpack. Tamara pointed at it.

"I brought that yesterday from Aaron's mother," she said. "Even back then, after his accident, she called me. Said that he had all sorts of documents left, but then it was so..." Tamara fell silent, shrugging.

Professor Peretz opened the backpack and removed a few notebooks from it. "This is material we worked on together. I'm surprised it stayed with him."

"'Analysis of viewing data of spiritglow clips,'" Professor Peretz read aloud. "Names of the monkeys, dates, physiological data, mood..."

"That's just a small part of the data we collected," Tamara said. "And the thing that interests you the most isn't here, so you'll just have to rely on my memory."

She paused as if waiting for her memory to catch up to her brain. "They showed lab monkeys videos that displayed an object or a fruit. The monkeys were supposed to choose that object from several different ones in front of them. And then they found out that in videos where the spiritglow was glowing in the background, the monkeys became really attached to the object shown. They developed a real desire for those objects. In the control observations, on the other hand, without the spiritglow in the background, the monkeys behaved normally and remained indifferent."

Surprised silence met Tamara's story.

"We knocked around an idea—to use the spiritglow in commercials," she went on. "A joke really. We were scientists, not sales people."

"That means you can shoot commercials with the spiritglow glowing in the background..." Peretz said.

"...And attach people to the products on an unconscious level!" Joel said. "That's insane!"

"It really is unbelievable," Tamara said, shy yet proud of the accomplishment. "Of course who would do that?"

"Such commercials could make people helpless," Professor Peretz said, jumping up from his chair, alarmed. "They could control us all."

"Are you sure about this?" Joel said.

Tamara nodded. "The impact of the spiritglow on the monkeys was clear. If the spiritglow glowed, they wanted whatever was shown. It didn't have to be food, either. It could be a book or a shoe or something a monkey wouldn't have any use for normally."

"So do you think it's being used in commercials?" Noa said.

No one had the answer to that.

"Listen," Tamara said, "all I can say is if they overcame the technical difficulties, it's possible. To us that was off limits. The idea reminded us of the 'twenty-fifth frame.'"

"But a thousand times worse," Joel said.

"What is the twenty-fifth frame?" Omer said.

"Ah, in the past, before the digital age," Joel said, "they used to screen a movie as a rapid succession of still photographs. The rapid succession created an illusion of motion. The ideal rate of projection was twenty-four pictures per second. But it turned out, and I'm talking many years ago, that the human mind absorbs much better than they thought."

He fell silent for a moment, then went on. "An advertising firm planted within every twenty-four frames one additional photo of a drink they wanted to promote. What happened was, the audience didn't even realize they had seen that image but their brains did! And they went straight to the snack-bar to buy the drink without realizing why."

Omer looked stunned. "That's real genius!"

"Later this was prohibited by law," Joel said, smiling.

"Real genius," Noa mocked.

"But we must understand," Tamara said, "that any comparison between this simple subliminal suggestion and the spiritglow ends here. For the effect of the spiritglow is a hundred times more powerful. The clips with the spiritglow, when they were viewed..."

Uncertainty clouded her mind, but after a moment, she spoke. "When I viewed them, I couldn't believe how strong their effect was. A drop of spiritglow was enough—"

Professor Peretz reacted. "We tried it on people too?"

Tamara looked him in the eye, her tone embarrassed. "You didn't know about it. We watched the clips without telling you."

The surprise on Professor Peretz's face was complete. His brow furrowed, his hand clenched to a fist and touched his lips. But after a few moments a smile appeared on his face. "He who hides things will have things hidden from him, no? Wonderful. Classic. Simply classic." He ran his fingers on his mustache and sighed. "Ah, I resemble Stalin a little, don't I? With all the secrecy and separation. Secrecy. I built an empire of secrets."

Tamara laughed a little. "Don't take it so hard. You only became that way towards the end. At first we thought you were charming."

"Research is supposed to be an edifice of knowledge," Professor Peretz said, "but ours was more like a maze, with me in the middle like Pacman."

Tamara nodded slowly as she cycled through memories. Joel turned to her. "You mentioned 'technical difficulties?'"

"The main difficulty was the amount of spiritglow. The quantity that was charged in the collector and arrived at the lab was small. It wasn't even enough for the experiments, so commercial use definitely seemed out of the question even if we thought that was ethical."

"Moral dilemma and technical difficulty are a well-known couple," Professor Peretz said. "Miss Dilemma and Mister Difficulty, walking hand in hand into the sunset: The lady is famously flexible, and the gentleman always finds a way."

"Yes, that's true," Joel said, "you see it everywhere nowadays." He turned to Tamara, businesslike: "Did you watch many clips yourselves?"

"The truth is," she answered with furrowed brow, "Gilli, Itzik and I watched maybe ten clips. Those who really experienced it often were Aaron and Michael."

"Michael?"

"He joined late, but pretty soon became involved in everything. He got along great with Aaron and led the research with him. They complimented each other very well. Aaron is a half-genius but scatter-brained, and Michael... Michael is an extraordinary project manager. One of those who know how to put everything together and see the whole picture. Organize everything."

"What does it mean that they led the research?" Joel insisted. "What did they know, say, as opposed to you?"

"Everything," said Tamara, shrugging. "Mikey and Aaron were the only ones who knew both the vein and the collector and participated in the biological experiments. Everything. More than that, Michael financed part of the special equipment for the research himself, and funded part of the expensive experiments. I have no idea where he got the money. He never struck me as being rich to begin with."

Stunned, Joel said nothing. Professor Peretz took advantage of the silence. "Hmm, ah, perhaps you should remind me who Michael is..."

An awkward expression colored Tamara's face. "He was a researcher, one of the closest to you."

Professor Peretz listened without responding, awaiting more words. "After your incident, he helped you a lot. They say he went above and beyond, with no regard to cost."

Professor Peretz rolled the name on his tongue. "M-I-C-H-A-E-L...?"

"Michael Lampston, Junior?" Tamara said.

Professor Peretz's eyes widened with astonishment. "Michael Lampston, Junior? From World Sales Corporation?"

Tamara nodded. Professor Peretz put his fingers to his forehead. "It was him... It was him who helped me! Who saw to all the cutting edge treatments and the airfare, and everything." He refocused his eyes on Tamara's face. "Are you still in touch with him?"

Tamara shook her head. "No, not anymore. After your incident, the contact dwindled. Then it was cut off completely. We were surprised he didn't show up for Aaron's funeral, but then I figured it was probably too much for him."

Joel, who was staring through the window during the exchange between Professor Peretz and Tamara, took a deep breath and held it in his chest. He raised his hands and gripped his hair in his fingers. "You're all out of your minds!"

Everyone's eyes turned to him in surprise. Anger stained his voice. "Don't you get what's going on here? The guy led the research into the spiritglow and today he has the world's most successful marketing company! And I'm sleepwalking here!"

His words were absorbed with haste.

"You know," Tamara said, "now more things become clear. After Professor Peretz's incident there was a very meticulous gathering of all documents and materials pertaining to the research. Private investigators and detectives and security guards. Every scrap of paper was collected, every floppy disk, every CD, actually every computer. We found it hard to understand what was going on. Now it's clear who arranged and funded that."

Professor Peretz emitted a long, despairing stream of air. "I don't know what to think anymore. Who is pro and who is con, who's good and who isn't."

"I do know," said Joel with gentle decisiveness. "But now I realize how complicated the situation is. That company is huge, and very rich."

"Maybe we should go to the police," Omer said.

"And tell them what?" Joel said. "I can just see it: the officer on duty receives the complaint and faxes it straight to the district psychiatrist."

"But it's all true!"

"You want to explain to the district psychiatrist about floating in the Great Spirit?"

Noa chuckled at the look on Omer's face.

"Explaining it to the psychiatrist is the easy part," Professor Peretz said, "the hard part would be explaining it to the parole board."

"But maybe the police can investigate the commercials?" Omer insisted. "We have to show them that there's something wrong with the commercials."

Tamara shook her head emphatically. "Even if they wanted to, they couldn't look into it. The amounts of spiritglow in the clips are minuscule, and there is no equipment that can detect it."

"What about the theft of your research?" Omer said, turning to the professor.

"They're stealing something from the tunnel, too," Noa said, supporting Omer for a brief second.

"Not really anything of value—" Joel began.

Anger began to boil under Omer's skin."They're taking the snowflakes!"

"Snowflakes?" Noa said.

"Yes, snowflakes," Omer said, exhaling in short bursts. "Snowflakes are memories. They go from us to the Great Spirit like diamonds to the bottom of the sea—"

Omer stopped himself, painfully aware of the disbelieving stares in front of him. Earlier when he'd tried to explain what he'd seen, he had received the same look.

"You didn't mention the snowflakes," Noa said.

"Hey, I forgot! Anyway, it was only two and half minutes," he said, bitterness spreading its thorny branches into his tone.

"Two minutes, twenty-four—"

"Nevertheless, snowflakes are nothing of value as far as the police are concerned," Joel said.

Omer jumped on his feet. "I have to get back into the Great Spirit! I need to ask them what to do."

Chapter 23

For a long moment Omer tried to understand what woke him from his sleep. He lay in bed motionless, with open eyes, and listened: nighttime silence and the hum of the refrigerator from the kitchen.

The room was too well-lit. A night lamp in the hall sent a glow of yellow underneath the door. His eyes fixed on the ceiling. A quick tremor went through him. It terrified him, filled him with sadness and despair.

The paralyzing sensation began to creep up his body. He tried to shout, to call for help, but his voice went dumb. He tried to stop the paralysis, wiggling his toes and fingers with desperate speed—but knew it was in vain. He shook his knees in a last, hopeless struggle. Motion became harder and harder, as though his muscles melted into the paralysis. Tears flooded his eyes. He felt them running backwards over his ears and into the pillow.

BCP—Body Cooling Phenomenon—there can't be any mistake now, can there?

And then he saw them—two diagonal cracks lighting the room with their yellowish glow. *Eyes. Terrible.* A black dot in the center of each. Fixed upon him, blinking, closer than ever. Close enough for him to notice the alligator mouth. He could feel the breath: hot, almost burning, horrible, inching closer.

"Town Man?"

The call from the other side of the room surprised him. The room seemed very large all of a sudden. Its floor glittered as though made of glass. At the edge of the room, in the midst of a clear cloud of light, stood an unfamiliar man, wearing a gray silk kimono. Woven straw slippers peeked from the gap between the edge of the kimono and the floor. *A short old man, very thin. His eyes were slightly slanted, Asian.* His skin color was indeterminate, devoid of pigment.

Although the man's eyes were looking at him, it was clear to Omer that the man didn't see him. Omer stood by his bed, afraid to move. He remembered that the creature was still behind him, waiting, staring at him with his yellow, slit eyes.

The old man's voice was a mixture of patience and curiosity. "Town Man? It's me, Moonlight."

Moonlight? Can't be, doesn't even look like him!

The old man advanced towards him with small, rapid steps. The aura of light surrounding him lit his way. The old man looked around the room, unable to hide his surprise.

"You're a child!" His expression changed, became worried. "You're afraid. Is it because of me? You don't recognize me, I'm Moonlight."

Then he fell silent. His gaze fixed on something behind Omer's back.

"Is this your dream?" Moonlight said, whispering.

Omer did not respond.

Moonlight now stood beside him, with Omer turned to the yellowing eyes in front of them. The glassy floor reflected a green hue from the creature's huge body.

"Fight or flight? No, you can't flee a dream." Moonlight said.

Moonlight approached the yellow eyes. The cloud that followed him was reflected in the creature's twisted body, breaking on its mail armor. Moonlight took two more small steps. The aura fell directly on the elongated mouth—on the wide nostrils and the whiskers beside them.

"A dragon!"

Resting on air, crouching comfortably. Its fore legs were small with large claws, the hind legs large and powerful, folded underneath it. Its body was long and twisted, its tail disappeared in the darkness. The creature's face no longer seemed evil; it seemed to Omer that it was bored.

"This is your dream?" Moonlight said, enchanted, drawing nearer.

Omer nodded, panting in relief.

Moonlight turned to a large window, its frame made of aged, cracked timber. Omer couldn't decide if it was painted blue or red. He stood beside Moonlight and looked out, blinded by the sunlight. A wind blew, and Omer knew it was cold although he couldn't feel the chill. They were looking out on a large, rectangular yard. The court of a temple: dark wood walls, pagoda-like roof, gilt edges.

A long, curved creature was winding in the courtyard, made of sheets of cloth underneath which the hidden feet of people peeked out. Its head was a wooden mask painted red and black. A ceremonial dragon, its lips golden and its teeth white and huge. The large head moved nimbly: bending forward, pausing, then leaping in amused ferocity left and right, to the quick beat of percussion instruments and the sound of bells.

"Dragons usually mean well," Moonlight said.

Dragons mean well.

They turned away from the window and returned to another part of the house. Omer recognized the living-room's floor tiles, but they felt strange, pebble-like. He took another few steps, enjoying the grainy sensation.

"It's interesting that you dreamed a dragon," Moonlight said. "Do you remember where you met him?"

"There," Omer said, pointing at the old painting from his grandmother's house without, his finger guided by his subconscious self. A yellowing parchment at the end of the hall. A bluish village on the banks of a stream. Above it empty space, from which the dragon went wandering, and above that, words in black.

"Learning Doing Prosperity Peace," Moonlight read, smiling.

Omer searched, and barely located the yellow eyes: small and distant, growing further away. A sudden joy flooded him.

"Come back!" he cried, smiling and waving, then burst out laughing.

The room was engulfed in silence. Omer lay in bed, the ceiling spinning around him. He focused his gaze on the lampshade in the middle of the ceiling. The room stabilized, his thoughts spun.

He tried to keep his eyes open, but they shut of their own accord.

"You disappeared for a moment," Moonlight said, walking along a path between two flooded fields. Omer followed. Thin green foliage stuck through the water, reflected in it.

Rice paddies. I disappeared?

"I think I woke up for a moment because I laughed," he said.

"Ah, that happens sometimes."

But why isn't he like he was in the floating?

"Why aren't you... Why don't you look like you did in the floating?"

Moonlight turned his head towards him without stopping.

"While floating in the Great Spirit you imagined me. In the dream exchange you see me as I dream myself."

"So this is how you really look?"

"More or less, I imagine. One doesn't dream oneself precisely." Moonlight smiled and pointed. "Here, do you recognize?"

"What?" asked Omer.

"Him, look carefully."

Something coalesced above the flooded paddies, like a round foggy stain.

Wait, that's a face, here are eyes and...

"I think I see a face, but it's very fuzzy."

"Because it's a dream through a dream," Moonlight said. "Try to see again, I will try harder."

Omer didn't need more than two seconds. That's Frozen Tundra Man!"

A large fur hood framed the reddened face, almost swallowing it, save for angry eyes, nose and mouth.

"Well, he's not hard to recognize," Moonlight said. "He's always sour and snowy. And this, look, is World Man."

World Man's face was young and serene. Moonlight became serious: "You must meet Qualia."

"Qualia?"

"You have to tell her," Moonlight said, offering no further explanation. "Who else did you meet?"

"Rain Forest!"

"Yes, dear Rain Forest."

The sight of Rain Forest's face amazed Omer—tiny-thin, dark, wrinkled as a raisin. Her eyes were closed, her hair gray, gathered in a thick pigtail on her back. A thin, long wooden pipe rested between her lips.

Whoa, she's like two hundred years old!

Moonlight walked along the narrow path between the rice paddies. He stopped and made a polite bow towards Omer.

"Welcome to my home."

A pebble path led to a porch made of dark wood. Moonlight bowed a second time and slid a wooden door aside, removed his shoes at the entrance, and entered in his white socks. Omer removed his sandals and looked at his feet with trepidation. They were clean, free of mud or dust.

The room was very tall and dark. Scant daylight streamed in through high, distant windows. A bulb dangled all the way from the ceiling, illuminating only the desk beneath it.

Something moved in the room, fluttering around.

Butterflies! Whoa, so...many! White ones. Here little butterfly. They seek light. Tons. Many on the windows. Want to get out? But also around the lamp.

Moonlight sighed. "Running away. They won't stay. Not even for a moment."

With a heavy motion, Moonlight dipped a paintbrush into an inkwell full of yellowing, milky ink, and began to paint a letter on a dark page. But even before he finished painting, its edges began to peel, lifting off the page. At the very moment he finished, the letter detached and rose to the window, disappearing among its countless siblings.

"These are letters!" Omer said. He brought his hand close to the bulb and the letters bumped into it, tickling.

Moonlight dipped his paintbrush once again into the strange ink, and began writing another letter. It began peeling as soon as he did.

"Letters outside the word are worthless!" Moonlight said, his voice filled with impatience.

"What kind of ink is that?" Omer said.

"It's moonlight."

Omer inspected the letter being written and noticed the tiny craters dotting it.

"It really is moonlight!"

"If it won't join a word, it has no value!" Moonlight said, and stopped writing the letter a moment before finishing it. It peeled from the page, but remained attached at the edge not yet written. It kept trying to detach, to take off.

"Maybe it doesn't want to be stuck in a word for its entire life?" Omer said. The letter's miserable attempts to detach disconcerted him.

"But what value does a letter have outside a word?"

Merciful, Moonlight completed the suffering letter with the touch of the brush. The letter waited for a fraction of a second, drying, then detached and fluttered away.

Omer stretched his palms to the sides. The letters curled around them, passing through his fingers, running along his arm, circling his neck and face. He closed his eyes, giggling. Then he looked up. The letters carried him up to the ceiling and brought him near the window. The view outside was strange, as though painted by children. Omer looked closer and noticed that everything was made of letters: the branches and leaves of the trees, the white picket fence, the house. Even the smoke rising from the chimney was made of tiny letters.

"What do you see?" Moonlight said from below, deep sadness in his voice.

"Everything is made of letters," Omer said. Moonlight's voice saddened him as well.

A wind scattered the letters. They fell like snow, but once they hit the ground they disappeared into it, leaving it bare.

"In the Great Spirit, every snowflake has value," Omer whispered.

He pushed himself away from the windowsill and was carried downwards. He drew closer to Moonlight and a stab pierced his heart. The old eyes were brimming with deep sadness. The lips struggled to smile.

"In the Great Spirit, every snowflake has value."

Moonlight took a dark sheet and placed it on the table. With a slow, long motion he dipped a brush, brought it to the center of the page and began to paint a letter, finished and put the paintbrush down.

The letter didn't move. It didn't detach from the page. Didn't even peel at the edges. Moonlight looked at it, astounded. He reached with a finger and touched it, rubbed it gently, tried to peel it, but it became one with the page, a part of it. Concerned, Moonlight wrote another letter, then another. They stayed put. He raised his gaze, and the joy in his eyes washed over Omer. He burst out in a rolling laughter.

Chapter 24

In his sleep, Omer seemed so peaceful, almost smiling. His mother sat on the edge of his bed and observed him with tender eyes. Her hand found its way to his neck. Omer opened his eyelids, heavy with sleep, and looked at her without moving.

"No chill," said his mother with great relief. She caressed his face, his brow and head.

Omer didn't respond; he needed time to recuperate. When he did, his voice was hoarse. "Is it eight yet?"

"Exactly a quarter to eight."

"I told Noa I'd meet her here at eight-thirty."

"She's already here, waiting for you in the kitchen."

He lay for another moment with no response, and then sat up. "But we said eight-thirty!"

His mother's lips curved into a wry smile. "Maybe she missed you!"

"Yeah, right!" Omer fumed, leaping out of bed, putting an end to that kind of talk. "Tell her I'll be right there, OK?"

He ran to the bathroom in his underwear, brushed his teeth and washed his face. On the way back he peeked around the wall—she really was there, a part of her ginger hair in his sight. He dressed as fast as he could and put on sandals.

Noa greeted him. "Hey."

"Don't ask what I dreamed about!" Omer said. "Amazing things."

"Well, what is it?" his mother asked.

"I dreamed about... all kinds of things. Even about the old painting from grandma's house."

His mother's eyebrows lifted with curiosity. "Really? What did you dream about it?"

"I dreamed about the dragon in it and—"

"There's a dragon there? Oh, right, there's a sort of a creature above..."

"Sure there's a dragon there," Omer said, irritated, "right in the middle, above the village. And at first it was kinda monstrous, but then..." He turned to Noa. "Didn't we say eight-thirty?"

"We did, but I decided to come early," she said, placing a finger on her lips, motioning for him to wait.

The secrecy intrigued him. "OK, bye Mom, we're going,"

Outside, Omer grabbed Noa's arm. "It wasn't just a dream. It was a shared dream, with Moonlight."

Noa stared at Omer, shock and anger shaping her face.

What?

She walked away.

"What is it?" Omer said, catching up as they reached their bikes.

"Joel sent us an email and asked that—"

"I didn't check my email!"

"...and asked," Noa grabbed Omer's arm, stopping him from turning back, "that we call him early. When I called, he asked that we come immediately because he has some troubling news."

Joel met them at the entrance to his apartment, barefoot and in shorts, a toothbrush in his mouth. He brushed vigorously, greeted them with a foaming mouth, and led them to the living room.

"Be right back." He apologized upon return. "Forgive me for the for the mess here, eh? I just sat up till the middle of the night entering data from Aaron's documents on the computer. Parameters from the experiments. And then I sat down and dissected and manipulated them and whatnot."

"Yes, and...?" Noa said.

"I found nothing."

Omer and Noa looked at each other, wondering.

"But at four-thirty in the morning Tamara called. She woke up and called right away." Joel waited another moment, gathering his thoughts. Again, Omer and Noa gave each other a glance. "She recalled something... but it would be best to wait for Professor Peretz, no?"

"Aw, come on!" Omer said. "Tell him again later!"

"But he'll really be here any minute. He called me from the road a few minutes ago."

Noa got up from the armchair and paced the room. "Tell him about your dream last night."

There was that tone again...jealousy?

"I think it was a dream exchange," Omer said.

"Dream exchange?"

"Right. A dream exchange with Moonlight."

"The same Moonlight you told us about before?"

"Perhaps we should wait for Professor Peretz, no?" Noa said.

"Okay," Joel said, "I get it."

At the sound of three gentle knocks, Joel leapt from his seat. Professor Peretz's bald head shone in the doorway.

"Omer says he exchanged a dream with Moonlight," Joel said.

"What?!" Professor Peretz said, stunned, hurrying in.

"It was incredible," Omer said. "At first it was like a regular dream, but it wasn't, and then I suddenly saw Moonlight, who didn't look at all like Moonlight in the floating! Not at all. Totally different. Because when you float you imagine the ones you're meeting, and in a dream exchange you see them as they dream themselves."

Professor Peretz's astounded gaze passed from one of them to the next. "I can't believe it," he said. "I would so like to..."

He fell silent for a moment. "Well, you have to tell me everything, to the tiniest detail. Who and how and—" Remembering something, he stopped and turned to Joel: "I've been in suspense since your phone call this morning."

Joel nodded. "I didn't want to explain on the phone or by email, but I think there's a real cause for concern." He picked up a sheet of paper with a printed colored graph. "Tamara called me early in the morning. She recalled something that, at the time, wasn't considered important because it was within the statistical error range, but today she realized that it might be valuable. At her direction I picked the oldest monkeys in the experiment and entered a certain criteria throughout the time period, and this is what came out: almost imperceptible, but there."

Joel laid the page before them. The graph showed a slight trend of decline.

"What was the criteria?" Professor Peretz asked in trepidation.

Joel took a deep breath. "Their body temperature. After a prolonged period, the videos with the spiritglow caused the monkeys' body temperature to fall."

"The Body Cooling Phenomenon!" Noa said.

Joel's eyes darkened with anger. "The Body Cooling Phenomenon. World Sales commercials are what causes it."

That's it! That's why I got it, too! All day in front of the TV. The commercials! Tons of commercials.

"Stop watching TV," his mother had said time and again. "You'll make yourself sick. Go outside and play."

Omer sat down heavily but no one noticed—the professor nearly collapsed.

Joel rushed over. "Professor Peretz, are you all right?"

The Professor's gray face leaned back into the chair, heavy.

"What have I done? Man has never known how to manipulate the metaphysical elements. To manipulate the metaphysical elements... When they learned to manipulate the physical elements they made the atomic bomb... now what? The Body Cooling Phenomenon, and who knows what the consequences will be..."

He stood up straight, weak but determined. "We must locate him immediately. I must talk with him. I'll demand that he stop. And if not, we'll speak with his board, and go to the police and—"

Joel's hand touched the professor's shoulder. "We must act prudently."

"How could I have been so irresponsible?"

"It's not your fault," Joel said. "You can't be responsible for someone coming along and—"

"Responsibility is not a piece of chocolate!" Professor Peretz said. "I can't take responsibility only when I feel like it. Responsibility is the axis around which the world is supposed to turn, and it's usually a bitter pill."

Joel stayed silent, preferring not to argue. After a few moments he opened his laptop and began going through the links. He found the page he was looking for and turned the screen to Professor Peretz.

"Do you know him?" he said.

"Know...? Ah, I'm not sure I remember..."

Omer paled, recognizing him immediately. He pointed at the image smiling from a corporate website. "That's World Man!"

Joel tensed. "World Man!?"

"I saw him last night!"

His words alarmed Peretz. "Last night?"

"Yes, World Man," Omer said. "I saw him in the dream exchange with Moonlight."

"Are you sure?" Joel said. "That's Michael Lampston, the owner of the World Sales Corporation."

"Yes, it's him," Omer said. "And I saw him before, when I floated in the Great Spirit."

"That's alarming. He managed to get into the Great Spirit." All stared at Joel. *Did he now believe—*

"What?" Joel said. "I keep an open mind."

"This indicates something worse," said Professor Peretz in an icy voice.

They raised their eyes to him.

"That means he knows how to find new veins. That means more spiritglow for commercials."

Joel turned to Omer. "But are you sure it was him? I mean, because it was a dream, and—"

"A million percent sure!" Omer said.

"Did you talk to him?"

Did we talk?

"Yes, no," Omer said, confused. "Only in the floating. We also laughed about something," Omer recalled. "But then there was like... a tension. Yes, when I told them that someone was using the spiritglow. He got close and there was this tension..."

Joel's fingers gripped the curls on his head.

"What a mess," he said, his eyes closed. "If you're really communicating with him this way, now he knows that someone knows."

"He'll look for Omer," Noa said.

Professor Peretz let out a short, dense blow of air. "This is not good. It's getting really dangerous. You're right. If he thinks someone is on to him he'll look for them. And if he looks he'll find."

Omer hesitated for a moment before he spoke, his voice faint. "But how will he find me?"

"If he looks he'll find," Professor Peretz said. "If he looks he'll find."

Chapter 25

Hadassa had to hand it to the researchers: they were thorough. The compulsions of the BCP patients weren't as random as initially thought. It wasn't just any brand of toothpaste they craved, and not just any make and model of automobile or hairspray or running shoes. Sales and profits soared for a number of companies, identified by their very success. Astounding sales figures in all sorts of industries gave the forensic accountants and financial detectives a great deal to work with. The companies that benefited from the Body Cooling Phenomenon seemed to have nothing in common, at first.

Hadassa stared in shock at the last page of the section on compulsions—except for one fact: they all employed the services of a certain international Public Relations/Advertising/Marketing firm:

"World Sales Corporation. CEO, Michael W. Lampston, Junior."

Chapter 26

Omer was well-practiced by now. Before Noa finished taping the last contact to his skull, he had closed his eyes and concentrated. Soon, the blue reflected in his eyes, and after a moment he felt a presence near him.

"Yaam! Town Man."

The presence responded. "Yaam, Mountain Trails."

Town Man saw him—wrapped in an orange monk's robe, holding a long walking stick.

"We've been waiting for you," Mountain Trails said.

Waiting for me? Who?

Another presence. "Yaam, Frozen Tundra Man."

The sight of Frozen Tundra's face brought a smile to Town Man's lips: the angry, flushed-cheeks, all wrapped in a fur coat.

"Yaam, Town Man," Town Man said. "Hello, Frozen Tundra Man."

"Oh, there you are, finally," Tundra bellowed. "You said someone is taking the snowflakes from the vein, and you disappeared!"

Mountain Trails nodded in agreement. "What you told us is terrible. And now it's also clear what is causing the blurs in the Great Spirit."

Frozen Tundra's face reddened with roaring anger. "But what are they doing with the loot?!"

"They are using it for advertisements," Town Man said. "They film commercials with it and it makes people buy their products."

"Commercials?!" Frozen Tundra choked with rage.

"Who are they? Is it known?" Mountain Trails said.

Town Man hesitated for a moment. "World Man. The World Sales Corporation."

The astonishment on Frozen Tundra's face made Town Man hesitate even more.

Maybe I'm wrong? Maybe it's not true?

"World Man? Are you sure?" Frozen Tundra said, his voice a painful whisper.

Town Man nodded. A sudden call startled him, far and close at once, out of place. "Omer?"

The voice reached him as through an oily bubble.

They're calling me! Something happened.

"I have to leave," he said. "Yaam, I have to leave."

Gradually, Omer opened his eyes, Professor Peretz's worried face was almost touching his own. The proximity of his eyes startled him.

"What happened? Professor Peretz asked, frightened.

"What?"

"Everything is OK, no? Hmm?"

Omer's gaze shifted towards Noa.

"Nothing happened," she said, "but you've been there for like six and a half minutes, so Professor Peretz was worried."

Omer's mouth gaped in surprise. "Six and a half minutes?"

"Do you feel you were there longer?" Joel said.

"No! It felt like I was there maybe half a minute. I met Frozen Tundra and Mountain Trails." He suddenly recalled, tensing. "I need to go back! I was just about to tell them about the cooling."

Professor Peretz nodded. Omer closed his eyes once again. The immense blue sparkled from one infinity to the next. Town Man dropped, approaching the river with blinding speed.

I wonder how they control it. Know where to float. Know how to get from place to place. Maybe it takes time. Rain Forest is like two hundred years old. I hope I see her. And Moonlight. Ha, a presence! No, two, three!

"Yaam, Town Man," he said.

"You disappeared on us again," Frozen Tundra said.

"Yaam, Sahara."

He saw her—in a black robe—in the veil that left a crack uncovered, from which a pair of alert eyes peeked.

Another presence approached him. Circled around him, as though trying to feel him.

"Yaam, Town Man," he said.

"Yaam, World Man."

Amusement danced in his voice. Town Man saw the familiar face immediately. World Man was almost within touching distance. Town Man, floated away a bit, frightened.

"It's good that you're back," Mountain Trails said to Town Man, "we were talking to World Man about—"

Frozen Tundra cried out: "You must stop using the snowflakes!"

World Man remained calm. "I'll look into it."

The cooling, I have to tell them about the Body Cooling Phenomenon, too.

Sahara approached World Man. "All that remains to the dead is the last journey of their soul," she said in a soft voice. "The end of their journey is what gives us life."

World Man kept his voice dry. "It's all a matter of belief."

Town Man's voice failed him. He tried to turn to Sahara, to Mountain Trails, to Frozen Tundra but it was as though he was blocked. He remained silent.

I'm afraid! Of him. But I have to tell them about the cooling, have to!

Frozen Tundra floated towards World Man, suppressing his anger.

"The snowflakes belong in the river!"

"I'm sorry that we don't share the same beliefs," World Man said with calm simplicity. "I don't believe that souls wander or go down to the river or whatever you call it. When a man dies, he dies. We just found a new energy within the earth, and this energy needs to be studied. We are not harming anyone."

The cooling! Say it now, now! The BCP!

"What do you mean, don't harm?" Mountain Trails said, surprised. "Look, it creates blurs in the Great Spirit! These blurs are dangerous to everyone!"

"Maybe so and maybe not," World Man replied, his voice cool. "And anyway, that may not be the reason. The subject must be studied over time, patiently. I commit to invest the resources to investigate what the source of this energy is, and develop it for the benefit of all."

"No!" Sahara said. "Let the souls go down the artery! Don't invest, don't develop anything."

Frozen Tundra fumed. "The essence of human beings' life experiences! All the memories, the knowledge. How can you do this?"

"Look," World man said, his voice stern and serious, "you yourselves don't agree on what goes through the artery! But as I've already said, we will study the subject over a peri—"

"To learn and to exploit are two different things!" Sahara said. "You must not interrupt the flow in the artery. You must stop using it!"

World Man hesitated for a moment, a very brief pause. "I'm afraid I can't make that promise."

Town Man, rolling in the tides of his emotions, remained silent, and the silence burned in his throat. Another presence approached World Man, strong and clear.

"Yaam, Qualia."

She had a low, quiet, smooth voice. Her black eyes were full of expression —curious, smiling. They were deep and dark as a pair of wells, and something shone in them, clear and opaque at once: an unattainable serenity. Her face was very fair, almost milky. Her long dark hair gave her face an ageless quality. Her smiling gaze turned to World Man.

"Even if you promise to stop using the artery, it doesn't mean you can deliver," she said.

World Man examined Qualia closely.

Tell her about the Body Cooling Phenomenon!

By now Town Man was already hating himself for his silence.

"You are violating a very delicate balance," Qualia said.

"Change is difficult," World Man said, a sympathetic tone to his voice.

Frozen Tundra could no longer hold back. "The snowflakes must reach the river! How dare you? Those memories must reach the river and dissolve into it! They are everything—they are us, they are you, they are all of existence, the past, the future..." Frozen Tundra floated around in intense agitation. "You take memories, or... or souls, and turn them into commercials!?"

He stopped in front of World Man, a strong, decisive presence. World Man did not react to the outburst. He remained silent. Then, for a short moment, he seemed detached, as though listening to something else.

"We make commercials to fund the research," he said, "and as I have already said, I don't believe in souls, or frozen memories, or snowflakes or... snowmen or snowballs."

"Yaam!" Frozen Tundra called out in wrath, and far away, and disappeared.

For a moment, World Man once again seemed attentive to something else, and then seemed to shake it off. "I must leave."

Say something about the cooling before he leaves!

Qualia alternated her gaze between World Man and Town Man. "I want to show you an artery."

World Man tensed. "The arteries can be seen?"

Qualia nodded. World Man seemed to be torn. "I would very much like to," he said at last, honestly, receding from them, "but I must leave."

The words choked within Town Man, wrapped in layers of fear and trepidation. They found their way, bursting out. "The spiritglow is causing the Body Cooling Phenomenon!" His cry was so powerful that it surprised everyone, even himself.

World Man stopped, looking at him with immense concentration.

Spiritglow, why did I say spiritglow? What a mistake.

World Man was suddenly very close to him. His presence became intense and oppressive, threatening. He floated about Town Man in slow circles, stressing every word as he whispered. "The spiritglow is causing the Body Cooling Phenomenon?"

Fear pierced through Town Man, fast and true as an arrow, spreading like cracks across thin glass.

"Why do you say that?"

Town Man did not reply.

World Man waited.

Town Man could not speak.

"I have to leave, but I'll look into this matter," World Man said, his intense gaze still fixed on Town Man. He receded from them. "I promise I'll look into it. Yaam."

Promises to look into it! So lucky I said it at the last moment. So scary. He was angry. Big time. Because of the cooling. Because I said spiritglow. Too bad I said spiritglow. Such a dummy. I could have said something else. He was really angry. But promised he'd take care of it. Promised. You don't promise if you don't mean to keep the promise. Scary. Was really angry. Said it at the last moment. The last moment. Spiritglow. Too bad that. What? What...?

The swirl of thought ended at once, replaced by an empty silence. Town Man noticed that Qualia's fair fingers were touching his arm. Her eyes examined him at length, attentive. Her fingers left his arm. Not far from him, Town Man noticed Sahara and Mountain Trails. Their faces beamed with worry.

"No use can come of evil!" Mountain Trails said. "What shall we do? I know we cannot do anything, but we must do something! We must talk to him, explain, persuade!"

"His reason no longer runs alongside ours," Sahara said. "He won't give up on the artery now."

Qualia's eyes remained fixed upon Town Man. Something in her gaze frightened him—the depth in her eyes drew him in. Their darkness left him no hold. And when she spoke, it seemed to him that her words surrounded him, wrapping him in a delicate veil, secluding him from the surroundings.

"Your potion is the Three Transparencies," she whispered. A hidden rustle accompanied her words. "The Three Transparencies... knowledge of them is vague. They were used thousands of years ago. The flow from them... was very strong."

Qualia extended her hand. Town Man hesitated. No choice left, he reached out. Qualia squeezed his hand. Her gaze seemed to fog for a moment, then it sharpened.

"Don't let go of my hand," she said in a deep and clear voice.

A sudden discomfort condensed within him, like a free-fall on a roller-coaster. He let out a long muffled cry, followed by silence and darkness.

"Do you see the presences?" Qualia said.

Town Man saw the presences, yet not like before, as human figures, but rather as subdued, blurred balls of light.

"I want you to see the flow," Qualia said.

The flow?

"But in order to see the flow you must hear it," she said.

"What is the flow?" Town Man said.

"The connecting flow," Qualia said. "When you hear it, you'll be able to see it. But in order to hear it, you must stop thinking."

Stop thinking. In order to hear. Stop thinking about what? About the flow. Hear. Connecting flow. Connecting what? And seeing. But first must hear. Stop thinking!

"I don't know how to stop thinking!" Town Man cried out in frustration. "The thoughts keep coming, from everywhere."

A hint of a smile painted Qualia's voice. "Think only one thought. Just one sentence. Think: 'Don't think.' Slowly. Over and over. Think only that thought: 'Don't think.'"

Don't think, don't think, how can I... Shh! Don't think. Only one thought. But how is it poss— Shhh, shut up already! Don't think. I can't do it. Words keep coming. Enough! Shut up, shut up, shut up! Don't think. Think it slow, don't think, don't think, don't think...

His thoughts slowed, dissolving into shreds of heavy cirrus clouds. Large spaces of quiet began accumulating between the thoughts. And within this quiet he managed to hear a faint rustle—thin, continuous, beeping lines.

"Now try to see it," Qualia said. "*Want* to see it."

At first, a single line appeared before his eyes: a faint line of red light, nearly invisible, and soon Town Man noticed dozens of red lines of light, thin as spider webs. Part of the flow lines passed between the presences, others disappeared far into the infinity.

"Amazing!" Town Man said.

"The Three Transparencies creates a strong flow," Qualia said.

Without saying a word, she was asking him to look at his own presence.

Myself. See. Want to see. Concentrate.

He followed the flow lines. Those that led to him were of a more vivid shade, clearer and stronger.

"The Three Transparencies creates a strong flow," Qualia said once again, "a flow of great power. Power that enabled those who floated through it to enter the river, the river of snowflakes."

"I thought that was impossible, that you freeze there," Town Man said.

"The Three Transparencies connection is strong enough."

"But why? Why did they need to go in?"

"In the river you can see things clearly," Qualia said. "That clarity is power."

Power.

"That is the reason the Three Transparencies were eventually hidden," Qualia said, "until the day you found them."

Found them? Who? Does she think I did?

Pale light rose and flooded the darkness. *Presences! So many!*

Blurry balls of light filled the entire space surrounding them, from horizon to horizon, connected through an infinite number of thin red flow lines.

"Where are we?"

"Always in the same place, Town Man. Same place, different dimension."

"But who are these presences?"

"All human beings are connected to the Great Spirit."

"These are people that..." Town Man said. "I mean, in the regular world? That aren't floating?"

"The Great Spirit is the shared spirit of all people," Qualia said. "The Great Spirit is the flow, is the entities. It contains all the experiences ever experienced, all the thoughts and emotions. The entities in the world aren't really separate. This separation exists only in the imagination."

The grip on his hand became stiff once again.

"Pay attention," she said.

Quick strobes blinded him, accompanied by noise and a trembling sensation, like rocks tumbling down a slope. Town

Man looked around, excited at the darkness surrounding him—a darkness infused with glaring strobes of invisible light.

"An artery!" he said, awe-struck.

The force of the artery pounded him, shaking him, drawing him in. Town Man floated towards it but was forced to stop every other moment, like a diver adjusting to the pressures of the depths.

"The essence flows through the artery," Qualia's distant voice reached him.

Essence. Essence of what? What is the essence?

"Don't be in such a hurry to reach the artery," Qualia said.

The density of the power became unbearable, like the blows of a smith's hammer beating metal around his body. He wanted to withdraw, but realized his wishes didn't matter. He advanced, washed along by the current, like a suicidal whale approaching the shore.

Something stopped him, held him, carried him away.

The familiar blue stretched far below, glimmering. Town Man noticed Qualia looking at him. Her black eyes filled with care, examining him. All around him seemed familiar and clear, but he knew nonetheless that something had changed.

Qualia's voice seemed to whisper in his ear. Her words surprised him.

"The change is within you." She motioned for him to come closer. "I want to pass through you. I want us to exchange a dream."

Town Man floated towards Qualia. Her eyes gazed at him darkly. "Now, don't think about anything."

Shoulder touched shoulder, knee touched knee. Sparks rustled around him. Town Man was sucked into a vortex, into a storm of disjointed flashes of color, of unclear fractions of sight, of dense, distant sounds.

Chapter 27

Michael Lampston passed the guard with a polite smile. He climbed the first staircase with a measured step, but as soon as he was out of the guard's sight he was no longer able to contain himself and began running up the tunnel. Only at its outer entrance did he stop, panting, leaning against the wall. His hand closed around a rock outcropping and tightened around it, and his throat released a short scream of rage and frustration. He forced himself to calm down—closed his eyes tight, took a deep breath and held it in his lungs, then stood up straight and crossed his arms on his chest.

Only after catching his breath did he exit the tunnel, feeling calmer. The light of the setting sun caused him to narrow his eyes to a thin slit, and to wonder for a moment as to the location of the temporary office. But he soon remembered and turned left, beyond the small gravel hill.

The office door was open. As he placed a foot on the metal stairs, his eyes met the ever-tense gaze of Security Officer Dan Gerryowen hunched over the table alongside the local security officer, his hands stretching the site map to the sides.

"Are you done?" Gerryowen said in his thick voice.

"More or less," Lampston said. "Can I use your sat-phone?"

"Of course," Gerryowen said. He drew a small, sophisticated device from his belt, punched in a few numbers and handed it to Lampston.

"You can go into the other room," he said. "It's empty and secured."

After closing the door behind him, Michael Lampston stood beside the barred window. Half his face was painted red in the setting sun. He turned his back on the window and turned to the center of the room. His jaw tightened. He looked at the telephone, rolled it in his hand, looked at it again, and finally put an end to his hesitation and dialed a long number. Upon hearing the female voice on the other end, soft and clear from the other side of the globe, a smile thawed on his face.

"Hi, it's me," he said.

Her words turned his smile into a short laugh. He closed his eyes for a moment. "And how are my sweet twins?" Something in her reply softened his gaze, his face radiated. "What did you talk about?" His smile broadened. "Tell them in a few days, before their birthday, like I promised them."

But then, as though remembering something, the smile faded from his face. His brow furrowed. He tried to keep his voice cheerful. "Make sure the girls don't stay in front of the TV, OK? As little as possible."

Her laughing response weighed heavily on him. He closed his eyes. The smile in his voice became half-hollow. "It's not... you're right, maybe I'm exaggerating a little but it's not... it's not the programs, it's the commercials. No commercials, understand? In the near future." He regretted it, and had to keep his anger in check. "I didn't mean only in the near future... just have them watch less, please? It's important. I'll explain when I get back, OK? In a few days."

He hung up, tossed the telephone on the table and stood once more by the barred window.

At the hotel, he was greeted by Amina Aziz, Deputy CEO of Marketing for the corporation, summoned the night before. Her smooth, dark face betrayed no sign of her fifty-two years and her energetic gait carried her full frame with ease. She approached Lampston, a smile decorating her face. "Nice haircut."

They exited the hotel into the outer lobby facing the noisy street.

"As per your request, I mobilized the crisis team," Amina began. "They will follow any mention or item about the corporation. The focus will be on Internet and TV. I asked them to scan as many scientific publications from around the world as possible. Irregular material will be passed to me immediately."

Michael Lampston nodded, and, in response to her questioning gaze, explained with matter-of-fact directness. "There's a certain chance that rumors about us will be circulated, about our conduct, or some environmental harm. The likelihood seems slim, but I prefer that we be ready."

Amina Aziz lifted her eyebrows. "It's best if our responses are ready in advance, and as precise as possible. It's best if we know as early as possible what the rumors will be." Lampston preferred not to answer. "Is it us or one of our clients' products?" Again, Lampston shook his head. "The question of whether the rumors are true is secondary," Amina tried after a short while. "What we need to care about right now is do they have any proof one can sink teeth into, meaning scientific studies or known figures—"

"Flat out no," Lampston said. "No proof and no nothing."

"Then there will be no crisis to manage," Amina Aziz said, shrugging. "No significant news outlet will disseminate unfounded rumors about us. And what doesn't exist in the media just doesn't exist."

Lampston stared. *Is she kidding me?* "And in case something is published?" Lampston said.

"Spins," Amina Aziz said matter-of-factly. "Distract the public from the topic, and the topic from the public." Her brow furrowed. "It will be important to prepare in advance in order to choose the right strategy. Choose between accepting or rejecting."

Michael Lampston cocked an eyebrow.

"In the accepting spins, we turn to the public and say: 'You're right, we've made a mistake, we'll change, blah blah blah.' And right away we fire some executives, change some procedures, and the public forgets about the incident. In a rejecting spin, on the other hand, we need to bombard the public with confusing and irrelevant statements until it becomes exhausted and drops the subject. After all the noise, we return to square one.

Perhaps if I knew the nature of this upcoming challenge—?" Amina said.

"Thank you," Lampston cut her off, ending the meeting. "You've been most helpful." She had indeed, like a mirror held up to his own ambition.

Security Chief Dan Gerryowen awaited them both in the lobby, sunk into a black leather recliner. When Lampston entered, Gerryowen nodded towards him. Lampston bid Amina Aziz farewell and sat beside Gerryowen.

"Two short updates," Gerryowen said. "Dr. Pok is very ill. He's hospitalized in serious condition."

"What? Since when? What happened? Heart attack?"

"Apparently something septic, or a complication of a bad flu. Or maybe Strep A. He's in intensive care."

Lampston remained silent for a few moments, his brow wrinkling. "Phew, poor guy," His voice was soft, and he balled his hand into a fist and propped his chin upon it. "I hope he'll be all right."

"They don't expect him to make it through the night," Gerryowen said, and then raised a quick eyebrow. "although there are always miracles."

His voice was flat and dry, as always, and his face expressionless. Lampston took a long look at this face, at the spherical head. "We must make sure to cover all the hospitalization costs."

"Of course," Gerryowen said, "hospitalization costs, funeral arrangements when the time comes, and of course security for his room."

Lampston fell silent again, for a few moments. "You wanted to brief me on something else?"

"A report on Professor Peretz as you requested," Gerryowen said.

"That was fast."

"Every two months we run a thorough check on him," Gerryowen shrugged.

"I didn't know that."

"You're not supposed to know," Gerryowen said. "The last check was about three weeks ago. Nothing unusual was detected—he hasn't done anything unusual, hasn't met anyone unusual, hasn't made any unusual statements and hasn't even searched online for anything that can interest us."

Michael Lampston pursed his lips and lowered his brows. He remained like this for a moment, deep in thought. "Could you isolate Professor Peretz? So that we can verify that it's not him making the waves."

Gerryowen didn't look enthused. "It would be best to avoid that."

"Just for a short while, for a day or two, and without making a scene."

"OK. Possible."

"And without hurting him."

"Of course."

Chapter 28

The old thermometer—hanging from a bent nail on Professor Peretz's balcony wall—indicated 27C. Professor Peretz eyed it with concern: hot for early morning. He inspected all the birdcages lining the shaded porch. The tiny water trays were all full. Professor Peretz addressed the birds by name. When he got a response from any of them, he chuckled and replied with fond words.

When he raised his eyes from the last cage, he noticed a courier company's van on the narrow street below him. From the vehicle, which stopped in front of the entrance to the building in which he resided, emerged a tall man in a brown uniform, with dark sunglasses. Professor Peretz approached the edge of the porch to see better. The brown-clad driver scanned the street with his eyes, and suddenly he raised them, catching the gaze of Professor Peretz.

Professor Peretz felt his heart skip a beat. He retreated in alarm, his breath heavy. Then he advanced again and peeked, trying to stay hidden. The van was still parked there, but the driver was no longer beside it. Professor Peretz remained silent, listening to his galloping heartbeat, trying to figure out what scared him so.

The sound of steps rose from the stairwell. Professor Peretz grew tense as he waited. The steps stopped, and the ring of the bell followed.

Professor Peretz froze for a moment. He took quick, hushed steps towards the door and stood by it, confused. He was afraid to even look in the peephole. Three knocks followed. "Professor Yitzhak Peretz?"

A strange sense of despair overcame the professor, like a rabbit in a snare.

"Yes, I'm coming," His voice was faint, but refrained from opening the door. After a couple of moments, as though coerced, he laid a heavy hand on the doorknob.

The man in the brown uniform seemed taller and broader up close. The sunglasses covered his eyes even in the gloom of the hall. "Are you Professor Yitzhak Peretz?"

Professor Peretz nodded. The man smiled. "May I see some identification? I have a package for you."

Professor Peretz nodded once again. Keeping an eye on the door, he walked to the cabinet by the kitchen door. He withdrew his wallet and returned to the tall man by the door. As Professor Peretz handed the man his ID card he endeavored to keep his hand from shaking. The man looked at the picture and at Professor Peretz's face.

"Thank you," he said and handed Professor Peretz a flat rectangular package. "Please make sure everything is sealed and undamaged."

Professor Peretz nodded and the man handed him an electronic signing pad. "Sign here, please."

Professor Peretz signed. The man in the brown uniform turned around and closed the door behind him.

His eyes closed, behind the closed door, Professor Peretz listened for the steps pattering down the stairs, even after he no longer heard them. Only after long moments had passed did Peretz turn to the dining table and place the package down. A large, red-white sticker bore the sender's address. A PO Box, with no sender's name, postmarked Denmark.

Professor Peretz shook the package. It made no noise, packed tightly. He sat down, wiped the cold sweat from his brow with a blue napkin, and with a sharp knife cut the adhesive tape. It contained a yellow document folder. Attached to the cover of the folder was a piece of paper torn from a writing pad.

The handwriting was distorted and barely legible.

Yitzhak hello I don't ask that you forgive me I do not deserve forgiveness I wanted to contact you a long time ago but didn't have the courage and now I no longer need courage but maybe grace

I wronged you I made an irreparable mistake I was in a crisis and I cooperated

this doesn't lessen my guilt. All that is left for me is regret.

I was poisoned they were afraid I would talk. We won't meet each other in heaven we will surely reach different places

You will never forgive me Yitzhak but I do beg your pardon.

Lester Pok

The paper became heavy in his hands. Professor Peretz laid it down on the table. His breath shortened and accelerated. He took a deep breath and held the air in his chest, trying to get his respiration under control. Now he noticed that both his hands were shaking.

With slow deliberation, he opened the cover and glanced at the first page. The top edge of the page showed small, precise cuts and tear marks of a shredding machine. Professor Peretz ran his finger along them and shuddered, almost hearing the sound of the shredder. The page bore no title. The paragraph at its top seemed to be a continuation from the previous page. But his eyes immediately spotted the initials "Prof. Y. P."

Within an hour Professor Peretz had read all the documents in the folder, like a hungry lion devouring prey. He read in rage, in frustration, in pain. When he finished reading the last page he closed the folder, turned it over and rested his elbows on it, laying his cheeks between his palms, looking at the tears that stained the cardboard cover.

After a long while he rose from the chair and washed his face. The walls closed in on him, suffocating him. He put on his shoes to get out of the house, see the sun, see plants and dogs and cars. When he stood at the entrance to the house, on his way out, he looked again at the folder on the table. He hated it but could not ignore it. He took it with him.

At the public park near his home, he walked on the grass, and finally sat down on a shaded bench. A congested feeling built in his head, becoming denser. His fingers found one of the first few pages: a printed list of seven psychiatric medications and dosages. Underneath the list was a note in parentheses: "*Follow dosages strictly.*"

Professor Peretz's finger moved to the lower half of the page. There, in handwritten blue ink, was the note: "*given to the patient without his knowledge by M. L. Evident changes observed. Suspicion and inability to trust, anger, confusion, temporary loss of orientation. After three months diagnosed as suffering from severe 'nervous breakdown.' Urgent psychiatric intervention required.*"

Professor Peretz turned his eyes aside, distraught once again. He returned his gaze to the folder and leafed on. "*Patient is aware of his condition and is fully cooperative. He realizes and dreads a descent down a slippery slope of depression. He is trying to fight it.*

"*His explanations are as fascinating as they are bewildering. He speaks of a new energy he discovered. Flows through a vein in the ground and can't be measured. Is transferred with special stones (/) Three Transparencies (?) which can be used to connect to some Great Spirit.*"

"*Must be isolated insofar as possible from difficult memories that may cause deterioration in his condition. The need for stabilization is critical. The memories trigger anxieties.*"

Professor Peretz skipped to the bottom of the page. "*It is imperative to achieve complete insulation of the patient from any memory relating to research he conducted. Isolate him from any term, data, definition or names of people connected to the research. Hypnosis will be used as well as medical hypnosis and electro-therapy.*"

The congestion in Professor Peretz's brain compressed into pulses of pain.

"*Lately he is frightened. Speaks of darkness and despair.*"

Professor Peretz could no longer read. The letters became blurred, flashing before him. He averted his eyes and closed them.

"*Patient's condition continues to improve. He reads a lot, rests, smiles often. Has resumed eating regularly.*"

Professor Peretz's hand turned pages as though possessed. His eyes stared at the words, stormy thoughts elsewhere. A headache pulsed like a continuous thick line.

"*It seems that the most efficacious treatment is a combination of hypnosis and shock therapy. Patient still displays some curiosity as to the notion of The Great Spirit, but does not respond to the terms spiritglow, Three Transparencies, veins.*"

His gaze moved to the last line on the page, and he kept staring at it for a long while:

"*Patient does not respond to the name M. L.*"

PART FOUR

Chapter 29

As Omer opened the refrigerator and chose an apple, a short dizziness overcame him, as though the house had turned on its axis for a moment. He peeked out the kitchen window and calmed down: everything was in place and at peace. On his way out of the house he stopped at the doorway and turned the alarm on. He left, slamming the door behind him. He took a few steps and stopped, bewildered. A thick silence surrounded him, absorbing the bird chirps and the hum of the cars from the street. The sun was glared in an unusual way.

Omer's bicycle lay beside the entrance path. The metal parts flashed blades of light at him. He walked over, but as soon as he tried to ride, he was forced to stop. The ground seemed to swarm around him again. Dizziness made opening his eyes difficult. He let his bike drop and stood up, trying to balance himself. All he wanted to do now was go back inside and lay down.

The paved path twisted under his steps. He stumbled like a drunk towards the front door, grabbed the knob and felt around with the key till it slid into the hole. Short, broken chirps rose from the alarm system. Omer did not remember the numbers, and his hand tapped them mechanically. He went inside, lay on his back and closed his eyes. The apple dropped from his palm and rolled to the center of the room.

The dizziness decreased, stopped. He rose to a seated position without opening his eyes. His palms gave him a strange, warm, sandy feeling. Cautious, he opened his eyes and looked—short, soft, light-hued grass covered the plain that surrounded him on all sides, moving in gentle waves under the slight breeze.

Not far from him a single tree stood out, small against the flat landscape. Omer stood up and strode towards it. He felt the hot sand against his feet. When he drew near, he saw how large the tree was: a huge, bottle-like trunk, narrowing as it rose to delicate foliage.

He was filled with sudden joy.

Baobab!

He rushed to the trunk, wanting to pat its bark but then noticing a figure sitting at its roots. He stopped. A black-skinned old woman, her hair curly white and very short, sat with her back to him, upright, her legs stretched forward, her bare feet dusty. Her wispy, tiny body was wrapped in blue cloth and one shoulder bore a gleaming red stripe, its edges adorned with white flowers.

The old woman patted the ground beside her. Omer sat, looking at her worn palm, the deeply wrinkled face, the shut eyes. In her other hand the old woman held a rolled-up piece of cured meat. She brought it to her mouth and nibbled. She turned her face to Omer, leaving her eyes closed.

"Town Man..."

Her voice sounded amused. Her smile revealed a single tooth.

"Moonlight told me you are young, but it is still surprising."

Qualia!

A walking cane lay across her lap: a long branch, stripped of bark and scoured. Along its shaft, at regular intervals, black circles were burned into the wood.

Why doesn't she open her eyes?

A laugh line crossed Qualia's face. She raised her walking cane and pointed forward:

"The river brings life to this valley."

Only now did he realize that they were sitting at the edge of a shallow body of water.

"And life, as we know, brings suffering," she said, opening her eyes.

Omer's hand tightened in fright around a clump of sand—Qualia's eyes were clouded, covered in a horrifying, thick crust. She shut them half-way.

"River blindness is indigenous to this place. Like the river itself."

Omer's heart pounded in his chest at the sight of her eyes. He tried to look away but couldn't, as though hypnotized. Qualia laughed. Her rapid smile, like a little girl's, calmed him.

Qualia reached out a black, wizened finger and touched his forehead:

"You're a coward."

Her finger traced slowly down his face: his nose, lips, the edge of his chin, his neck. Finally the finger stopped at the impression between his ribs.

"A coward who isn't afraid to decide," she said in a curious tone. "Interesting. An excellent combination."

She gripped her walking cane, stuck its tip in the ground, and stood up with surprising agility.

"Only rarely is blindness a gift," she said, and began receding with a light gait over the sandy ground.

Omer stood up quickly as well.

"Because that allows you to enter the Great Spirit?"

Her clouded, half-shut eyes no longer scared Omer. He walked beside her.

"I wasn't asleep, you know?" he said. "The minute I left the house and wanted to ride I felt dizzy, and then I saw you."

"It was important for me to meet you," Qualia said. "I made an effort so you would hear me, so that we could exchange a dream although you were awake."

Omer looked back, amazed at the pace of their walk: he could no longer make out the large tree.

"There may be a way to retrieve the transparencies," Qualia said.

"Really?"

"Yes, and only you can walk this road."

Omer stopped. He noticed that his laces and socks were full of little thorny balls. The thorns scratched his legs, marking them with white, dry lines. He tried to remove them but they were too sharp, and were stuck too hard.

Distress engulfing him, Omer raised his eyes to Qualia. "Because I enter the Great Spirit through the transparencies?"

Qualia nodded.

They stopped and looked—they were standing on the edge of a desert. The vegetation thinned and a wide plain of pale land stretched before them, strewn with little pebbles. The air around them was scorching. Far on the horizon Omer noticed tall, darkened mountains, their peaks adorned with a white crown of eternal snow.

"The transparencies were created in the previous time," Qualia said.

Previous time?

"When men knew how to turn thoughts into dew."

"Into dew?!"

"Thought dew," Qualia said.

She opened her clouded eyes and raised them to the mountains.

"Where the desert meets the mountain,
At the hour when day meets night,
Heat meets cold,
Man meets stone."

She returned her gaze to Omer.

"They knew how to think one thought together for an entire night. Thought it with all their might. The thought tightened and condensed until it became dew on the rock. And a moment before sunrise a drop trickled. One each night."

"And these drops created the transparencies?"

"Night after night, for years, to cast one Three Transparencies stone," said Qualia.

"And there are four of them," Omer said, and walked away, as though driven. He stopped and crouched on his knees, carefully examining the soil. He raised his head and looked around. Giant trees surrounded the hill on which he stood, and around them rose the mountaintops.

He dug in the earth with a broken twig. "This is where he found the box with the transparencies."

The twig hit something. Omer pulled out a small box made of stone from the earth. He removed the lid. It was empty, but at the bottom he noticed the symbol—the circle, the spiral lines, the letters.

"There were tablets here too," he said.

Qualia dug next to him. Her fingers felt something, and she withdrew a large, thick stone slab from the soil. Her palm passed over the slab, feeling lines of letters and symbols. Omer reached out and touched the tablet. It seemed to be soft, made of sponge. "The tablets also told of the Three Transparencies, but he couldn't decipher it all."

"The viewers of the transparencies..." Qualia said, her palms moving over the stone slab.

"Who were they?"

Qualia shoved the stone tablet with a gentle motion back into the earth.

"They are the ones who viewed the Great Spirit through the transparencies. They saw beyond the dimensions, saw the essence. Four viewers looked after four castings. Nomads. Loners. When one of them would reach the midpoint of life, he would seek out a replacement, and train him for years to enter the Great Spirit through the transparencies, to look without being blinded by the power. Only then would he pass it on to his successor, and wander away."

Qualia smoothed the earth, hiding the edge of the slab.

"The viewers through the transparencies believed that power without preparation is a trap. Power without preparation begins like a candle and ends in a fire."

Using her walking cane, Qualia rose from her crouching position. Omer stood beside her. "The transparencies have so much power."

"The castings themselves have no power," Qualia said. "They are like all the stones lying around here. The power is in the clarity of flow to the Great Spirit."

Far on the horizon a ruined structure rose to the sky: the lower remnants of an enormous pyramid. Thick vegetation grew amidst the wreckage, huge rocks lay around it. Omer shaded his eyes with his hand. Qualia stood beside him, clutching her walking cane.

"Clarity of thought is always power. Clarity of thought is a line—a clear, precise, thin line. And in the Great Spirit this line spreads like a fan of lines. Remember... it has been only a few days since you've known the Great Spirit, you and World Man, and you can already do things others do only after years. This is thanks to the powerful flow of the transparencies. And you will be able to see and do things we never will, like entering the river itself, touching the drift at the bottom."

Drift.

"Drift?"

"Leftovers," Qualia said. "Memory refuse that does not enrich the Great Spirit."

A tiny smile rose to her lips:

"Do you know what the most important moment in life is, Town Man?"

He looked at her, wondering. Her clouded eyes opened half-way. The smile on her lips died away.

"Death," she said. "The moment we're never ready for. But there is something within us that is always ready: the memories. Waiting. Organized, ready to crystallize at the moment of death to a spiritual kernel that will pass into the Great Spirit."

The snowflake.

Qualia nodded.

She can hear my thoughts!

Qualia's dead eyes danced. "In the river, the spiritual kernel disintegrates. The important memories fill the river, and the rest fall to the bottom as memory refuse. The viewers of the transparencies knew how to fill themselves with this refuse."

Fill themselves with refuse?!

"It enabled them to see the essence of things," Qualia said. She began to walk again.

The remnants of the giant pyramids seemed so near. Qualia climbed the stone stairs. Her walking cane made a knocking sound every two steps. Omer hurried to catch up and walk beside her. The size of the rectangular blocks on both sides of him was astounding. The persistent crumbling-sprouting of forest flora filled the cracks between the stones.

The stairs they were climbing led not up but down, descending into the pyramid. A quick glance backwards showed him the distant entrance, a glaring square of light through which they had entered.

The growing gloom weighed Omer down. Qualia's staff clicked against every second step. The descending corridor turned narrow and dank. The smell of ancient dust floated through the air. The clicks echoed and reverberated from every direction. When he looked back, he could no longer see the entrance.

The clicks of the walking cane ceased. Qualia stopped. They stood at the entrance to a large, dark room with a low ceiling. Anxiety clawed at the walls of Omer's mind. Qualia's voice reached him as though from afar.

"The viewers of the transparencies made sure not to meet outside the Great Spirit. They believed it would be safer."

Omer did not want to enter the room. Pressure rose in the pit of his stomach, compressing his chest like compact air. A repugnant smell reached him from within the room, overwhelming, sharp and pungent.

"But eventually," Qualia whispered, "something caused them to meet outside the Great Spirit, despite the caution."

Get out of here!

Omer failed to escape.

She's blocking me!

"Someone caused them to meet," Qualia said.

Her words pushed him forward as though they were hands. A stone platform occupied the center of the room. An elongated stone coffin sat on top of it. It emitted a horrifying smell, causing Omer to gag.

Get out of this dream!

Tremors shook him from the knees to the neck, sticky sweat covered him dripping from his fingertips to the floor. Qualia laid her hand on the coffin lid. Omer shuddered. He wanted to get out of there, to escape, run all the way up the stairs to open air.

Get out! Right now, out of this dream!

He stood there rooted to the ground, unable to move. Qualia indicated the coffin with her chin:

"He took over one of the castings by force and cunning. But he wasn't ready! Wasn't ready for the power and lost his bearings, and began to search for the others."

She circled the dais, and pushed the stone lid with two of her fingers. Desperation ran in needles from Omer's feet to his chest, his hair stood on end from fear.

Don't open it!

The heavy coffin lid moved a bit, a muffled screech of stone on stone. A murky wave burst out: a miasma of solid stench. Through the crack, Omer saw black, dusty hair adorned with colorful beads. A scream rose in his throat, compressing like a glob, piercing his gut, head and eyes. His vision blurred.

"One by one he found the other viewers of the transparencies." Qualia's whispering voice carved through the air. "Found and eliminated, and gathered the transparencies, until he had all four."

Qualia pushed the coffin lid further. The friction of the stones sharpened Omer's sight for a moment, and a wizened mummified corpse appeared before his terrified eyes. Its face was turned towards him: two dark holes for eyes, a smile with lipless teeth.

Omer couldn't even scream. He jumped back, sweating all over, his breathing heavy. His knees barely carried his body. The scream compressed his throat, choking him. He retreated till his back hit a wall. All he wanted was to keep pushing against that wall and disappear into it.

Qualia approached, her eye sockets empty black holes. Her hand extended to him, fingers like coiled wire, shiny and twisted. Omer pressed against the wall with all his might, felt the stones at his back creak, tumble...

Omer opened his eyes. He lay on his back, on the floor in his home, panting like he'd run a marathon. He held his breath and gritted his teeth, trying to relax. He released the air slowly, his heartbeat shaking his chest.

At the last moment. Lucky I got out.

His head was so heavy he had difficulty lifting it. He didn't dare close his eyes, not even to blink. He looked at the strange light entering the house through the kitchen windows. Pink. He succeeded to lift his head, barely, as though it was stuck to the floor with chewing gum. The entrance door was half-open. Through it, Omer noticed the cloud of smoke engulfing the house. The entrance door itself also looked strange: made of metal, painted blue.

Knocking and squeaking sounds filled the air. The noise came from directly below him, underneath the floor. He lifted his head a bit more, looked, and recoiled: his shoelaces and socks were covered in hairy little thorns.

The knocks and squeaks intensified. Omer tried to crawl on his back and get away, but couldn't. He was glued to the spot. The knocks vibrated beneath him, toward him, like metal worms. Out of the corner of his eye he saw the bitten apple rolling away. He bent his knees and tried to push himself back as the bristles of the thorns stuck to the floor. A loud crack sounded: pieces of floor-board flew in all directions, and a large hole appeared in the floor. Something extended outwards, bright orange, elongated. It grabbed Omer's leg and pulled him in with astounding force.

He needed a few moments to readjust to the darkness, and another few to get used to the calm that enveloped him, and the sense of security. Warm tranquility pulsed through his body. The source came from his arm: Qualia held him. Her clouded, half-shut eyes locked his. Omer's lips curled into a smile, threatening to burst into laughter. He walked, leading Qualia towards the stone coffin. There was now no fear in his eyes as they took the shrunken corpse in, its lips pulled into a morose smile, its eye sockets empty. In the wizened face, in the preserved gaze, pain and fear pooled.

Omer turned to Qualia, a question forming on his face. Qualia pushed the stone lid of the coffin, and there, Omer saw a large dagger, stuck in the middle of the chest of the desiccated corpse.

"Power is always in demand, Town Man," she said.

By the hilt of the dagger he saw a large, round pendant made of silver attached to a long chain. The pendant was almost white in the glare. At its center was the symbol—a circle containing spiral lines, symbols, and letters.

Power is always in demand.

Omer inspected the shrunken corpse in detail. Eventually, he pushed himself away from the coffin and turned around.

Now he has them. But there may be a way. She wants me to do it! That's why she made such an effort, so that I would hear her. Me.

Omer's posture straightened. A strange tremor ran through him, which brought a combination of feelings: courage, fear, pride.

"What do I have to do?"

"Go down to the bottom of the river and fill yourself with refuse," Qualia said. "Pass through World Man and flood him."

Flood him.

"We'll help you get rid of it later," Qualia said. "We'll perform a purification ceremony on you."

"And World Man?"

"He won't be able to deal with the refuse outside of the Great Spirit."

He'll give the transparencies back?

"He will have to get our help," Qualia said.

Power is always in demand.

"I'll do it."

Her clouded eyes examined him with calm curiosity.

"It will be much more difficult than you think, Town Man."

"I'll do it."

Chapter 30

Joel was having trouble driving and digesting Omer's explanation at the same time.

"Now let me get this straight," Joel said, looking at both Omer and Noa in the back seat, in the rearview mirror. "Michael Lampston has the Three Transparencies stones."

"That's right."

"And your dream people want him to give them back."

"They're not my 'dream people.'"

"Okay," Joel said. "I'm trying to keep an open mind here. The 'people in this other dimension' need you to help get the stones back."

"Exactly."

"And to do this, you need to eat a bunch of garbage?"

"Refuse," Omer said. "They call it 'refuse.' At the bottom of the river."

"And this refuse is...?" Joel said.

"He told you," Noa said. "It's extra memories the Great Spirit doesn't need."

"Oh, the Great Spirit again," Joel said, hitting the brakes, pulling up to the curb across from Professor Peretz's apartment building. For a moment, it didn't look like Joel was capable, or willing, to open the car door.

Joel sighed. "Okay. Let's just say for argument that you're not having an hallucination of some kind. I find it hard to believe Michael Lampston can be forced to return the transparencies."

Before Omer could answer, Joel got out of the car and headed for the crosswalk. Noa and Omer followed. As they waited to cross the street, Joel suddenly began patting his trouser pockets.

"I left it at the gas station!" he said. "My phone."

"In the car," Noa said. "You used it in the car."

"Whew, right," he said. "OK, so go on up. I'll be right there."

Noa and Omer crossed the street toward Professor Peretz's apartment building. Noa's red hair glittered in the sunlight: unkempt, bouncy, glistening. It reminded Omer of something. *The glitters of the river.*

"You know...?" he said.

"What?"

She took another two short skips and stood in the shade. Only then did she turn her head towards him. "What?"

"Uh... just... nothing," he mumbled, the moment gone. He broke out running towards the lobby.

"You jerk!" Noa said, laughing, running after him.

Omer galloped into the lobby, but slipped and fell on the first step, and Noa ran past. Omer jumped right up and, running up the stairs, caught up with Noa but could not pass. She blocked him, left and right. Their running became a wrestling match—panting-shoving-pulling-laughing. Her knee brace scraped and rattled against the rail and Omer hesitated, then pressed hard against her once more. At the turn of the stairs he seized the opportunity, reached past Noa and held onto the corner of the rail. Noa crashed into his barricading hand at full speed but couldn't break free, trapped in Omer's arms, bodies against each another, faces so close. Omer felt Noa's rapid breath on his face, saw the whiteness of her teeth between pale lips, and saw a single red hair stuck to a sweaty cheek. Through the lenses of her glasses he saw her eyes—narrowed into thin slits of laughter and exertion. The slits widened, filling with a curious, questioning look.

An unclear, joyful excitement flooded Omer all at once, shaking his chest and pushing him away, forcing him to burst into a renewed, laughing run up the stairs.

Noa, recovering, set out running after him. But suddenly, a few steps before the floor of Professor Peretz's house, her sharp eyes spotted the danger: the door of the apartment across the hall was ajar, and in the opening she saw the worried face of Varda, the elderly woman they'd seen before, Professor Peretz's friend and neighbor, with her hand motioning to Noa: *no!*

"Wait!" Noa said.

But it was too late. Omer had already pressed the bell. He turned to her with a triumphant look on his face and only then noticed the fright on hers. The glee vanished from his expression.

The door to Professor Peretz's apartment opened half-way. At the entrance stood a muscular man, broad and tall. His face was coarse and unsmiling. His penetrating gaze scanned them at length.

"Yes?"

Omer's heart sank. He lowered his eyes before the tough gaze.

We're toast.

Omer and Noa remained like that for a moment or two, paralyzed with fear, Varda peeking out from her own apartment.

"We're collecting donations for the blind." Noa stammered with false gaiety. "You can give twenty or fifty or a hundred."

The overgrown man did not respond. His thick arms remained crossed on his chest. His black shirt smelled heavily of cologne. Omer couldn't lift his gaze, and focused on the man's black leather shoes. After a moment the mocking voice of another man rose from inside.

"We gave at the office."

The man leaned against the doorpost, fixing them with his baleful glare."You heard him."

Noa pulled Omer to the apartment across the hall. Their ears remained alert, awaiting the sound of a door slamming shut, but none was forthcoming. Noa pressed the bell button, and Varda opened the door.

"We're collecting donations for the blind," Noa said. "You can give twenty or fifty or a hundred."

"Oh, a donation, yes," Varda said. "Come in, come in, let me find my purse..."

Her hand pulled them in forcefully, drawing them beyond the half-open door. "We must find Yitzhak, warn him!"

"Who are these people?" Noa said.

Varda shrugged. Her speech was rapid and tense.

"They entered with a key, that's why I didn't call the police. Maybe he gave it to them. And he's not answering his cell either."

"We tried calling from the road too," Noa said.

Omer tensed. "Joel!"

"Right!" Noa's face went pale. "Quick, before he comes."

But before they could leave, they heard his footsteps coming up the stairs. Noa pulled out her phone and dialed. Tinny music came from the stairwell, and then Joel's voice. "Uh, No-ah?"

His voice was close by, only a few steps from Professor Peretz's apartment. Noa whispered. "Stop! Don't go in there. There are people there! I'm serious. Keep on going like you're here to see someone else and pretend you don't know us." She hung up and went out into the hall with Omer.

Joel stood in front of Professor Peretz's apartment, bewildered. The door was closed. He looked at Noa and Omer coming out of the adjacent apartment and did as instructed—walked past them and down the hall, feigning indifference.

Noa and Omer hurried down the stairs. When they reached the street, they turned the corner around a hedge to watch the building. Joel emerged and walked toward his car.

Noa and Omer ran down to the next corner and met him there. Joel's sweaty face showed grave concern. "What was all that?"

The two teens jumped into the car.

"People were in Professor Peretz's apartment," Omer said.

"What people?"

"Scary people."

"We saw one, but there was another one there," Noa said.

"But what people? What are they doing there?" Joel said, pulling over, taking out his phone.

"I guess they're waiting for him." Noa said.

"And apparently they got in with a key, so maybe they know him," Omer said.

"Although they didn't quite seem like friends of his," Noa said.

"He's still not answering," Joel said. "Voice mail. I hope he's checking—"

"Don't leave a message!" Noa said.

Joel hung up, touching the phone to his forehead. "You're right. This isn't good. We need to find him. I'm surprised he isn't calling us."

"We need to stake out the street so that if he comes back..." Omer began, then fell silent. His eyes fixed on a distant point in the park.

Isn't that something?

He pushed his head closer to the window, surprised.

That's him, isn't it? Yes! "Ha! That's him, isn't it? There, sitting on the bench! Ha, I rule!"

Omer was about to call out, but Noa stopped him at the last moment. "Don't shout! What are you, stupid?"

Omer held his shout, embarrassed. Noa got out of the car, circled it quickly and knelt by the driver's-side door. "Wait for us there, on the other side of the hill. We don't want him on the street here."

She rose from her crouch and climbed the grassy hill with ease. She did not approach Professor Peretz directly, but made a wide detour, using the trees for cover. Joel drove to the agreed-upon spot and parked, leaving the engine running.

Noa and the Professor walked quickly to the car. Peretz's eyes looked frightened, with added exhaustion and a measure of disorientation, as though in shock. Joel greeted him with a calming smile, but Professor Peretz did not return it.

"Did you see them too?" he said.

"No," Joel said.

Professor Peretz remained standing by the open car door. Beads of sweat condensed on his face and forehead. His eyes blurred at the sight concerned faces around him. His hands tightened on the yellow document folder. He raised it. "This is my lost life."

A car passed by—a new model, long and dark. Joel tensed. When he noticed an old man driving, he relaxed a bit. "It's dangerous here, we'd best leave. Let's go to my place."

Professor Peretz did not reply. Another car passed. At the top of the hill, two men walked towards them.

"We've got to get out of here," Joel said.

Only the sharp sound of Noa's voice seemed to penetrate Peretz's isolation. "Professor Peretz, we're with you! Let's go."

Clutching the yellow folder against his chest, Professor Peretz lowered his head and got into the back seat of Joel's car. Noa hurried in after him.

Professor Peretz whispered as the car moved. "A lie! It was all a lie. It was all a lie."

When they reached Joel's apartment, Professor Peretz leaned against the doorjamb. "I'm a bit dizzy. I think my vision is a little blurred—"

"Sit down!" Noa said. "That's not good, maybe it's a heart attack."

"No... it's a... thought attack," Professor Peretz said, indicating the folder. He handed it to Joel, sat on the sofa and closed his eyes. Bitterness filled his voice. "This morning I received this. The black hole of my life, in a yellow folder."

And so he remained for a long while—slightly hunched, unmoving, his expression a sad mask. He did not hear the rustling of the pages, the angry whispers, the broken-off words, choked-off with disbelief. He remained frozen, almost calm, until the moment Noa got up and walked over to him. She sat beside him and laid her hand on his. Something twitched in his face at that moment. A tremor ran through his lips and cheeks. It seemed as though his emotions, and the pain within him, were trying to flow once again, to flood his face. His breathing was interrupted.

"Since this morning I've been falling in a dark hole. I'm falling incessantly," he said, his eyes closed. His hand tightened around Noa's. "Marta sensed it! She sensed that what I was going through wasn't real, didn't make sense..."

Professor Peretz fell silent for a moment, then cleared his throat. "When she became sick due to what I was going through,

I felt guilty. And when she passed away I felt a hundred times guiltier. I felt that I had left her alone..."

Professor Peretz cried. At first it was a silent cry, to himself, and then it burst into deep, choked-off sobs. His shoulders hunched, his head bowed. He swayed to and fro.

Omer found it hard to look at Professor Peretz, so he moved his gaze to Noa. She placed her other hand on his arm. A large tear trickled down her cheek, leaving a shiny trail behind, until it was gathered into her lips.

She's so pretty.

Professor Peretz took a deep breath. When he spoke again after a few moments, he did so with bitter calm.

"Today, I realized how brilliant Michael was. While we studied the trees he already saw the forest. He was the first to realize the possibilities that lay in the spiritglow, the first to think of the commercial value. And once he realized the commercial value..."

Power is always in demand.

"I have to run away," Professor Peretz whispered.

Joel approached and knelt beside him. "We need to act."

"They'll find me, they're like wolves," Professor Peretz said.

Joel refused to agree. "Omer exchanged a dream with Qualia. She says there's a way to force Michael to return the transparencies."

Why is he saying these things he thinks are fantasies?

"That's right, right?" Joel asked Omer.

Something genuine awoke in Professor Peretz's face.

Omer hesitated. He looked at Noa, then Joel.

"Tell him what you told me," Joel said.

Which you didn't exactly believe...

It's something, Joel's look said. *For him...*

"Qualia says there's a way to force Michael to cooperate," Omer said. "We need to transfer memory refuse from the bottom of the river to him. He won't be able to get rid of it without help from others."

Professor Peretz tensed. "Can she do this?"

"I'll have to do it," Omer said.

Professor Peretz leaned back. "The circle of wolves is drawing closer. If they reached me they'll reach you." After a moment, his eyes re-focused on Omer, and he added in a soft voice: "No one can help you when you're alone in the river."

I know. On my own.

Chapter 31

Although he needed more rest, Professor Peretz refused to remain behind. The four of them had agreed to meet in the grove and continue from there. Professor Peretz and Joel reached the meeting spot first.

The sun beat down on the dusty leaves. Joel walked a short distance from the trees in the grove, shaded his eyes with his hand and looked at the dirt trail.

"What I mean," he said, throwing a quick glance at Professor Peretz, "is that even if he returns the transparencies and they stop using the spiritglow, the Body Cooling Phenomenon won't stop. What has infected people isn't going to evaporate. It has become a part of them."

Professor Peretz sat atop a large rock beneath one of the trees. "You're thinking too literally. This isn't a virus, this is..." Peretz gestured with his hands, palms up, in little circles, indicating the whole world, the vapor of the air, the essence of life.

Joel's eyes sparkled with excitement. "Amazing, this business. You know, I think I can fit some scientific logic to the Great Spirit. Maybe the feelings and thoughts that burst out of us, that create an aura around us, are energy. Admittedly, it's another energy, unfamiliar to us, but energy nonetheless, whose source is life itself. Under certain conditions, after all, energy can become matter and vice-versa, and that's what happens here as well—at the moment of death the psychic energy becomes matter, of a sort unfamiliar to us: the spiritual kernel, the snowflake. This kernel passes through one of the veins to the Great Spirit and dissolves back into energy. But then what's this 'refuse?' I have a problem with that. Ah, there they are!"

But it was only Omer on his bicycle.

"Finally!" Joel said. "Where's Noa?"

Omer's eyes beamed with annoyance. "I don't know what's the matter with her! She said she'll be delayed and that she'll get here on her own."

Joel raised his eyebrows. "Delayed? That doesn't sound like her."

Omer shrugged. "I think she's a little ticked off, too."

Joel drew his cell phone from his pocket, then paused. "What's she upset about?"

"I don't know. She said she needed to do something she didn't want to do."

Joel swallowed hard, dialed and waited. "Hi, where are you? No, he told us but...uh, yes, OK... She hung up," Joel said, "and she's ticked off."

"Told you."

"Shall we wait for her?"

"No way! If she wants to come, let her. We don't need favors from her. Besides, she knows the way."

They crossed the grove, and under the cover of the last trees they stopped and observed: the thorn field was abandoned as always. They crossed the tall thicket and thorns with careful steps, trying not to leave a trampled trail behind them. They followed each other as they skipped over the stones filling the dry well. Through the hidden aperture in the wall, they squeezed into the tunnel.

The tight tunnel no longer scared Omer. Every curve, slope and turn were now familiar and clear. Not far from the entrance, Joel stopped, stuck his hand deeply into a crack between layers of rock and took out an elongated, dust-proof plastic pouch. He opened it and peeked in: the light from the headlamp washed over the two packed floater devices. Joel loaded them into the backpack he was carrying and kept on moving. Before long, they were able to stand upright and advance.

"So the problem with the refuse is this," Joel said in a troubled voice, turning his head towards Professor Peretz and Omer. "The energy becomes matter, which passes through the veins to the Great Spirit and dissolves back into energy. But it's not a clean dissolution, a division with leftovers, which is the refuse. The important memories, the unique life experiences, pass into the Great Spirit, to which we are connected at all times. The general life force. And the refuse? What does it carry?"

Death?

"And is it matter or energy?" Joel said. "An enormous amount of unimportant memory paste, of thought particles, that go down to the bottom of the river, and then what? It couldn't be just for nothing! What is this refuse?"

"It could be that the refuse is potential," Professor Peretz said, breaking a long silence, "that it is the possibility of a billion future experiences."

"Potential." Joel said.

"Perhaps that is the reason that those who viewed the transparencies filled themselves with refuse," Professor Peretz said. "Perhaps through it, they could view experiences not yet experienced, see things not yet created. That is why they had to be purged of it immediately, because this potential, outside the Great Spirit, is illogical knowledge— it could have devastated them."

They fell silent as they stopped in front of the circular chamber. Joel shook off his thoughts and entered. He unburdened himself of the backpack and passed one of the floaters and the tube of contact gel to Professor Peretz. When they finished preparing Omer, Peretz knelt beside him. Joel waited for them with the connecting tube. It seemed to Omer that the look in Peretz's eyes asked him to reconsider. He cleared his throat "No one can help you there."

Omer shrugged with obstinate simplicity and motioned for Joel to connect the tube.

The sparkles of the river flashed at him almost at once, glittering far below him. The rustle of a light wind rose in his ears. Town Man spread his arms to the sides. He could feel the wind, enjoy it.

Such fun!
He concentrated and listened, but felt no presence nearby.
Better wait for it.
Calm enveloped him—no tension, no concern. He was ready, filled with an odd impatience. The river glittered far below, golden red. Town Man laughed, filled with joy:
Like her hair!
He descended towards the river. The flashes intensified, nearly blinding him. His feelings sharpened, and the beauty of the river grew deeper, more compact, until he found it hard to descend against this viscous density, like between two magnets repelling each other.

As though a line was crossed, the thickness vanished, and so did all the beauty. The river changed, became enraged. A fierce wind blew in his face, raising a freezing spray that reached him—a warning.

He slowed down but didn't stop. The storm grew stronger. The wind whistled, deafening, powerful and freezing, wrestling with him. Town Man did not back down.

And again, as though a certain line was crossed, as though the storm remained above him, the river surface turned quiet and smooth, disturbed only by tiny ripples.

He was within touching distance of the river, filled with renewed peace of mind and great concentration. He refrained from entering the water, dithering. His gaze sharpened, penetrating the clarity. Far in the depths of the river he noticed a gray stain taking shape, growing clearer. To his astonishment, he recognized his own face—not as a mirrored reflection—he himself, different, separate.

Am I already in the river?

He focused his gaze further on the image deep in the river, scary and intimidating. He noticed that the face—his face—bore a painful expression. The wide-open eyes feared to close: they were trying to hint something to him.

Town Man recoiled but did not retreat. He noticed something coming out of his image deep in the river: a transparent density. The wave rose, and drew closer. Town Man's image in the river began to dissipate. He took a last glance at it and noticed the calm on its face. At that moment he realized what the approaching thing was: fear, reaching out to him from himself in the river.

Run away from it? Run away from the fear? Absurd. Like chasing courage.

Town Man waited in terror. The wave of density approached with accelerating speed, full of silent force. A moment later, it reached the surface of the river. With a sickening, bubbling sound, it crashed against him, blinding him.

When the blindness subsided, something about the river changed. Either Town Man's vision had become sharper, or the river itself had become clearer. It was as though he was above an endless chasm.

He tried to organize his thoughts. He tried to silence or isolate or ignore the fear. But the planted seed began to sprout and grow in his mind. He had only a short time to decide; if he didn't enter the river now, he wouldn't dare do it later. He drew closer, within touching distance, and then stopped, hesitant.

At that moment he realized that he was too late. He shouldn't have hesitated. Now he couldn't overcome the fear. This realization pained him, filled him with rage, built up a scream within him. He tried to relax, but the anger burning within him lit a flame of self-hate and despair.

The scream grew stronger and stronger, until it finally burst out. "No!"

In boiling anger, he leapt toward the river.

The surface of the river shut before him and took on a hard glaze. The river filled with scorn, mocking him.

Town Man reached out and touched it, appalled. He stood on the river's surface, got down on his knees, feeling it with both hands. Despair flooded him.

It doesn't want me.

The thought was painful. Town Man remained like that for a moment, his hands flat against the surface of the river, and then raised a hand and struck with all his might.

"I want to get in!"

His own shout re-lit the inner burn, turned his his fears into determination. He struck the cover once more. Something was lit beneath—a pair of yellow, elongated, familiar eyes.

The dragon from the dream!

And at once he remembered. *They have good intentions.*

"Help me get in!"

The yellow eyes looked at him with disinterest.

Town Man did not give up. "Help me get in!"

For a long moment, the creature continued to look at him with no interest and then, it reached up with heavy laziness, and pierced the cover with the tip of its pointy tail. Town Man leapt and grabbed the rough tip with both hands. He held on and did not let go even when he was drawn—sucked into the river, his arms nearly ripped off. He gritted his teeth.

Long, burning lines cut into his flesh and penetrated his body through his fingernails, through his ears. They burned in his lungs, sawed at his teeth, clawed into his spine. He was completely paralyzed. He felt nothing but his palms, tightening around the tip of a rough tail with all his might.

The pain subsided. Town Man's fingers remained bent, but empty—the creature and its tail disappeared. He succeeded in moving his limbs. The pain was replaced by a sense of flow. His body became a net—the river not only surrounded him but flowed right through him.

Town Man raised his hands over his head, spreading them to the sides, reveling in the flow. He made his way down with feathery slowness. The flow was not uniform, but made of thousands of ultra-fine, delicate flows, and these infinite flows, passing through him, connected him to everything and everywhere in the world. He felt himself glow, his spirit sharpened, and he belonged to everything, and everything belonged to him.

He circled himself, joyful, powerful, glowing.

Power without preparation is a trap.

The sudden thought made him pause.

Gotta be careful with this.

Town Man came to his senses. He focused his thoughts and directed himself towards the riverbed, sinking slowly towards an immense purple surface, a dark desert stretching from one horizon to another. The more he descended, the lighter the purple, glowing, as though giant projectors lit the riverbed. It seemed lumpy all of a sudden, like oily purple bubbles. Now, up close, Town Man saw that the purple desert was actually very deep.

The refuse!
He approached within arms-length.
I need to enter it!
In amazement, he passed his hand over the purple. The bubbles felt his hand, responding, rising to it. He held his hand still for a moment, and the bubbles pushed against it like puppies to their mother. Town Man smiled. He lowered a finger toward one of the bubbles, and it rose and touched him.

He screamed and recoiled, shaking his hand in agony. The purple was absorbed like ink on paper. Town Man's finger was stained from the inside. He forced himself to relax, to think with a cool head.

You touch the drift and it fills you. Nothing to be done about it. That's what needs to be done. Fill up with refuse.

Reluctant, he lowered his hand to the purple bubbles rushing toward it. He descended until he touched them. They were quick to be absorbed into him, staining him from the inside— the fingers and palm, the hand and entire arm. The purple invaded his chest, stomach and legs, coloring his field of vision.

Everything turned purple.

The bubbles soon stopped edging at his finger, refrained from being absorbed into him. Then they began shying away. Town Man's purple body no longer scared him. On the contrary, he was pleased with himself.

Now I need to go up.

He feared he would have difficulty rising, that he had become clumsy, but once he tried to move, he was glad to see that his movements were as light as before.

Strange thoughts flooded him. At first he paid no attention, but the further he got from the riverbed he noticed that he was having trouble concentrating. Unfamiliar idea shards wove into his thoughts: meaningless words, noises, images.

It's the refuse. Ignore it. You have to concentrate.

Town Man advanced upwards. The alien thought fragments wouldn't let go; they hummed around him like bees around a hive. He had trouble concentrating, and became thought-drunk. He could no longer see the bottom of the river.

Sharp pricks of pain in his fingertips woke him, returning him instantly to focus and alertness. He was approaching the upper part of the river. Recalling the pains of entry, he tensed, preparing to cross the painful part as quickly as possible and reach the river's surface. The pain increased, becoming sharp stabs, reaching every part of his body.

Advance, don't stop. Advance, don't stop. Advance.

The long burn stripes hit him once again. He twisted at their touch, as though he was being deeply cut all along his frame. He could barely go on.

Advance! Don't stop! I won't make it. I won't make it, no! Don't think, don't give up.

He was completely blocked, stuck under a load too great, which he was trying to lift too high, unable to let go or go on. A sharp contraction stabbed his chest, taking his breath. Town Man gritted his teeth hard, holding a terrible scream within him. He strained all his powers, his force of spirit and the will to keep progressing. Long cracks appeared in his hands.

I'm disintegrating!

The panic damaged his focus. He noticed himself begin to retreat.

No! Don't go back! Don't give up! Hard!

The effort became unbearable. He balled his hands into fists with unrelenting force. He bit his lip, his head exploding with pain, noise, and effort. But the retreat did not stop.

"No!"

"Omer!"

The voice was clear, but could not locate its source, nor could he answer.

"Omer!"

This time he saw her, approaching him like a bird of prey descending on its quarry. Her red hair turned as dark as soil.

Agony twisted her face and body. She approached, trying to tell him something.

He trembled. Her hand fastened on his with great force. Her voice slammed him from dream to reality.

"Omer, are you all right?"

What are you doing here? How did you—? Is this all a dream? A regular, nothing dream, like all the others, not real? Not connected? The Great Spirit? The Great Nothing?

"Omer, are you all right?"

Town Man nodded heavily. Noa's face was pale and fatigued, like a person coming inside from a winter storm. Concern was evident in her eyes, decisive and resolute. "We're getting out of here in one shot, OK? Are you ready?"

New strength flowed through Town Man. He nodded. Their eyes met for a moment, and it seemed that at that moment their wills, thoughts and strengths joined as well. Noa raised her eyes upwards and they began to move. Her red hair covered both their shoulders.

The pain increased. Town Man could already see the surface of the river. He pointed upwards. Noa did not respond, staying focused. They crashed hard against the cover with their heads and shoulders. Noa sustained most of the blow and barely held back a cry of pain. She placed her hands flat against the transparent cover. Her voice betrayed great fatigue. She spoke with clenched jaws, her eyes narrowed. "What is this thing?"

"Didn't you run into it when you came in?"

"No."

"It's a sort of coating on the river."

"How do you get past it?"

"You can't pass it without help," Town Man said. "You need help. When I entered there was this creature that—"

"You ready?" Noa cut him off, her voice rough and decisive. She tightened her grip around his waist again.

They gathered momentum with a slight descent. Her hand gripped his, and he strength flew in both directions. When their eyes met, his gaze was clear and strong.

"Ready."

The trace of a smile appeared on Noa's lips. Town Man missed that smile.

"Let's go!" she said.

This time, they hit the cover with more force, and to their surprise, it didn't stay hard, but flexed around them, stretched, rose with them like the crust of old paint in a forgotten can, soft and heavy. And as it stretched, it made an ugly sound of liquid ripping. The crust rose but did not break.

We won't make it! I don't have the power. Maybe we need to go down...

"Omer, now!" Noa said. "Don't give up!"

Her voice penetrated him like a jet of scalding air. It circled through his body and hammered at his brain. They retreated, surrendering to the heavy crust.

"Omer, don't give up!"

Town Man recognized the edge of tears in her voice.

Because of me?

Something awoke within him. *Don't give up!*

Her grip on his waist loosened, and he tightened his hand around her body with all his might. Her eyes were exhausted, but she seemed to recognize something in his expression and draw strength from it. Her hand tightened around his waist once more, and the trace of a smile resurfaced on her lips.

For one more moment they waited, hesitating. Neither would have the strength for another attempt. They tightened their holds on each other, concentrated their thoughts once again, their wills. Riding their joined force, they burst upwards yet again.

The heavy crust stretched above them, but did not burst. Their faces twisted from strain, their eyes turned to narrow slits, their jaws tightened. But the crust did not yield either, and every passing moment sapped more of their strength. Their progress slowed, until it stopped.

Despite all this, their unified thought remained sharp, persistent and focused. And at a certain moment, like a finger sensing a fault in a smooth surface and stopping at it, the density of their thought found a weakness point at the crust and created a tiny opening in it.

"Now," Noa shouted. "Hard!"

They remained stuck in the crust, squeezed, pressed on all sides. And then, their shouts burst out, carrying the remainder of their strength with it.

A velvet silence enveloped them. Far below, the river glistened, in all its thousands of flashes.

We made it!

Town man raised excited eyes at Noa. She wouldn't look at him. Her profile disappeared in the mass of red hair.

"Noa, we made it!"

The excitement in his voice sounded hollow. Noa kept looking at a vague, distant spot. Only after a long moment did she turn her face to him. Her eyes brimmed with tears.

What? Crying? Why?

Town Man wanted to ask but the words wouldn't cross his lips. It seemed to him that she too wanted to say something, but remained silent. Another moment, and then she moved away, disappearing.

Town Man stared long and hard at the spot. The velvet silence around him turned suffocating, stressing his solitude. He lowered a thoughtful gaze to the river, to its golden glimmers.

Such strength she had.

"Yaam, Qualia."

Town Man jumped. He hadn't sensed her presence. "Yaam, Town Man."

She looked like she did in the dream exchange: a tiny old woman, her skin black, her hair white. She looked at him with her clouded, half-closed eyes. Other presences surrounded him.

"Yaam, Rain Forest. Hello, Town Man."

"Yaam, World Man."

A pulse of fright ran through him.

He saw them: Rain Forest Woman and World Man, floating in a seated position, legs folded, moving closer to each other, faces lowered and hands in their laps.

World Man raised his smiling eyes. His gaze pierced Town Man like a bullet. Town Man wanted to run but didn't know where to go.

Mockery.

Shoulder touched shoulder, knee touched knee, elbow to elbow. Rain Forest and World Man's motions ceased. World Man's eyes turned serious, then he lowered his gaze.

The disintegration began: tiny spherical sparks flew. Rain Forest and World Man became two bustling clumps, rustling with countless colorful little balls. The two attached, pressed, resisted and finally combined into one big shapeless mass.

Town Man watched the display in fascination. Qualia approached him. "You're a very brave coward, Town Man."

The shapeless mass divided once again into two separated rustling clumps. They tightened and soon took on distinct shapes: Rain Forest and World Man once again.

Now me, before he leaves.

Town Man approached World Man. Not surprised, World Man motioned with his hand, inviting Town Man to sit beside him. There was no mockery in World Man's eyes now, only smiling curiosity. Town Man sat cross-legged. He placed his hands in his lap and lowered his gaze.

Now, don't think. Don't think about anything.

Shoulder touched shoulder. Knee touched knee. Elbow to elbow. Town Man was drawn into a powerful vortex, noisy, flashing, twisted...

And at once, it all stopped. The tumult was replaced by full silence. And fog, dissipating. Town Man listened to the silence within him.

Everything passed to him?

Like the waking pinpricks of a numb arm, rustles began flickering in his mind: vague shards of foreign thoughts. He raised his eyes to World Man's face and recognized deep surprise in it.

"I... There's a lot of noise? Inside me. I don't know, I'm hearing a lot of..." He fell silent again, looking around in wonder. "And I'm also seeing all kinds, all sorts of strange sights."

Qualia approached them, her calm, clouded gaze focused on World Man. "It's the drift raging within you, World Man. From the bottom of the river. Remnants of memories."

Qualia turned to Town Man.

Letting me tell him.

"Uh, it's the refuse from the bottom of the river," he said. "It's what's left of the snowflakes that melt in the river."

World Man listened, fascinated.

"It settles and collects there, and then I went down and it filled me—"

"You entered the river? To the bottom?"

Joy passed through Town Man. He nodded. "And now that we've done the passage, it's passed to you as well."

Town Man fell silent.

"Memory refuse," The eyes of World Man filled with wonder. "Noise, I feel as though there are a million voices inside me. And flashes. Sort of flashes of images, like..."

He fell silent for a moment, a smile touching his lips: "Like I've had one drink too many. Actually, one bottle too many."

World Man's smile widened. A warm, pleasant smile. He focused on Town Man. "But entering the river, going down till... what was it like?"

Town Man thought for a moment. "Mostly painful. But only at first. And when you get filled with refuse that noise inside of you begins."

I'm beating around the bush and not telling him, Town Man thought in growing frustration. *I have to tell him. He has to give it back!*

World Man's gaze clouded and cleared, glassy and crystallized, like moving clouds reflected in the windows of an office tower.

"Way to go, really, for daring to go in," World Man said with sincere appreciation.

Warm fondness filled Town Man. For a moment, he tried to sound decisive, but instead stuttered. "You can only go into the river, uh, with the transparencies. Only you and me. But now we need..." He fell silent, raising distraught eyes to Qualia.

"The transparencies must return to their place, World Man," Qualia said.

World Man's gaze sharpened and instantly turned wild.

"The transparencies are a magnifying glass," she said, "with which to look at the Great Spirit. Now they are concentrating sun rays and scorching the world."

Not a muscle moved in World Man's face, but a clear shadow passed over it. He turned bitter, furious, vicious. "You ambushed me. The transparencies in exchange for removing the refuse. Control of the transparencies, this is what it's all about, huh?"

Power without preparation is a trap.

Qualia remained calm, her voice softened. "We are not enemies, World Man. We don't want the transparencies for ourselves. They need to return to their place."

"Oh, this is ridiculous!" World Man said. "A man cannot unknow what he already knows. You understand that nothing will prevent me from returning to take them."

"Then help us find a solution," Qualia said, "you can—"

"I have no such intention," World Man said. "The transparencies stay with me."

His voice was calm, but the intermittent cloudiness of the refuse filled his eyes, the one that screens the thought process with noises, fragments of images and shards of foreign thoughts.

How is he staying focused?

"The transparencies cause damage, World Man," Qualia said. "The Body Cooling Phenomenon, the blurs in the Great Spirit."

"You treat these things as facts," World Man said. He spoke in a moderate tone. It was evident he was battling on two fronts, trying to calm his swirling thoughts as well. "It was only a few days ago that we heard these rumors, and I promised to check everything. But you have to understand, it's always the same—some news story pops up and everybody jumps on it. If the use of the transparencies has side effects then they need to be dealt with, but there's no need to shut down everything right away."

Qualia lowered her eyelids over her clouded eyes, as though closing off, accepting the verdict. This scared Town Man. World Man saw it, too. "I intend to keep using the transparencies.

They are a natural resource and I have them! But as I promised, I will investigate the issue to the fullest extent. And if need be...I swear! I'll stop using them."

Qualia's blackening lips stretched into a sad smile. Her eyes shut completely. She nodded. "You are unearthing a large boulder from a mountaintop, World Man. When it begins to slip, will you be able to stop it?"

World Man did not reply. He looked at Qualia and Town Man for a long moment. His expression was sharp and alert. Then he began to float away. "I need to leave. Yaam."

Power without preparation!

Qualia's voice was commanding and pleading. "World Man!" World Man stopped.

"I don't know how the drift will impact you when you are outside," she said.

World Man's face changed, as though purified. The anger vanished from it, replaced by a sort of grateful warmth. After a moment he turned, drifted away and vanished.

At once, the refuse stormed within Town Man. The same, unfamiliar voice fragments and image shards swirled inside, blinding him. Qualia's voice calling his name reached his ears. She was far away, motioning for him to come. His thoughts sharpened for a moment.

Calling me to get free of the refuse.

Chapter 32

Michael Lampston's eyelids lifted with slow cautiousness. He remained motionless for a long moment, deep inside Site 2, listening to the silence around him, to the silence within him, in tense concentration. Beside him stood Ernest Cole-Angel, worried. Their eyes met. Cole-Angel bent towards him.

"Is everything OK, Michael?"

Lampston waited a few more seconds, raised an eyebrow, and then let out a short laugh. "Of course everything is OK! Everything is fine. I just needed to make sure that the noise... How long was I floating?"

"Three minutes and ten seconds," Cole-Angel said, looking at a stop-watch.

Lampston rose from the folding cloth chair. The floater was still on his head. A tube connected the floater to an anchor in the wall, long enough to allow Lampston to stand up straight.

"You had to make sure that the noise...?" Cole-Angel said.

Lampston dislodged the tube from the wall, lost in thought. A clarity of mind filled him, along with unexplained happiness. His senses were sharper than ever before, his mind alert and attentive. He replied to Cole-Angel's question with a dismissive wave of his hand, and carefully removed the floater from his head.

But as he looked at Ernest once again, he noticed something strange—something was distorted in the man's face. A thin, beeping sound, almost inaudible, made him freeze. Lampston closed his eyes and listened. The beeping was indeed there, a precursor to the noise. He opened his eyes and met Cole-Angel's gaze.

"I might have to go back to float at once."

"What? Now? Why?"

Lampston did not respond. He remained focused on the sounds within him. Now he knew for certain that the noise was approaching. He was terrified at the thought and tried with all his might to control himself. "Listen. I'll explain everything later. I promise. Right now I need your cooperation. OK?"

The inner noise continued to intensify. A cacophony of beeps, rustles and creaks. Tiny glimmers began to accompany the noise. He knew that these would soon become flashes, obscure image fragments.

Ernest Cole-Angel looked into the a glassy expression in Lampston's eyes, coming and going, closing off the man's gaze for a moment and then vanishing.

"I think," Cole-Angel said, "that perhaps it would be best if you rested a bit because you look—"

"We have no time!" Lampston fumed. "I've been set up. I was loaded with refuse from..."

He fell silent for a moment, reached out and laid a hand on Cole-Angel's shoulder. "Trust me, Ernest, I know what I'm doing."

"I'm not sure it's a good idea in this state—"

Lampston screamed in a voice not his own. "I know what I'm doing!"

He fell silent, astonished. His own scream revealed to him what he was so afraid of. He took a deep breath, letting a smile spread across his face.

"Ernest, please, trust me," he said in a quiet, pensive voice.

Lampston arranged the floater on his head. All that time, he kept trying to ignore the noise, the fragments of thought and shards of images making it difficult for him to stay focused. He finished attaching the connecting buttons and approached the socket.

"Michael, stop!" Ernest Cole-Angel said, compelled to intervene. "I know you'll get angry, but I can't let you connect like this. You must rest. You—"

"If you don't want to help then just step aside!" Lampston hissed. His time was running out. When a strong, gentle hand gripped his shoulder, holding him back, a sense of fright and rage swirled within him.

"Ernest, don't you dare."

"I can't let you do this," Cole-Angel said in a resolute tone.

Michael Lampston ripped himself from Cole-Angel's grip with a wild shoulder motion. The ferocity of the action unveiled the pent-up anger within him. He tried to relax and make his movements seem cool and collected.

The coolness with which he dressed his rage was only paper-thin. When he felt Ernest Cole-Angel's restricting hand on his shoulder again, he lost control and struck with force.

Cole-Angel tottered. He stumbled, but immediately lunged at Lampston once again, pushed him away from the socket and held him tight.

Lampston's next blow was no longer intended just to push his friend-turned-enemy away. Turning ninety degrees inside the hands embracing him, he sent a massive punch into the bottom of Cole-Angel's ribcage. The man groaned in pain and collapsed but would not let go. Another blow loosened Cole-Angel's grip. Lampston broke free and collected the dropped floater from the floor. He moved away and once again tried to arrange it on his head.

Cole-Angel got off the floor, but instead of attacking Lampston again, he turned to the nearby metal table and grabbed the comm device on it.

"Gerryowen, can you hear me?" he yelled into the device. "Can you hear me? Come in!"

Lampston crossed the few feet separating them. Cole-Angel didn't try to escape. but shielded the comm device with his body, preventing Lampston from snatching it away. A few seconds passed from his call to Gerryowen, very long seconds for Cole-Angel.

"I hear you, Ernest."

Michael grabbed the flexible antenna and tried to break it..

"Get here right away, with a medic!" Cole-Angel said. The device was snatched from his hand, smashed against the corner of the metal table and thrown across the room.

Michael Lampston's heart exploded against his chest. The noise that flooded him was a bit muffled, but the flashes intensified. They became so blinding as to make it hard to walk. Hands grabbed him. His mind cleared as he met the chilly gaze of Security Chief Gerryowen.

Lampston turned to him with forced calm. "I was set up. I need to go back to float, to remove the refuse from me!"

"Who set you up?" Gerryowen said.

"A few in the Great Spirit," Lampston said, not liking Gerryowen's matter-of-fact tone.

"Why?"

"They want," Lampston said, stopping himself from mentioning the transparencies. "They want us to stop using the spiritglow."

"Why?" Gerryowen said. "What's their problem?"

I'm being held and interrogated!

"Get your stinking hands off me," he said. "You are out of your minds!"

The grip slackened. Ernest Cole-Angel approached him, his gaze soft and concerned. "Michael, something bad is happening to you—"

"Nothing is happening to me. Step aside."

"Maybe like you told us happened to that professor," Cole-Angel said, "that he went crazy from the floating, had a breakdown—"

"He didn't go crazy," Lampston said, "he—"

"Maybe you really should rest a bit," Gerryowen cut him off in a severe, harsh tone.

Gerryowen's grip tightened around him again. Something cold and damp wiped Lampston's arm. Alarm rose through his body, brought on by an approaching needle.

"Wait!" he said, trying to shy away from the needle. "Listen!"

Gerryowen signaled with his eyes and the needle stopped in mid-air.

"They want us to stop using the spiritglow because it causes the coo—" Lampston fell silent. Again, an instantaneous thought crossed his mind, an instinctive warning. "It's causing blurs in the Great Spirit."

The noises and fragments had turned into a storm. Gerryowen's voice no longer penetrated the thick screen. A sharp jolt surprised his arm. There was nowhere to escape. He stumbled, but was caught, carried backwards and laid back.

Chapter 33

Hadassa was surprised by the personal stories contained in the report. Amid the facts and figures and medical findings were several hundred pages of personal accounts of the disease from all over the world.

That's good, Hadassa decided, though she couldn't bring herself to read them. *It shouldn't all be statistics.*

She could write her own chapter. She'd start by saying that, in some ways, Ari's last days had been the best of their lives together. He insisted she go to work as usual, then tell him all about her day in the minutest detail—every conversation, every encounter, moment by moment, as if he were living his life through her, the only way he knew how.

He stopped telling Hadassa his dreams—he could see they only upset her. They'd also removed the TV from his room, opting for the radio instead. Gradually, Ari's cravings subsided, and his insatiable desire for a certain orange juice, a specific brand of pain reliever and a single type of paper towel disappeared. He spent more and more time asleep, or in a trance—Hadassa refused to call it a coma—where she could not go. She wished she'd had the courage to question him about that world the way he questioned her about her day in the so-called real world, but that wasn't in her, and she knew he saw her skepticism in the corner of her mouth and the arch of her brow.

Still, Hadassa told herself, years later, alone in the secret reading room, *I could have played along.*

Chapter 34

Omer opened his eyes to a narrow slit. The beam of a flashlight illuminated the tiny chamber. He was reluctant to open his eyes further. A stranger sat in front of him, looking at him: a young boy. Out of the corner of his eye, Omer noticed the silhouette of another person, standing.

I'm awake, or am I?

"He's opened his eyes?" came a whisper.

It's Joel.

Joel bent down, bringing his face closer. Professor Peretz's voice came from the side. "Omer, are you OK?"

The professor's kind, pleasant voice made Omer glad and at ease.

"Hey, are you OK?" Joel said.

Omer did not respond. He was exhausted, as though a great weight had been poured into each of his limbs. There was another thing as well: a sort of distress, a slight depression. He opened his eyes fully.

I know this kid!

The strange kid held a floater in its limp hands, thin and bald, staring at him with blue eyes through glasses.

God, she shaved her head!

"Noa!" Omer said, hardly believing it.

"Ha!" Joel said. "He didn't recognize her."

Omer couldn't take his eyes off Noa. Her lips curled downwards, pressed together. There was a moisture to them.

Professor Peretz approached, concern in his voice. "Are you OK? You look tired."

Omer nodded and rose to his feet. "I'm fine."

Joel packed the floaters with haste and scanned the room. "Come on, let's get out of here," he said. "We'd better fly."

A heavy silence enveloped them as they walked through the tunnel. When they emerged from it, Noa drew away from the others and walked alone.

Noa and Omer soon parted with Professor Peretz and Joel, who rode off in Joel's car. The two teens rode their bikes, Noa pulling away and riding before him alone, thin as a rail, almost vanishing in the bluish blackness of the evening. *Silent. Not looking back.*

At first, Omer tried to ride beside her. He remained behind, looking at her—she seemed so different without her mane of hair, a small head stained with sticky mousse.

Delicate neck. Fragile frame. Like Samson after he was cut. But what courage she has. If only I had half of it.

Soon they left the fields and moved to the asphalt road. At the entrance to her villa neighborhood, Noa stopped, not far from her home, next to a small playground. She leaned her bicycle against a lamppost and sat down on the yellow plastic seat of a merry-go-round. Omer sat two seats away.

The silence between them dragged on. She refrained from looking at him, fixing her eyes on the grass instead. He couldn't avoid looking at her again, mesmerized. A drop rolled down her nose, and his heart missed a beat. When she finally spoke, her voice sounded steady, but different, low and quiet.

"I'm a little depressed," she whispered, her eyes on the grass. She cleared her throat and sniffed. "I'm cold inside. And I'm also a little afraid. My mom will blow a gasket when she sees it. My dad too."

Because of me.

She dared not touch her head. He wanted to reach out for her, but couldn't muster the courage.

"And then at school—"

"You saved me!" Omer said, choking.

Another tear rolled down her nose. She hesitated for a moment. "I don't regret it, you should know that," she said, "But..."

She fell silent, her smile hiding sadness as she removed her glasses and wiped them with her shirt. She put them back on and looked at him. Her blue, moist eyes examined him.

"It's just, I feel a little stupid, and..."

Tears and a smile. Like a rainbow. Her mom will blow a gasket.

Her hand slapped the knee brace with a sort of despairing rage. "With this stupid thing on my leg all the time, and now..." Her hand passed over the side of her head. "Now this... I look like some sort of a lizard, you see? An ugly lizard."

What?! You're so beautiful!

He couldn't get the words out. They stabbed at his throat, fighting to emerge, but his obstinate mouth remained dumb.

Noa was silent. She wiped her nose and eyes with the short sleeve of her shirt and got up from the yellow plastic seat. She adjusted her glasses on her nose and walked over to her bike, pulling it away from the post.

"Noa!"

She stopped for a moment, looking at him. He lowered his eyes.

"You..."

Well, tell her already! Dummy.

"I... I would have stayed stuck there..."

Noa smiled. It seemed as though she was a bit more at ease. She got on her bicycle and pedaled away, turning to a side street and disappearing. Omer remained seated for another long moment.

He rose from the carousel seat, turned heavily to his bicycle and picked it up reluctantly. A long line of street lamps flickered at once, coming to life, although it was not yet completely dark. The sky was still lit in dark blue and violet purple.

He rode on the sidewalk, listening to the dull roar made by his off-road tires, to the squeak of the left pedal, creaking down, creaking up. In no hurry to get home, he made a wide detour through the commercial zone and Joel's neighborhood.

His ride was slow, painted with sadness. He reached a pedestrian staircase and didn't even attempt to ride up, getting off his bike and pulling it along. He passed the locked gate of his school, mounting again as he turned and rolled down the gentle incline. The cars on the road had already turned on their headlights. He crossed an intersection and rode in front of a giant billboard, slowing before its blinding light, then stopping altogether. He stared at the soundless advertisements, meaning to keep riding, but the beginning of an ad glued him in place. The screen was flooded by a powerful darkness, like that of an eclipse. At once, the sign was lit again, displaying city information.

Omer shook off the overwhelming emotions and hurried away.

That was one of their ads! I can tell!

He turned into a quieter street, and from there into Joel's street, where he stopped. Next to Joel's apartment building he noticed two large SUVs. Both had tinted windows, with their parking lights on. Omer approached them, pedaling with slow curiosity.

One of the vehicles tilted as several people boarded it. The doors slammed, the headlights turned on and it lumbered away with surprising speed. The other vehicle waited. Next to it stood a tall, bulky man in an expensive suit who spoke on a cellular phone. Omer stopped pedaling, letting his bike roll on its own. A wordless warning flickered in his mind, igniting a sense of danger.

The man finished talking, opened the door and laid a foot on the runner board. Omer passed near him. Their eyes met. The sense of danger compressed into Omer's mind and formed a clear sentence.

We gave at the office.

A single heartbeat seemed to suck all the blood from Omer's body. A sudden weakness made his arms go soft. He passed the tall man as his feet fumbled at the pedals. The blood re-flooded him all at once. His face and chest flushed, pinpricks in his armpits. Cold sweat covered his head. He rode on from there, the man's eyes stabbing the back of his head.

But despite the storm of fright, Omer managed not to look like he was fleeing the scene. At the first available turn, he climbed left, into a narrow pedestrian lane. He crossed a little park as fast as he could, and only then did he dare turn around and watch the car drive away. He realized who the people who boarded the car were. *Perhaps forced on board.*

Fear seeped into Omer like water through a test-tube full of sand.

A sharp squeal made him jump. It was followed by laughter from children playing ball in the park. He kept on riding and left them behind as he entered a quiet side path. Dizziness overcame him, forcing him to stop and get off his bike. Nausea spread through him, and a strange faintness that made his knees go soft. He tried to walk beside his bike but lost his bearings. The path twisted under his feet, swaying, eluding him.

Qualia, calling me to exchange a dream.

In the last moments of consciousness, with strange, cool calmness, he hid his bike among large bushes before collapsing beside them. His gaze turned through the thin branches of a thorny shrub to a nearby streetlight. A small fracture in the cover of the light focused an orange beam straight at his face. The beam became stronger and stronger, so blinding that he was forced to close his eyes.

Chapter 35

A weak light source, smoky-gray, low to the ground, revealed the front of a round, wooden stage. Golden bars enclosed it like a circus cage. Omer observed it, hidden in the dark. On a low and narrow bed, in the center of the cage, lay a striped, tiger-like figure, breathing deep in sleeping.

Omer approached the cage with cautious steps over rustling, gravelly dirt. The sound of breathing was interrupted. Omer stopped. A muffled voice replaced the breathing, heavy and labored, yet familiar. "Town Man..."

World Man...? Where?

"Town Man..." it called out again, weary.

Where is he?

Omer drew nearer to the cage, stepping into the lit area. The striped creature sensed him. It didn't seem threatening, in fact there was something pathetic about it. It lay in a twisted pose, its large head hanging back to the side of the bed. Omer couldn't see its face, but a small tranquilizer dart was stuck in its furry arm, its tip a tuft of red cloth.

Knocked out, but don't get too close. They have long arms with nails the size, actually claws, long as a finger. But where did he call me from?

Omer turned his searching gaze from side to side. His eyes filled with darkness, and he returned his gaze forward. The cage was now illuminated by brighter light, from a higher source. The golden bars gleamed.

Ha! I thought it was a tiger.

On the narrow bed in the middle of the stage, in the clear light, lay a man in tailored office garb. He was lying in an uncomfortable position, his head tilted backwards, hanging off the edge of the bed, a tiny syringe in his arm. With visible effort, the man raised his head. Omer recognized the face: World Man, like and unlike. His face was drained of vitality, turned off somehow.

World Man's eyes turned on Omer and were filled with amazement. "You're a boy!"

His head slumped backwards, stopping in a twisted position. His face was once again hidden from Omer.

He's uncomfortable like that!

In desperate frustration, Omer searched for an entrance to the cage, a space between the bars.

Where's the entrance? He needs something under his head, a board or something soft. He must be uncomfortable. Crooked like that. Can't he move?

"We're in deep trouble," World Man said. From the side, only his pale cheek could be seen, moving with his heavy breathing.

Omer circled the cage in slow, measured steps. His hands gripped the golden bars. He could see World Man's face again, which gave him an exhausted smile.

"That's better," World man said, closing his eyes for a long time.

Fell asleep, huh? Oh, that's silly. We're in a dream anyway. We're in deep trouble.

World Man's eyelids cracked open. "I'm under double check. The transparencies. When I could give them back, I didn't want to. Now that I want to, I can't." He tried to lift his head, exerted all his power to lift his shoulders a bit, but failed. He slumped back with a sigh and released a short, despairing laugh.

The laughter fragment struck Omer, penetrated him, echoed inside him. His hands tightened around the bars.

No entrance? How can there be no entrance? If there were one I'd go in. How can there not be one? In every cage. To bring in food, or to clean. Double check. Maybe from above? No, smooth, can't climb it. How can there not be?

"Where's the entrance?" Omer said.

World Man lifted a bewildered gaze towards him, and his eyes passed from bar to bar.

"It's your dream!" Omer said. "There has to be an entrance!" World Man's gaze stopped at a certain point. "There?"

At the spot he indicated Omer saw a small, square entrance. He approached, reached in and slid an inner bolt. The entrance was small and forced him to squeeze in, crawling. His outstretched hands felt the touch of dirt and gripped the edge of an outcropping of rock. He pulled himself forward, as though he had escaped a fox's den. He rose and stood upon light-hued soil covered with dry leaves. He was surrounded by many trees, their tops swaying gently in a light noon breeze.

World Man sat not far away from him, in the sun, on a group of low rocks. He wore shorts, and sandals on his feet. With a red pen-knife, he peeled an apple. The peel curled under his hands into a large dangling spring. When he was done, he raised the peel-snake to his mouth and chewed it with amusement.

"I love the peel," he said, smiling, and cut half of the apple off, handing it to Omer. "Want some?"

Omer took the half and bit. The apple had a cardboard-like texture. He wanted to throw it away. Not far from them stood a large warehouse with a red shingle roof. He pointed at the warehouse. "You see," he said, "That's the warehouse where they come with the car." He turned his finger to a large hole in the ground, lined with stones, hidden in the thorny thicket. "And that's the secret entrance. This is where you connect with the main tunnel."

World Man stood next to him, surprised.

"This..." he said. "I had no idea."

"It's old," Omer said.

World Man inspected the lined hole with his eyes.

"Deep, huh?" he said, his arms folded on his chest.

"Very," Omer said.

World Man stood at the very edge of the hole. Omer joined him, standing next to him.

"Ready?" World Man said. Omer hesitated. World Man's gaze was warm and sympathetic, as though they had known each other for a thousand years. He extended his hand and

World Man grasped it. He jumped into the hole, pulling Omer with him.

The fall was long. *Long and dark. And dizzying.* Distant laughter reached Omer's ears: children at play. An orange beam of light blinded him, emerging from the broken corner of a streetlamp. The sounds twisted and swirled, and vanished along with the light beam.

The fall slowed to a stop. Omer followed World Man out of an elevator into the softness of a carpet in a wide hallway. An opulent lobby, its walls pale marble. The entrances to the elevators were all empty, and each entrance revealed a dark pit.

World Man approached one of the entrances and peeked in. "Dangerous, huh? Have to report this."

Omer was careful not to approach the entrance. He looked to the sides. "Wow, they're so fat!"

In a large aquarium, built into the wall, eleven fish swam around, floating. They were chubby, fluorescent yellow, with blue stripes. A violet light illuminated them from beneath.

Huh, check that out! They can close their eyes. Strange fish.

"Sometimes I feed them eggs," World Man said, tapping the glass pane twice with his finger. "Usually they jump."

World Man left the aquarium behind and turned to the end of the hallway, to huge windows overlooking the abandoned streets of a large city. Omer stood next to him. On the road below them, two long blue SUVs passed by, windows tinted.

Omer tensed, pointing at them. "Look, there! In the cars, they kidnapped them, they're taking them, you understand?"

World Man pressed his face to the window like a curious child. He flattened his palms against the window panes, following the vehicles until they disappeared behind the highrise buildings.

He detached from the window. "I know where they're taking them. We need to free them."

He set out, Omer following him. They ran down a nighttime street, crossing abandoned roads, passing by dilapidated buildings and public parks. The grass trampled under their hurrying feet. Above, the treetops shook in a fierce wind.

They ran across an abandoned warehouse and stopped in front of tall wooden doors. An iron bolt echoed. They exited the warehouse into a field of low-growing clover, awash in sunlight, slick with the nighttime rain, and ran through it, jumping and slipping, laughing. Their shoes kicked up clumps of mud every which way until they stopped before a white picket fence.

"Can you hear that?" World Man said.

Omer heard girls giggling. They sat at a table, drawing.

"Twins—aren't they cute," Omer said.

"You can see them?"

Omer hesitated. "Uh, yeah, no? You can't see them? Drawing."

The effect of his words upon World Man was harsh. He almost collapsed. He knelt, his hands clutching the white fence. "My girls. I can't see them. Do you understand? Do you see what that means?"

The girls stopped drawing and looked around in alarm, their eyes filling with tears.

Crying! How do they know? They feel. Well, he's the father. Must be some kind of sense. His dream. Tell him? Better not. No, no way, I have to.

"They're crying," Omer said, regretting it instantly. World Man's face distorted with pain. Terrible sorrow caused his frame to collapse sideways.

"You have to help me, Town Man," he said, his voice weakening.

"I'll help!"

"You have to tell them to get the refuse off of me," World Man whispered. "You have to persuade them, explain to them. They'll believe you."

"Without returning the transparencies?"

"In order to return them! There is no other way." His hand trembled. He was hard-pressed not to collapse completely onto the ground. "The truth is... the truth is that I am very scared. When I came out of floating, I couldn't manage to explain to them that it was because of the refuse. I threw a fit, and they... are strong." His face became a mask of wonder. "And what if

I can't explain it to them, Town Man? They'll think I'm crazy... The truth is that I'm trembling with fear."

The truth is. Is he speaking the truth? The truth has a certain color...no, not color. What's the word Dad uses? Yes: hue. There's a taint of death in a lie. There's a hue of life in the truth. From some book about a heart. I'll help him. I'll explain to them. She'll believe me. They'll take the refuse off of him. But if he's lying? Because I'm a kid maybe he thinks. Maybe this is a mistake. Qualia knows better about this than I do.

"You have to return the transparencies," Omer said.

World Man's expression became quiet and calm. "I can't get to the transparencies like this, Town Man."

A hue of life. I have to help him. He's telling the truth. Or he's trying to cheat. But I feel the truth! A hue. No! I can't. I have to get out of here. Have to escape.

Omer turned his back on World Man and set out running fast, with all his might. His rapid steps clicked like pebbles falling in the dark. His running turned soft, floating, so fast. But not fast enough to elude a shout. "Omer!"

He knows my name!

Omer stopped. World Man was lying back at the center of the stage in a twisted position. Golden bars rose around him, polished and gleaming. Omer couldn't make out his face, only a cheek. Omer circled the cage, his hands grasping the bars. His eyes met those of World Man.

"How do you know my name?"

"We're sharing a dream. I must have felt it," World Man whispered, closing his eyes. "You should know, I'll return the transparencies if I can. You should know that."

He'll return them. I know. There's a hue of life in the truth. I have to help him. I'll help him.

A pale orange beam of light blinded Omer again. He raised a hand to shield his eyes, looking at the streetlamp through his fingers.

The sound of children arguing passed near him. Between their words, a basketball bounced with a whining twang. The voices sounded close by, but seemed to belong to a different world. The arguing voices receded.

Omer rose to a sitting position. A distressing pressure rose in his chest. He stood up, checking his balance, and turned to his bike. He began to ride, his thoughts floating behind him, as though he were riding ahead of them. He knew his thoughts were there, but couldn't find them them. Images emerged from behind, swerving around and bypassing him, seen for a moment and vanishing—blue cars, tinted windows, Professor Peretz's smile, a tiger, a golden cage, fat neon fish, a peeled apple.

At the first intersection, he turned toward his home. He rode, now on the shoulder of the road, now in the middle of the lane, detached from his surroundings. A police cruiser passed. A female officer gave him a stern look and drove off. The anxiety continued to compress in his chest.

A loud honk made Omer jump on his seat, and he almost shouted. An older woman reprimanded him with an angry hand-gesture as she sped by. Omer turned the bicycle to the side of the road and stopped for a moment. Then, with no clear purpose, turned the other way and rode towards Noa's home.

Noa's mother opened the door for him. She was tall and pale, her hair red and curly, reaching down to her shoulders. She smiled at him and nodded, holding a crumpled white handkerchief. She remained standing at the doorway, her blue eyes piercing him, angry and withholding, her face a hidden storm. Omer looked down.

"She's in the garden," the mother said in a quiet, precise voice, and moved aside to let him through. Not daring to look up at her, he passed her by, the chilliness of her eyes like thorns in his skin.

Noa sat in a far corner of a large wooden deck. She looked so odd with her shaved head. *Like a matchstick.* Her thin arms hugged her knees. They were bare. Unshielded by the mane of red hair. Her chin rested on her knees, her eyes staring at the shadows between the branches of the hedge. She did not turn her head at the sound of his footsteps, staying as motionless as a hunched statue.

The side of her face captured his attention, for the first time so sharp and clear. Her small, precise head seemed vulnerable to him. He sat beside her in silence. Noa turned her face to him for a moment. Her lips didn't lift in a smile for him. Her eyes were wet. She returned her gaze to the shrubbery and motioned forward. Omer remained silent, suddenly sorry he came.

But after a moment, she turned to him again, as though sensing something. "What happened?"

Omer reclined towards her. "Professor Peretz and Joel were kidnapped."

"What?!" Noa said, having to lower her voice. "How do you know?"

"I saw," Omer whispered. He peeked backwards for a moment, making sure they were alone. "When I rode home I passed by Joel's house, and I saw them being put into cars. But after that, I had a dream exchange with World Man."

Noa's eyes went wide with shock. "And what did he want?"

"He asked us to help him get free of the refuse."

"In exchange for Professor Peretz and Joel, instead of putting the transparencies back?" Noa said.

"No, no way!"

"So will he let them go or not? And return the transparencies?"

"He can't. They imprisoned him or drugged him or something."

"World Man? Who did?"

The question, so simple and obvious, surprised Omer. He thought for a moment and then admitted. "I don't know."

Noa passed a hand over her bald head, rustling across the tiny stubble. Her motion, short and natural, caused an unexplainable acceleration in Omer's heartbeat.

"But he's the head of their corporation," Noa said, "So how?"

"It's because of the refuse," Omer said. "They think he's gone crazy or something. I guess he talked nonsense and made a scene."

"He actually told you this?" Noa said.

Omer nodded. Noa's hand stole over her head once more. The prickliness of the stubble was so familiar to Omer. He wanted to reach out and trail his fingers behind her hand, but didn't dare.

Her voice turned rough. "Do you believe him?"

"Yes," Omer said, "It's for real. And I told him I'd help him." On Noa's look, Omer was quick to appease her. "But I can't do anything anyway. I need to tell Qualia about this. She'll know what to do."

They fell silent at the sound of steps on the wood planks. Noa's mother placed a watered plant at the edge of the deck, looked at them briefly and returned indoors.

Awkwardness crippled Omer, clutching something behind his ribs. "I should go."

Noa pierced him with a strange look. "But what about telling Qualia?"

"I hope she'll exchange a dream with me," he said. "I don't know how they do it."

"You're gonna wait for her to exchange a dream with you?"

"What am I—"

"We're going there tonight," Noa said. "Can you get out of your house without anyone noticing?"

I shouldn't have told her.

Omer shifted in his seat. "I can, uh... get out, say through the window, but I think—"

"At midnight sharp be at the corner of my street," Noa whispered with sparkling eyes. "We can do this."

"Yes, but at night? I don't think it's—"

"And don't you dare go to sleep, got it?" She stood up in a springing motion, barely able to contain her renewed excitement. "Come on, come on, go home so your parents don't get upset with you, too."

Chapter 36

Later that night, Omer biked to the meeting-point a little before midnight. A small delivery truck sped down the road, passing Omer with engine roaring, blowing hot exhaust. It drove away, taking its noise and smoke with it. Omer tried to pick up the pace. The creaks of the left pedal accelerated. He turned into the temporary road to the new neighborhood being built, having decided to take a shortcut. The whine of the tires changed into the whispering rustle of dirt. He rode for a few minutes alongside housing developments, and began to regret taking the shortcut. The clear street lighting was replaced by moonlight, pouring a sickly pallor on the skeletal houses and the new sewer trenches.

Omer slowed down. He rode a little longer and suddenly stopped, scared.

What was that?

He held his breath and waited. He looked in fright at the dark between the houses. The motion he had seen did not repeat.

Am I imagining?

He remained standing for a few moments, staring in concentration, then decided to ride back to the road. He turned his bicycle and laid one foot on the pedal, but froze again.

A headlight!

A beam of light moved over one of the houses.

Security guard? No, it's them.

His heart raced. He turned his bicycle around once more, but waited again. The beam of light turned out to be the reflection of the moonlight from a metal insulation sheet. Something inside him urged him to escape and he did so at once, pedaling for all he was worth, narrowing his eyes so as not to see anything but the path. Within a few moments, breathing heavily, he reached the lit portion of the street. He did not slow down or look back. He rode to the agreed-upon street-corner and stopped there, drenched in sweat.

He waited by his bicycle and, in a fit of anger, he pushed it away from him, dropping it on the road. He began pacing the sidewalk. Pain pounded in his head. He ripped a branch from a nearby bush and crumbled its leaves. He walked in circles as though seeking a place to stand. At last, he sat down on the curb and waited, restless.

He heard a bicycle approaching and rose to his feet, annoyed at her tardiness, but when he finally saw Noa, he burst out laughing. "What's this?"

Noa rode hunched over on a small children's bicycle like a circus clown. Colorful tassels dangled from the side of the handlebars. She stopped beside him, a full head shorter.

Omer laughed. "What's up with the bike?"

Noa's bald head gleamed at him with red stubble, matching the embarrassment on her face. "I'm such a moron! I forgot to put mine outside in the evening and then I couldn't 'cause it would've made noise."

"Whose is this?"

Noa shrugged and set out riding, rotating the small pedals rapidly. She was uncomfortable, her knee brace not adjusting to the sharp angle.

At the last intersection before the fields they turned left, riding down the road alongside the sidewalk. The street lighting hid the darkness of the fields to their right. Omer switched gears on his bicycle, the chain rattled and engaged. He shot a quick glance backwards. Noa, riding slower, was left a little behind him. He slowed down, and after a moment looked behind again—a car followed, approaching. Omer left the center of the road and stuck to the shoulder. His ears caught the sound of the car, overtaking him with a purring roar. He glanced and his heart skipped a beat. A large, blue SUV.

His jaw tightened, his body hunched. It seemed to him that the vehicle was slowing down. He didn't dare look. The car advanced and passed him.

Gotta warn her. Escape to the next street. No, we can't, they'll notice!

The vehicle's brake lights came on, strong red. Despair pressed into Omer. He wanted to stop but did not press his brakes.

That's it. We're toast.

The vehicle signaled and turned, entering a side street and disappearing. Weakness shook Omer's body. He kept riding downhill, his movements automatic. He heard Noa approaching him, overtaking him. He saw the nape of her neck, her bald skull gleaming in an indeterminate color under the orange streetlights.

Maybe it wasn't them?

Noa crossed the sidewalk, leaving the paved road. The little wheels of her bicycle raised a plume of pale orange dust. Omer rode behind her. His eyes stuck for a moment to a white stripe in her shirt. The stripe became less and less visible. The two riders became two gray bodies, moving along a pale path in the sylvan light of a partial moon.

Is it waxing or waning? Some light. You cut it upwards diagonally and then you can tell by the shape you get. So what is it now? Waxing. Full of spots. Craters. Took a lot of meteors. Like earth, but no atmosphere.

His fright subsided. He looked at Noa, smiled, touched the gear lever with his thumb and accelerated, catching up with ease. Her knee brace flashed quick fragments of moonlight at him. Omer saw the brace and was filled with remorse.

I'm such an idiot.

"Wanna switch?"

"No."

Her neck and bald head, slick with sweat, glistened in the moonlight and filled Omer with awkwardness.

"Come on, what do you care? I wanna try the little one, too."

Noa stopped pedaling. Her bicycle kept moving forward on inertia. She looked at him, panting, contemplating. She pulled the small handle and the bike stopped, raising dust.

"Here, take it," she said. She got off the small bicycle easily and stood beside it, holding the handlebars. So different without the mane of hair, so different in the moonlight.

She's so beautiful.

"Well?"

Omer got off his bike. Their hands exchanged handlebars, and in an instant of touch exchanged finger heat. Noa got on Omer's bike and began to ride. He heard the chain rattle as it moved between flywheels.

"Wow, what a difference!" she said.

Omer got on the small bicycle and burst out laughing. "How can anybody ride this?"

He turned the small pedals and built up speed along the gravel road. He tried to pop a wheelie. A thin line of joy hit him, and turned silver in the moonlight. Rustling on the gravel, fragrant with dust, the joy melted into him.

A quick flash of light, somewhere in the fields, caught the corner of his eye and focused his attention. The happiness that had collected within him was gone. He looked at the fields as he rode, but the light did not flash again. His bicycle drifted to the dry weeds on the side of the road. He righted his course, but when he looked at the field again he saw something there: like a dark puddle in the middle of the silvery field. It was the figure of a man kneeling, and not far from him another, and another. Now he could see that they were armed with rifles, waiting. He realized that he and Noa would not be able to escape. His bicycle bumping as it rolled over obstacles. His legs were scratched by the thorns as he rode straight at them, lost.

"Omer!"

His foot pushed the pedal backwards, and the rear wheel broke its spin, dragging in the dust. The bike stopped in a thicket of weeds and thorns. He raised surprised eyes at Noa's distant voice. She stood by her bike on the gravel road, close enough for him to make out her silhouette but too far to make out her features. He returned his frightened gaze to the field and saw only silvery land bathed in tricky light. The figures were gone. Like the SUV.

Figments of imagination.

"Omer, are you OK?"

What's happening to me?

A sharp metallic click made him leap. Noa stood her bike on the kick-stand. She approached him with walking-galloping steps.

This is going to be tough if you don't know what's real and what's not—

"Omer?"

"It's, it's OK, Noa!" he answered, tense. Noa stopped. Omer turned his small bike around and advanced toward her.

"Are you OK?" she said.

He shrugged, his gaze leaving hers, turning aside. He jerked his head up at footsteps in the dry grass.

Or is that more nothing? Like the gunmen and the SUV...

Noa's warm hand covered his holding the handlebar. A strange sensation passed from his palm to his entire body, sending shivers through him.

"I'm okay," Omer said before she could ask again, looking up at her—taller than him by half a head. He could not see her eyes—the reflection of the moonlight sealed her glass lenses.

They rode again, and soon saw the first trees of the grove, tall and dark, alongside the path. The trees, few at first, thickened into a dark mass—tall, deep, uninviting.

They rode by moonlight. Omer had difficulty recognizing their location, so he rode behind Noa. When she stopped, he stopped beside her, exactly at the right spot, to the right of the narrow path running through the woods. Noa jumped off her bike and led them on foot. At the trees, she hesitated, as though the deep darkness intimidated even her. She took another step and stopped again, listening.

Omer stood a few steps behind her. "I heard it too!" he whispered, taking half a step back.

Something rustled again by one of the trunks. Noa did not move. "Probably a mouse, no?" she said, half to Omer and half to herself.

She turned her and pushed her bicycle to the hiding place. She was tense and attentive, but not at all prepared for the terrible assault: a creature burst at her. Noa's scream was sharp and piercing.

"Ahhh!"

She ran, breathless. Omer screamed himself, and took cover behind one of the trees. The creature, beating its powerful wings, flew past Noa, escaping at low altitude to the open field.

Noa remained frozen with fear. She hugged herself, pressing shaking hands to her shoulders. "So scary! I freaked out."

"Partridge," Omer said under his breath from his hideout.

"Stupid bird!" Noa said.

Omer chuckled. "Partridge."

The shrieking call of a bird of prey broke out somewhere in the sky: once, twice, three times.

"I hope to God he eats her now," Noa said.

"I think she's a little big for him," Omer said.

"So he can eat only half of her for all I care," Noa said, pulling a tiny flashlight from her pocket and turning the end, focusing the beam. For a moment, she lit up the area around them, checking something, and then began advancing along the path between the trees. Omer walked behind her, nervousness weakening his legs. Noa's scream still echoed in his head.

She sure got scared. Well, it did fly straight at her. I would've fainted. Partridge. Must've been scared too. Silly. They hunt them. Wonder what they taste like. Probably like chicken. Well, it's like a little chicken. Plump though.

A sudden hunger overtook him. He picked up the pace a little and sniffed the air—a distinct, clear, powdery scent. He sniffed again: the rich, enticing fragrance of cocoa.

The darkness thickened, enveloping him, isolating him. The scent was sharp, almost visible. Omer had no problem following it. After a few minutes, he noticed a low bush with green leaves and small, brown fruit. He knelt and sniffed—the scent of chocolate. He reached out with a finger and touched the fruit. It melted and left thick brown juice. Omer brought his finger to his mouth.

"Did you hear them?" Noa whispered in his ear, her voice soft but excited. She stood next to him, listening with a curious ear. Omer remained stunned. The scent vanished, along with the bush and the brown fruit.

Where was I? What was that?

Pain, sharp and burning, pulsed in the side of his head. Omer extended a finger and touched. A long scratch appeared above his ear. He put his finger in his mouth, and his tongue twisted with the saline taste of blood.

Noa lit the flashlight again and began walking.

Scratched by a branch. Gotta be careful. What's happening to me?

"Watch out for the hole." Noa leapt over a narrow ditch and illuminated the ground with the flashlight for Omer's sake.

"Huh, you hear them?" she whispered again, stopping.

Omer heard them. At first one barking yowl and then many yowls, long, distant.

"Jackals," Noa said.

Omer nodded. "Far away."

The distant howls ceased. Noa listened for another moment, lit her flashlight and continued to walk. Omer walked beside her, staying close. A small glade let the moonlight into the heart of the grove. Milky night-time light, hiding and illuminating. A canine figure frolicked in the middle of the glade. A jackal. It rummaged in the weeds in search of something.

Omer extended two fingers and touched the painful scratch at the side of his head, feeling the swelling. When he lowered his fingers he saw they were dark, stained. The jackal in the center of the glade froze in place. One of its forelegs remained raised. Its tail dropped. It sniffed the air, searching.

The pain in the side of Omer's head worsened. Something warm dripped onto his neck. Omer quickly reached out to touch—something thick and smooth.

This is going too far. I need to bandage it.

The cautious jackal advanced towards them, sniffing. Omer motioned towards it. Noa caught the gesture and stopped, looking at the jackal with disdain. The pain in the side of Omer's head intensified. He noticed that the sleeve of his shirt had turned completely red.

It wasn't a jackal but a dog, a wild dog, one of those who ran away from the surrounding villages. It advanced further, fur shaggy, filthy, its frame large and slim, its proud, thin tail raised. Its eyes met Omer's—wild, dark, unfriendly. Its neck bore the remnants of a thick, blue collar.

Blood streamed from Omer's head, flowing over the length of his arm, dripping to the ground from his fingertips. He raised a frightened hand to the wound to stem the flow. The quick motion intimidated the wild dog for a moment, but in an instant a furious glint lit in his eyes. It bared its teeth and emitted a gurgling growl.

Stay upright, Omer thought. *Stay taller than the beast. That way it won't dare.*

The dog's feet moved in place, preparing, a last twitch of muscles prior to attack. Its eyes, mesmerizing in their power, locked onto Omer's. Its tail leveled parallel to the ground. Its yellowing teeth showed, and after an instant twigs flew under its leaping legs—

The dog disappeared. The glade disappeared.

Nothing. Another hallucination. Another nothing to scare you to death.

Noa led on, illuminating the path with her little flashlight. Omer's mind could not fathom the change. His thoughts remained completely frozen. Only after a few moments did he dare look to the sides, and backwards: complete darkness. His hand felt his neck: dry as a bone.

A dog's bone. I'm going crazy. It's the refuse. It stayed inside me! I'm going crazy.

A halo of silvery light illuminated the trees ahead of them. Noa turned the flashlight off and stopped.

"Wow, look how beautiful that is!"

The small valley at the edge of the grove was entirely flooded by the cold moonlight. Noa crossed the trees' shade line, entranced, bathing herself in the glow. She raised her hands to the sides, laughing.

The rustle of the dry weeds changed, softened by the dew. The moisture also changed the scent of the dust raised by their feet. Omer followed Noa, making sure to stay close. They passed a group of low, familiar rocks. Omer stopped and examined them with surprise.

Funny, this is where he sat! With the pocket-knife, peeling an apple. Peeled it to come out like a spring coil. A peel snake. Like the peel. Want some?

"Noa," Omer said

Noa stopped and turned to him.

Omer pointed at the rocks. "This is exactly where he sat!"

"Who?"

"What do you mean who?"

"Who sat here? You said this is where he sat."

"World Man," Omer said "You know, Michael Lampston from the corporation."

Noa's astonishment was complete. "What? When was he here?"

"In the dream exchange," Omer said, "When—"

"You showed him the entrance from the well?!" Noa said. "What are you, a moron?"

A wave of sudden rage flooded Omer's entire body, condensing into his head. "I didn't bring him! It was in a dream, he came on his own! Like you can decide what happens in your dreams, right? Yeah, right!" His throat caught, his eyes filled with tears and he fell silent.

Noa's breathing became short and rapid. Her silence grew longer. She tensed, and turned away from him.

"If he set a trap for us, then they saw us already," she said. Her voice was different, scared. She waited for another moment, hesitating. In a low voice, almost whispering, she turned to Omer. "I'm sorry. You're right. You can't decide what happens in dreams."

The compact rage in Omer's head dissolved, deserted him, leaving him empty. The emptiness brought fatigue, a weakness that took over all his limbs. He remained standing, wordless, powerless.

Noa turned and walked. She reached the blocked-off water cistern, stood on the ledge stones and waited for a moment. In two cautious steps, she entered the hole. She passed between the stones and dirt, pushing the tall thorns aside with her hand. She approached the narrow, hidden entrance, knelt beside it and crawled in. Once inside, she lit her flashlight.

Omer approached the tiny hole. A thorn scratched his arm. A vague feeling coursed through him, a bad feeling, sour, worse than anger: hate. He hated the night, the walking, the crawling ahead of him. He knelt and squeezed into the entrance and noticed the lit headlamp left for him there. Noa waited for him a few feet in, a small backpack on her shoulders.

The bluish light of the headlamp projected onto the floating dust like moonlight into marshlands fog. The weakness in Omer's limbs made it difficult for him to advance, made him feel like he was crawling and drowning at the same time. But the unclear anger gave him strength.

He struggled to understand his actions there, crawling in the dust through the narrow tunnel. Quick images flashed through his brain—a bicycle, Joel, Professor Peretz. He was filled with anger towards them, knowing that it was only due to them that he was there. The dust filled his lungs, like smoke in a smoker's chest, turning into muddy sludge within him. It burned his eyes and ground his teeth down.

He was no longer crawling. He hadn't noticed when he stood up, but now he was walking along the tunnel. A bluish light flashed for an instant from up ahead. Noa's headlamp, making sure he was following. His anger toward her grew hotter and hotter.

It's all her fault, for having to meddle in everything and drag me into danger in the middle of the night.

The tunnel deepened. Omer lost all sense of time and place. He no longer walked on his own; his legs carried him as they willed. He reached the spot where the tunnel forked left and right. He tried to go right, but against his wishes, he turned left. When he looked back, he could no longer see the fork. The pale blue light flashed at him once again from up ahead. Things became clearer in his mind—he realized that Noa was controlling him, dragging him somewhere. His anger turned to hate towards her.

I must be wary.

The bluish light flashed again.

Leading me.

The hue of the headlamp's beam changed from one moment to the next, turning purple. Everything around him became purple: the light beam, the walls of the tunnel, the dust on the ground, the fine particles floating in the air.

He almost bumped into Noa as she knelt and pushed wood boards aside. Underneath the boards, an entrance appeared.

She wants to force me to go in there. He had to run away, this was his last chance. He saw her dangling a thick rope and rappelling down on it. This was the moment he had been waiting for. She couldn't see him. He tried to bring himself to turn around, run, get away.

But he failed. On the contrary, he approaching the hole, reaching out to grab the rope. It was clear to him that he wouldn't make it in his condition, that he would fall and break every bone in his body.

He looked back, catching sight of the sway of the thick rope. He hadn't even felt himself descending. Noa walked ahead of him.

She is controlling me completely!

Lost, he followed her with his eyes on the ground, searching. He picked up a stone and held it, for self-defense. Something was about to happen—something catastrophic, horrendous. He was about to be hurt. His hand tightened around the stone. Her headlamp flashed. She turned her head for a moment, her face carrying a mean expression.

I hate her. I'm frightened of her.

He walked behind her with his back to the wall of the tunnel, keeping a safe distance. The stone remained primed tight in his hand the whole time. He knew for certain that he was about to be attacked. He prepared himself. He wasn't scared anymore. The anger and hate gave him strength. The purple grew darker and obscured the details.

Noa disappeared around the corner. Omer advanced, peeking. She fiddled with something. An aperture opened in the wall. She knelt by the hole, holding a long tube, her back turned to him.

This is my last chance to escape!

He hoped he could do it by running fast, and if not, he planned to strike. His limbs refused to listen, he couldn't move away. On the contrary, he was controlled, drawn into the tiny chamber. He stood with his back to the wall, pressed against the corner: tense, ready, alert, animal-like.

The purple darkened further. Bright flashes shot through it. Omer had a hard time seeing, but Noa turned towards him. There was something in her hand, something threatening, multi-armed. Her lips moved. Her mouth twisted into a smile as she spoke, but nothing reached Omer's ears. Her hand rose, holding the evil arms.

In a moment or two, all will be lost.

His back pressed against the wall, his hand tightened around the stone. By now, only shadows surrounded him. She took another step towards him, and he attacked.

The muffled cry of pain she emitted froze his motion, cleared his mind. A frightened cry, full of shock. Her face twisted, trying to retreat, but her foot tangled in the backpack strap and she stumbled and fell backwards. Her headlamp fell off her head, its light focused on the ceiling. Omer's headlamp remained focused on her, blinding her with its bluish light. Omer took a step towards her and she crawled away from him.

He stopped. For a moment, they both remained motionless, set in a strip of light, in a frozen slice of time. Between them, a of fine dust of fear and wonder floated. Then Omer took small steps backwards, until his back touched the wall. His forehead turned downwards and illuminated the floor.

Something dropped from Omer's hand, hitting the floor with a clang. A choked sob followed. Sharp stabbing sensations pulsed in the side of her head, where she had hit a rock outcropping as she flinched away from his assault. He himself didn't hit her, since he struck the air like a blind man. She reached two fingers upwards and touched the line of pain. She lowered the fingers to see the tips were dark, stained.

Omer choked again. She rose to her feet, supporting herself with her hands. The side of her hand stung. She stood hesitating, analyzing him. His hands remained hanging at the side of his body. His head was lowered, shaking with ragged breaths. She stepped towards him.

"Omer..."

Her voice seemed to crumble the dam he had erected around his tears. They streamed out, unstoppable now, deep and painful. Omer tried to speak. "I..." he said, his voice breaking. "I'm sorry, Noa. I didn't mean to. I don't know what's happening to me." His lowered head moved from side to side. The beam of light from his headlamp drew a line between her and himself.

His suffering choked her throat. Her hands wrapped around him, hugging him.

"I really didn't mean it."

Her hand drew his head to her shoulder. His tears dampened her shirt. Her own tears ran down her cheeks.

The crying subsided, turned into sniffling, broken breaths. Omer's cheeks stung with embarrassment, and he moved back. Noa withdrew her hands from him.

"I keep imagining things," he whispered. "Seeing all sorts of...I don't know. I guess some of the refuse is still in me. I dunno."

He wiped his eyes with the end of his shirt, then his cheeks and his nose. He stood for a moment, confused and embarrassed. He shone around with his flashlight and found the discarded floater. He picked it up and sat down, leaning against the wall.

"I have this horrible feeling that I'm going crazy. And it's getting worse every minute. They have to get it off me."

The sting in the side of Noa's head became sharper. She tried not to touch the wound. An elongated red mark above Omer's ear fell into sight.

"You got a scratch," she said.

"In the woods," Omer said. "Am I bleeding?"

Noa came closer, took a better look and shook her head. "No."

She sat beside him. Omer laid the floater on his knee and spread its black arms around. His voice sounded hoarse as he spoke. "The truth is that I'm very scared. I don't know what happened to me, and I don't know what's going to happen."

Noa reached out and touched the floater's arms with her fingers. She lifted them, running her thumb along the attachment buttons. She turned her gaze to him. "Do you believe in Qualia?"

Their eyes met. Omer nodded. Her sharp gaze turned contemplative. "After this time, we can't come back here."

Chapter 37

Town Man waited. No presences around him, he focused his thoughts but failed to sense anything.

Now what?

Something dragged him backwards, as though a thin, long cable was attached to his body, shortening with dizzying speed. The pull intensified, growing in speed until he was pushed into darkness, like an accelerated particle in a long, sealed tube.

Qualia's voice rolled to him from a distance. "Town Man?"

"We need to get the refuse off of him," Town Man said. "Without that he can't return the transparencies."

Qualia remained silent.

Angry?

Town Man found it difficult to tell if he was still in motion. Another voice reached him. "We mustn't take the refuse off of him! We mustn't release him."

Frozen Tundra Man!

Frozen Tundra was asleep, covered in a thick blanket. His face peeked out from the blanket but his eyes were closed. "You don't hunt a seal twice. It's too big a risk. He's not stupid. We won't be able to catch him again."

"But he can't return the transparencies like this," Town Man said. "The refuse drove him crazy. They sedated him and locked him up."

Another voice, also familiar. "But maybe he's lying?"

Moonlight sat at his desk, his hands folded on the table-top, his head resting on them with eyes closed.

Asleep!

A pen dropped from the slack fingers. Underneath his eyelids the eyeballs moved in rapid motions. His mouth was ajar, relaxed.

"He really wants to give them back," Town Man said.

Frozen Tundra's voice condensed. "But how can we know this, Town Man?"

Because of how he lay there in the cage! Help me. Wanted to get back to his daughters. They were crying. Him too. Help me.

"He didn't lie," Town Man said, shaking his head. "He didn't lie, I felt it. We were in a cage."

Moonlight's voice grinned. "Feeling things is very important, Town Man. Perhaps the most important. But you should know that lies in dreams are different. They can be very difficult to uncover."

Maybe he lied? No, no! I felt it. Help me. But what exactly did I feel?

"It wasn't lies," Town man insisted. "There's refuse left in me as well and it's maddening. Those weren't lies."

Rain Forest Woman's voice whispered at him from afar, rustling through the treetops. "Are you sure you believe him, Town Man?"

Believe him? Yes. No?

"He didn't lie to me, I felt it."

Qualia's voice, sharp and clear, rolled quickly towards Town Man, and hit him like a whiplash. "Do you believe him?"

His thoughts froze. Although he couldn't see her, he felt her gaze pierce him, question him.

Suddenly, he was filled with courage. "I believe him."

His words created a maelstrom of distraught silences around him. Tension set its claws into Town Man, like the gentle stings of electric current. Frozen Tundra's sleep was disturbed. He turned once, twice underneath the heavy blanket. "You believe him, Town Man, and I believe in you. We must find a way to help. The question is what can we do?"

He believes in me!

"We need to get the refuse off of him," Town Man said, "so that he can function and return the transparencies."

"But how shall we find him?" Frozen Tundra asked.

How to find him?

Moonlight's voice said. "If he doesn't enter to float on his own we can't communicate with him, or even identify him."

"Maybe through a dream?" Frozen Tundra said.

"We won't be able to remove the refuse from him through a dream." Rain Forest said.

Confidence found its way to Town Man's voice. "We can do it through a different dimension! When Qualia took me to another dimension we saw all the entities there, even those not floating."

"In a different dimension you can see entities, but you can't identify them," Rain Forest said. "We won't be able to recognize World Man; there is nothing to distinguish him from the other entities."

Qualia's voice scratched the air. "There is something to distinguish him. We can identify him. He has the drift in him."

The cable that pulled Town Man backwards snapped. The rate of deceleration astounded him, emphasizing the speed at which he was moving before that. And with the decreased velocity, the darkness also lessened. Moonlight and Frozen Tundra disappeared. The silhouettes of Qualia and Rain Forest revealed themselves.

Rain Forest's voice was filled with tension. "But we can't identify the refuse."

"He can," Qualia said.

He is me.

"He can't move between the dimensions alone!" Rain Forest said.

"We'll transport him," Qualia said.

"It's too dangerous," Rain Forest said, shaking her head. "He'll have to float there alone!"

Qualia delayed her reply. She floated closer to Town Man. "The non-dangerous things are over. At this point, everything is dangerous." She kept advancing towards him, and when they were almost touching, she closed her clouded eyes to a couple of narrow slits. "But you've already faced dangers."

An electric current went through Town Man's body, sending a pulse of joy through him.

Me!

Qualia's eye slits filled his entire field of vision, as though projected upon a giant screen. Her voice sent shivers through him. "You will be able to identify him."

Only I know what the refuse looks like!

Their arms extended towards him. Town Man held on to the palms—one was soft, one calloused. Qualia's voice reached him from nearby, calm but grave. "Do not let go of our hands under any circumstances, Town Man."

Town Man's form was poured like a liquid through a thick mesh. For a moment, he spread over the mesh and then began dripping through it, coalescing beneath it. Imperfect darkness enveloped him. Two bright halos revealed themselves, vaguely spherical in shape, and in the center of each floated a clear dot of light.

Entities! Huh, I'm in a different dimension. Same place, different dimension.

More halos appeared: hundreds, thousands, countless. So many that he was blinded and dizzy.

But I'll find him! Gotta concentrate, try to see the...

The halos faded.

Why? I haven't found him yet!

The tiny dots of light that were inside the halos shone on in the darkness—countless, near and far, like stars in a dark, nighttime sky.

Qualia's voice reached him from all sides. "Now stop thinking, Town Man. Stop the thoughts."

Stop the thoughts. Don't think. See the flow. Yes. Don't think. Don't think.

Silence took hold. Town Man became more alert and focused than ever, looking and listening to the countless dots of light around him, trying to feel them, be part of them. Soon a soft noise seeped into him, a dry leaves' rustle in an incessant light breeze.

Red lines of light shone through the darkness—long, thin, crumbly, like wet cobwebs. Light lines filled the space from horizon to horizon, tremulous, pulsing.

An almost instant understanding washed over Town Man—an understanding of the power of the flow. It filled him with fear. He tried to concentrate, tried to see, to start seeking, but failed. He was blocked, wrapped in thin brilliant red lines.

Helpless, he called to Qualia. "How to search? What should I do to see?"

"You can't see here yet," Qualia replied.

"We need to cross another dimension. One with...other things in it." Rain Forest said.

The red lines of flow faded in the darkness, and along with them, the countless dots of light disappeared. The darkness itself seemed to fade to brown.

"From now on be very careful and attentive, Town Man," Qualia said. "We're entering a borderline dimension."

Rain Forest's voice betrayed tension. "You'll be floating there alone, but we'll try to help you."

Alone. Borderline. Border of what? Try to help. Try. Now search.

Town Man's form pressed into something thick, like a gelatinous mash. At first, he was afraid to try to move, but as soon as he did so, he smiled. His motions became very large for some reason. He couldn't see his hands but felt their power. He spread them to the sides and felt long, strong, broad wings. His legs became powerful as well, and their edges sprouted sharp claws. Power stunned him for a few moments. He floated in expanding, gliding circles. His feathers slid in the light brown liquid, producing an oily friction rustle.

His eyes became sharp, and recognized a red stain far away. He completed another circle of gliding and turned to the stain. It was square, like a red surface, hanging like a painting on a brown wall.

The closer he drew, the more clear the size of the red surface was—it stretched before him from one horizon to the other, shining in crimson. Town Man approached nearer and focused his eyes. The red surface turned out to be composed of countless thin lines of red light, and between the lines lingered tiny dots of light, surrounded by halos.

Something passed by him. Town Man couldn't hear or see, he just knew. *Something*. A frequency or a wave, or a pulse of condensation in the brown liquid. His sharp eyes caught nothing. He returned his gaze to the red surface, gliding above it in circles, ever larger, scanning it methodically.

Something passed by him again. He didn't know exactly where, but knew it was close. Town Man tensed, cautious and attentive but no longer frightened. His new power and the sharpness of his claws gave him confidence.

A tiny, purple, phosphorous dot shimmered in the red expanse. He looked at it, dazed, joyful. He tried to call Qualia and Rain Forest to tell them, but managed only to emit a sharp, discordant sound—the call of a bird of prey, short and clear.

"Go down to him and touch him," Qualia said.

Town Man descended further towards the red surface, deciding to increase his speed because of the distance. He gathered the sensation of his wings to his body and dived down in free-fall, his eyes focused all the while on the purple dot. When he felt he was close enough, he spread his wings back to their full length, stretching his legs forward to balance himself. He slowed into a gliding circle directly above the purple dot.

Town Man meant to descend further, but the strange thing was near him again. He tried to ignore it, but it was as though something within him realized the magnitude of the danger. He turned around and tried to look for the thing, tried to prepare for it, but didn't have the time—a split second later he felt a strong impact in his leg, and a condensed shock wave blew him aside, rolling end over end.

Town Man let out a sharp, long scream of rage. He scanned the surroundings with his clear, vengeance-seeking eyes, but nothing was there. Concern filled those eyes at the sight of the red surface, seeking the purple dot. He saw it, far away from him.

Town Man spread his wings once again to their full span. He was as strong as before, and even more so. His burning anger compacted strength into him. His claws tightened for a moment, and then erected like metal blades.

He was ready.

Qualia's firm words penetrated him. "Don't fight it, Town Man, it's not fighting you! Go down to the purple and hold on to it. You must get out of here at once."

Town Man clenched his claws. He remained furious but the thing was far from him now, and he decided not to waste precious time on the chase. The surface of red flow lines spread beneath him. He lowered and approached the surface with utmost caution. Now, from up close, the purple dot was not on the surface but rather inside it, deep in the layers of shining lines, between the dots of light and the faint halo spheres.

Town Man approached the flow lines. His sharp eyes examined the lines, calculating how to pass between them.

The thing was advancing towards him again, from his back. He turned around as fast as he could and set himself against it. His steel claws spread, waiting.

Rain Forest's words vibrated at him in the brown liquid, carrying a request, a demand. "Don't fight it, you can't, it has nothing to do with us!"

Two facts crossed paths in Town Man's mind—she was right, and he would fight. His body shook, not from fear, but rather from excitement. His senses could not locate the approaching thing, but his mind could—it recognized its location and manner of progress. Town Man began to move as well, priming his strength, aiming his claws.

The second impact was several times worse than the first. A mighty blow rippled through his neck. A compact shock wave accompanying the impact picked him up and blew him away, swirling the sights around him, the sensations, the directions. In an instant, Town Man became powerless. His limbs seemed to remain connected by string to his body. With great effort he managed to steady himself. He glanced towards the flow lines, and couldn't see the purple dot.

Rain Forest's words were charged with tense urgency. "You have to get out of here, Town Man."

"Find the purple and touch it," Qualia said.

Town Man unfolded his wings again. This time he felt the weakness spreading through them, but they held enough power to allow him to take flight, get away from the flow lines so as to enlarge his field of vision. Town Man resumed gliding in large circles, scanning the red surface in persistent rigor.

At last he noticed the purple dot and wanted to roar with delight, but instead let out a sharp triple-noted cry. He gathered his wings and lost altitude, spreading them once again only when his claws nearly scratched the red lines of light.

The knowledge that the thing was near him filled him with deep despair and terror. He remained staring at the flow lines, thoughtless, powerless. He surrendered to despair, gave up and went limp. Dropped himself into the flow lines.

As if he hit a high power line directly, powerful sparks exploded around him, passed through him. They enveloped him with a powerful noise, a sort of immense, ongoing metallic squeak. His body twisted from the noise. A desperate cry escaped his lips. Not the sharp screech of a bird of prey but a shout, a scream, in his own voice. With his last bit of force he looked around, searching for the purple dot. But he couldn't see it, and he realized he had lost all sense of direction. Everything around him was so tumultuous, and dense, and identical. Town Man could no longer bear the noise. All he wanted was to dissolve into it and disappear.

Qualia's calm voice held on to him, rescued him from his paralysis, flowed to him like breathing air. "Now reach it, Town Man."

He looked around and saw the purple not far from him. He advanced towards it with anguished slowness, stopping right before it. He knew for certain that the thing was moving towards him once again, approaching with haste.

Suddenly everything seemed hopeless, pointless. The noise began to daze him.

"Now!" Qualia said, "Touch it now!"

Town Man drew close to the purple and just as he touched, he was sucked away, rescued. The shining flow lines began to fade. Their horrible noise muffled.

And when he was safe, protected, out of range, he sustained the greatest impact of them all.

Chapter 38

Michael Lampston was hesitant to open his eyes. For a long time, he tried to figure out where he was. An indeterminate rustle enveloped him, muffled, prolonged, accompanied by a swaying sensation.

His left hand disappeared. Michael Lampston extended his other hand in a seeking motion above his head. He found it there, asleep, lying like an inanimate object, out of place, bereft of feeling.

The rustle surrounding him sounded familiar: dense, whistling. Although his eyes were closed, he could tell he was in a well-lit place. He opened his eyes with caution, and the place looked familiar: the bedroom aboard the private jet.

The sleeping hand began to awake, tingling. Michael Lampston sat up, placed the hand in his lap and traced gentle circles over it, massaging it back into life. Flashes of headache forced him to close his eyes every few moments. He refrained from lying down.

His shirt was dusty and worn. Two of its buttons were ripped, and on its side was a dry bloodstain. Traces of blood could be seen on the sheet as well. Lampston raised the hem of his shirt and examined his body. He saw no cut or wound, only scuff marks on the side of his torso. He remained staring at the bloodstain for a moment, then stood up.

He reached the hull of the aircraft in a short step and pulled the curtain aside. A blinding sun blazed at him from the wing. He lowered his gaze. A desert of clouds bloomed far below. Lampston walked to the tiny bathroom and looked in the mirror. Rough bristles sprouted on his shaved head and face, as though he had aged ten years. His eyes were sunken and tired, dirt in their corners. Dust stained his cheek and ear.

He removed his shirt and put it aside. He washed his head, face, neck and shoulders with warm water, and dried himself with a soft towel. From one of the shelves next to his bed, he pulled clean clothes and got dressed. He walked to the door and stopped, hesitant. At last, he opened it with a decisive motion and stepped out.

Ernest Cole-Angel sat in front of a laptop computer at the far end of the flying office. He rose from his armchair, face beaming with deep joy:

"Michael, I'm so glad to see you like this!"

A smile tugged at Lampston lips.

Security Chief Gerryowen turned in the leather armchair. His eyes examined Michael Lampston with curiosity.

"Good morning," he said, smiling. "How do you feel?"

"Like I slept in a cement mixer," Lampston said. He walked over and shook hands with Cole-Angel and with Gerryowen, turning back to Cole-Angel.

"Is that from me?" he said, embarrassed.

Ernest Cole-Angel brought a cautious finger to his forehead. A blue bruise mark stood out next to his eye. "Next time try to leave a scar."

Michael Lampston remained embarrassed, shaking his head. "Listen... I owe you guys a huge apology—"

"Oh, nonsense," Cole-Angel said.

"No, wait, really!" Lampston said. "I owe you a huge apology and a huge thank-you. I really mean it."

"The important thing is that you're OK," Gerryowen said. His gaze, piercing and curious, remained focused on Lampston's face the whole time. He raised his eyebrows. "You look a little tired."

"I am," Lampston said and turned to the coffee machine, filled a porcelain cup halfway, added cream and stirred.

"You should call your wife," Gerryowen said. "She's called several times already."

Lampston came out of his reverie. "Oh, yes, she must be worried."

An air-pocket shook the plane. Michael Lampston stumbled and grabbed the tall coffee table. Ernest Cole-Angel walked over to him. "Try to rest for a few days."

"I second that," Gerryowen said.

Michael Lampston steadied himself and sipped from the fragile cup. A brief smile crossed his face as he nodded.

"I will," he said. "I think I'll take the old wooden boat out to sea tomorrow."

"That's exactly what you need," Ernest Cole-Angel said.

"Is it ready? Equipped?" Gerryowen said.

"Yes, I suppose so," Lampston said. He turned to the soundproof phone booth at the fore of the plane. On his way, he motioned for Gerryowen with a tilt of the head to join him there. Gerryowen rose from his couch and caught up with him near the booth.

"We can drop the surveillance on Professor Peretz," he said to Gerryowen. "He has nothing to do with it."

Gerryowen was in no hurry to respond. It seemed that his curious eyes, focused on Lampston, did most of the listening for him. A strange smile rose to his lips. "OK."

The gaze intimidated Michael, charging him with tension. He masked his feelings with a smile and a careless look. "Silly that we even suspected him."

Gerryowen nodded with an almost imperceptible gesture of assent. "OK. Excellent."

Michael Lampston closed the isolating door on himself and filled his lungs to relax. Gerryowen was not someone to play games with. The world was a poker hand to him and he always seemed to win. Michael didn't have a chance, not in his present state.

I shouldn't even try.

Lampston looked at the flight data monitor through the glass pane: five hours and eleven minutes to landing. ETA: twenty-two minutes past midnight.

He took his phone out of his pocket and glanced through the contacts. The number for Joshua Peled, the director of Site 1, caught his eye. He waited until Gerryowen sat back on the couch to dial.

Three rings sounded, and at last Peled's sleepy voice came through the receiver. "Yes, hello?"

"Joshua, it's Michael. Can you talk? It's important."

Joshua Peled's voice turned alert. "Hang on a moment," he said, and after a few moments added: "OK, go ahead."

"Do you know the emergency diamond-gathering protocol?" Lampston said.

"Of course," Peled said, business-like.

"It needs to be executed urgently. At once," Lampston said. "The two diamonds, the collector and the decoder. To the main office. You with me?"

"I'm here."

"Urgent secured courier, to be handed to me personally, and no one else."

"Understood," Joshua Peled said.

"And Josh," Lampston said in a pleading tone, "this is strictly between you and me, OK? Top secret. You don't report on this to anyone. If there's a problem you talk to me. No one but me. OK?"

"Loud and clear," Joshua Peled said, "you can count on me."

"I know. See you."

Lampston shut the phone and closed his eyes for a moment. Gerryowen sat on the couch with his back to him, paging through a magazine.

Since when did he ever read a magazine?

With renewed urgency, Lampston located the number of Sergei Barilov, director of Site 2. He waited again: Gerryowen had turned around and was looking at him. Lampston pretended to be on the phone, listened, smiled, said something and laughed. Gerryowen looked back at the magazine. Lampston dialed Sergei Barilov's number.

When he finished the conversation, his heart pounded against his ribs, his head sweating and his hands cold.

This is how your father failed, isn't it? Something more important than success, something more important than money... the old man tried to tell you...

Michael Lampston dialed his wife.

* * *

Ernest Cole-Angel looked out from the window of his forty-first floor at the distant, noisy street. He turned away from the window and approached the desk. It was ten past three in the afternoon and, at his firm request, no calls were passed through nor any appointments allowed in. He needed a full hour of quiet.

But he didn't get it. The encoded cell phone rang with an unidentified call. Ernest Cole-Angel took it. Gerryowen's heavy voice rose from the telephone. "He has the transparencies."

"Excuse me?"

"He has the transparencies," Gerryowen said. "All four. The one here he removed from the safe, and he received the other three in special deliveries, and disappeared."

"Emergency diamond gathering..." Cole-Angel said. "Strange, he actually looked perfectly fine."

"He fooled us both," Gerryowen said "We need to act quickly. Although it's regrettable that I didn't get word earlier, I suppose we can still find him."

Surprise filled Cole-Angel's voice. "You think? I imagine he planned this and that he knows what he's doing."

"I'm not sure he's capable of complex planning right now," Gerryowen said in a chilly voice. "I don't think he'll be hard to locate. It will be a lot more complicated to get him to understand that we're on his side."

Ernest Cole-Angel remained quiet.

"If you hear anything, let me know immediately," Gerryowen said.

"OK, I'll—"

But Gerryowen had already hung up. Ernest Cole-Angel put the telephone down, turned to the window and stared out of it for a long time. He returned to the table, sat down and laid his head between his hands.

Ten minutes to five the cell phone rang again.

"Partial success," Gerryowen said. "The package has been recovered but its owner is in the wind."

Confusion ran rampant through Cole-Angel. "What? How?"

"The briefcases have a homing device, so we had no problem arriving at where it was hidden," Gerryowen said. "Lampston... we haven't been able to find yet."

A strange sadness crept into Ernest Cole-Angel's body. He took a deep breath and tried to sound business-like. "Where did you find them?"

"Hmmm, let's leave that for later," Gerryowen said.

Ernest Cole-Angel remained silent for a moment. Gerryowen was pulling his "need-to-know" routine. "It's depressing for me to think what he's going through. He probably thinks everyone is out to get him."

"I'm glad to hear you say that," Gerryowen said, relief in his voice. "It's weighing on me as well. We must make every effort to get him out of this. Maybe we should consult with experts."

Ernest Cole-Angel concurred. "I'll take care of it. I'll assemble a professional team to help us with this issue."

"Excellent," Gerryowen said. "And perhaps you should talk with his wife as well."

"I already thought of that," Cole-Angel said. "I intend to fly out to them tonight."

"That would be best," Gerryowen said with what Cole-Angel thought was genuine warmth in his voice.

* * *

Gerryowen's thick fingers carefully raised one Three Transparencies stone in front of his face: simple, rectangular, milky translucent. He stared at it long and hard and finally returned it to its black velvet bed, placing it alongside its sisters. He gazed at them with childish wonder. At last he forced himself to close the metal briefcase and carry it to the place that had become the most secure in all headquarters: the vault in his office. He placed it inside and shut the steel door behind it without triggering the locking mechanism.

His encoded cell phone rang. The screen showed Ernest Cole-Angel's number. Gerryowen peeked at his watch: seven minutes before nine in the evening. "Have you landed already?"

There was a strange sound in Cole-Angel's voice. "He has the transparencies," he said.

"What do you mean?"

"You have replicas, two euros for the four," Cole-Angel said with bitter gaiety. "Paper weights. He showed me the models a few days ago on the plane, and now they're not here."

Gerryowen barked. "Hang on!" He unlocked the vault, removed the metal case, slammed it on his desk, and opened it in a rage. "OK, what?!"

"Look if one of the stones has a crack in one of its corners," Cole-Angel said. "I accidentally dropped it and it cracked."

Gerryowen took the rectangular stones in his hands. The first and second were flawless. In the third, a tiny crack.

He kept gazing at it for another moment, dazed. Then he snapped out of it, burning with fury. Gerryowen hung up and hurled the telephone to the corner. He pulled out a sealed plastic bag from the desk and tore at it bag wildly, removing another mobile phone. His hands shaking in rage, he knocked a battery into it. The phone lit up, and after a few seconds it connected to the network. Gerryowen dialed and pressed "call."

"Pick up, pick up, pick up..."

The recording struck him hard. "The number you have dialed is not available or is outside the coverage—"

Gerryowen let out a choked-off scream and hung up, refusing to believe, and immediately dialed again: the message repeated.

His pent-up anger drove him out of his office to the elevator lobby. He stopped for a moment in front of built-in aquarium and stared at length at the two large blue fish with yellow stripes. He closed his eyes and remained like that for a long moment. When he re-opened his eyes, they already had a different look: after the storm.

* * *

The pilot of the tow-boat, which security officer Gerryowen so desperately tried to reach, glanced at the global positioning screen. He corrected the bearing of his vessel by two degrees east and increased speed by one knot. From a sealed pouch, he removed a cell-phone. The screen announced the device to be out of range. The pilot turned it off and put it back.

The tug-boat's twin massive engines were operating at high RPMs. The vessel moved rapidly, with no headlights or markings. From time to time, the pilot illuminated the stern of the craft with a flashlight, looking at the thick, taut tug-rope. Tied to its end was an old wooden boat. Michael Lampston's old wooden boat, gliding on the water, crossing the dark waves.

Chapter 39

A distant engine hum droned in Omer's ear. It seemed like a crop-duster plane, but the droning was too uniform, neither rising nor diving, neither approaching nor receding. Monotonous.

A lawn mower? Impossible at this hour.

He got up on his knees and peeked out the window. A pale blue began painting the horizon, merging like dust in the darkness of the night, coloring a new background for the stars. Dizziness lowered him on his haunches, wondering. He leaned against the wall.

They're calling me. Her or him.

He lay back on the mattress, on his stomach, and closed his eyes. His hand hugged the pillow. The engine drone sawed in his ears again, becoming muffled every few minutes, then rising. The world moved underneath him again, but softer this time, in a wave-like motion, lifting and dropping, carrying the scent of the sea, of saline spray. He tried to respond to the call, to merge, to listen, but it was as though his thoughts were consumed in an empty expanse, sensation-less, devoid of imagery, out of time.

Warm light flooded the room. Omer got up on his knees again and looked at the window, seeing the top third of a huge, burning, red sunrise. It painted everything it touched red: house walls, sidewalks, window panes, and also his room and his face, and the white stripe of his pajamas. The red of the sunrise changed in hue, becoming more yellow, blinding.

Omer closed his eyes, drifted on the wavy motion, and listened to the droning of the engines, once again dizzy.

It's him. Calling me. He's sailing.

Crash!

Omer woke up, his heart pounding, his breath trapped in his chest. He dared not move, but remained on his back. The silent light of early morning painted the room in a soft and calming shade. He released the air from his lungs and dared to look to the sides.

He recalled the humming and the wave-like motion.

He was calling me to exchange a dream. Or maybe it was nothing? Interesting. A striped pajama! Yeah, right! I don't even have one.

He let out a short laugh.

Huh, isn't that weird? You can't even see the sunrise from here. What a dream.

Smiling, he got up from the bed and walked to the doorway of his room, listening to the sound of morning tunes emanating from a radio in the kitchen.

Is she still at home?

He turned to the bathroom, closed the door behind him, looked in the mirror and was surprised—his face returned his gaze, but was different: dimmed, emptied. Sudden despair condensed within him, and he lowered his gaze. He washed his face and looked again: the facial features showed wet emptiness. But in his eyes he saw something else—resisting, burning. He tore his eyes away from the mirror. He wanted only to get away from there, to get out.

Their hands met at the doorknob as they pressed it from both sides of the door. It opened. Omer's mother looked at him with surprise. In her hand she held the green plastic watering-can.

"What are you doing up at this hour," she said, running a caressing hand over his head. "How do you feel today?"

His thoughts were somewhere else:

Was I really called or did I just dream it?

"Much better," he said.

"I made an appointment for eleven-thirty, OK? I have a few errands to run and then we'll go."

"A doctor?"

"Yes, of course."

"No! What do I need a doctor for?"

"This is not up for discussion!" she said. "Yesterday, you slept almost all day! And you sweated and you were in pain! Maybe it's the flu, but if it's something else we need to know."

She turned away from him, fear apparent in every movement. Omer remained standing as his mother marched away. The sound of the watering-can being filled reached him, and he walked to the house's main entrance, which stood wide open. Tiny puddles of water glistened on the patio, near the watered plants. He walked a bit further and sat on one of the stairs, laying his chin on his knees, his arms hugging his legs. His eyes stared out at the row of flowers next to the entrance path. A large bumblebee crossed the garden, humming.

Its hum changed, becoming monotonous, mechanical. Omer's heart picked up speed. He covered his eyes with hopeful lids, and was rewarded. The hum of the engines resumed its sawing in his ears. The sound grew louder as he concentrated on it, became clearer. But the patter of slippers and the pouring of sprinkled water mixed into it.

Not here. Gotta go away from here.

He quickly got up from the step and went back to his room. He changed his pants and while putting on his sandals pulled a t-shirt from the closet and slipped into it. He opened the door a little and peeked. Once the coast was clear, he left the house.

When he reached the paved road, he began to run. He didn't know where to but he wanted to get there already. He crossed one intersection and then another. He slowed down and began to walk, gathering his breath. He passed a closed grocery store with crates of fresh bread stacked in front of it. A truck unloaded vegetables in front of the store next door.

He passed another intersection and walked by the new little fountain. Suddenly, he stopped and turned back: the sound of leaping water called to him. He drew closer and touched the water.

Pleasant.

His fingers glided over slimy moss under the water level.

It's already grown.

He sat down on one of the benches surrounding the fountain, then lay down on his side, placing his head on his clasped hands. He closed his eyes. The humming was still there, as was the motion of the waves, carrying spray and a scent of the sea with it, and the worried voice of World Man rose in his ears. "Can you see where we are?"

Where is he?

Omer's fingers tightened around the wooden bulwark of an old boat. He pushed his legs forward and balanced himself against the bulwark to counter the sway of waves. A large wooden board was set in the middle of the boat, resting against the bulwarks. Upon the board was a body covered in a gray blanket.

"We're on a boat," Omer said, staring at the blanket.

"Yes, on a boat. "I've been on this boat for an hour now. But where are we, what do you see around us?"

Above Omer stretched a clear, star-laden night, around him glimmered dark water in partial moonlight.

"Nothing, just the sea."

"Hmmm, odd," World Man said.

They sailed and bounced between waves of medium height. Omer noticed elongated bodies frolicking in the water around him.

Dolphins!

They were observing him with eager curiosity. Their small eyes remained fixed on him as they leapt out of the water. They accelerated, sped away and then slowed down, whistling. As he followed them, a low, wide, rubber boat appeared not far in front, dragging the boat they were in with a thick rope. He returned his eyes to the blanket on the wooden board.

That's him. Here.

"Are you under the blanket?" he said.

"Huh? How do I know?" World Man said. "I have no idea where I am."

Omer got up from the bulwark and staggered to the board. He reached out and touched the blanket, but for some reason let go and moved away. The whistling of the dolphins grew louder and less amused. He was filled with an unclear terror as he leaned back on the bulwark, his hand tightening around a thick rope surrounding the boat.

"I'm not there, eh?" World Man said.

What's wrong with you? Stupid coward. Pick it up!

Omer drew closer again. The dolphin whistles grew angry anew, but he refrained from listening to them. He reached out, hesitant, scared, and with a quick motion he pulled the blanket off and drew back.

"Ah, finally!" World Man said. He was lying on his back, nearly paralyzed, unable to move. But a smile shone on his lips and eyes. He took a long look at the sky. "Look, what a night. The truth is that I'm pretty messed up. I feel terrible. Here, look." World Man nodded to his hand. "This is from the refuse."

On the inside of the arm, near the elbow, a dark spot the size of a coin took its residence. World Man turned his hand a little and the spot shone in the moonlight like dark, purple glass.

"But they cleaned you from it!"

"Maybe they didn't get everything off," World Man said, tilting his head aside. "There are more in other places." He revealed another spot on the neck, and another, smaller one, on the side of the forehead, shining and reflecting like a mirror. "I can feel it inside me too," World Man said, "Flowing like mercury."

"We have to do something!" Omer said. "They have to get it off from you!"

"Now it's a little more complicated, isn't it?" World Man said, bitterness tainting his voice. He tried to look to the sides, but the pain was unbearable. "You really can't see anything around here? From here, I can only see the sky and... uh, what are those jumping things?"

Omer looked around in a full circle. "Dolphins, and other than that nothing. So that's why they sedated you again?"

World Man made a dismissive gesture. "Ah, I'm such an idiot. I didn't think he'd find out. With all his spies. He figured out I took them right away."

The transparencies! He figured it out. But who is "he?"
"So he has them now?" Omer said.
World Man rejoiced. "In his dreams! Here, look at this."
With the fingers of one hand, World Man managed to unbutton and raise the hem of his undershirt. A cloth belt was fastened around his waist, with a hidden pouch.
"Touch it," World Man said.
Omer passed his fingers over the cloth belt and felt three rectangular bulges.
"There's one missing," Omer said.
"Of course!" World Man said. "A smart chicken never lays all its eggs in one basket."
Then which basket does it hatch in?
The boat struck hard on a large wave, which caused World Man pain. He grimaced and clenched his teeth, then looked aside, tilting his head as far as possible.
"Can't see anything around here," he said. "I wonder what he's trying to do. I'll probably be picked up by another ship."
"But then they'll find them on you, won't they?" Omer said.
World Man's eyes widened. It seemed that the idea never occurred to him.
"You're right," he said. "Help me, we'll get rid of them right away."
Omer shook his head.
"Then you throw them away," World Man said.
"Me?"
"Yes, you."
"Throw them here? In the middle of the sea?" Omer said.
"Better, isn't it?"
He's right.
Omer extracted one transparency from the cloth belt. It looked completely black, to Omer's surprise. He saw himself reflected in it by the starlight, perfectly clear, albeit tiny. He grimaced, and saw the whiteness of his teeth reflected.
"Do it!" World Man said.
Omer clenched his fist and threw the transparency overboard. The sound of it dropping cut through the tumult of the waves.

"Another one!" World Man said.

Omer reached for the cloth belt, then withdrew. "Do you think I really threw it? This is a dream, isn't it?"

World Man froze for a moment, contemplative. "I don't know. I hope so. I don't want to die."

Omer pulled the second transparency out of the pouch and threw it into the sea. "Neither do I."

Something moved underneath the board World Man was on. A quick, short movement.

Rats!

He pulled his feet away in horror.

"Something is moving underneath you."

"What is it?" World Man said.

Omer recognized another slight motion. He kept his distance but tried to look. "Uh, there's a blanket there or something, and underneath it something's moving."

"So move the blanket," World Man said.

Omer shook his head—one blanket was enough—

In great agony, World Man twisted and inched to the edge of the board. While suppressing a shout of pain, he slid his hand into the narrow gap between the board and the bulwark. His fingers groped after the blanket but it was too far down. He exerted himself and his fingers stretched like the eyes of a snail, until finally they grasped the blanket. With the last ounce of his strength, World Man swept it back.

Omer found it hard to believe his eyes and for a moment was rendered speechless.

"Professor Peretz! Joel!" he said at last, breathless.

They can't hear me!

"Professor Peretz?!" World Man said.

"Yes, they're here, underneath you," Omer said. Upon seeing Professor Peretz's frightened eyes, Omer's enthusiasm turned to anger. "You lied to me! You lied, you promised you'd let them go."

"I tried!" World Man said. "I specifically told him to leave them alone. Do you think I knew he wouldn't listen to me? I'm stuck here myself, aren't I?"

Omer remained silent. World Man took a deep breath and closed his eyes for a moment. Once he regained his composure he called down. "Professor Peretz?"

The professor's eyes froze.

"He can hear you!" Omer said.

His excitement infected World Man. "Professor Peretz, it's me, Michael Lampston."

Professor Peretz's rapid breathing ceased. For a moment, it seemed that his heart had stopped beating as well. The sudden combination of the voice and name stunned him. He did not respond, remaining silent for a long moment. When he spoke, his voice sounded flat and dry, and abrasive as broken glass. "What do you want?"

The words hit World Man like ice bullets. His smile died. He tightened his jaw and closed his eyes hard. He didn't open them even at Joel's angry voice. "Where are you taking us?"

Waves crashing against the side of the boat sent a fine water spray into World Man's face. He pursed his lips, tasting them. The glassy purple stain on his forehead glistened in the moonlight. "I'm not taking anyone anywhere—"

"You're taking us on your victory lap!" Joel said.

"If anything, it's my funeral procession," Lampston said.

Omer cringed. His hand tightened around the bulwark.

"The refuse is breaking me down from the inside," World Man said. "It's twisting my thoughts. It's breaking my body down. It's causing a..." He fell silent, taking a deep breath. "I know that something bad awaits me because of it. Someone. And that someone is... me. Me, but different. Insane. Waiting for me with open arms."

"Good God..." Professor Peretz said.

The board on which World Man was lying began to shake. Omer looked underneath where Joel strained against the rope that bound his hands behind him. Omer reached down to help, but his fingers passed through the ropes as though they were air. He turned to World Man. "He's loosening the rope. Help him."

World Man, a spark of hope in his eyes, came out of his self-pity. With a scream, he shoved his hand hard into the space between the board and the bulwark. "Guide me! Which one of them?"

"Joel, but you won't make it like that," Omer said. "Tell him to get closer to you."

"Joel, do you see my hand?" World Man said, ignoring his pain. "Get closer, I'll help you untie the rope."

Joel's movements stopped at once. He looked at the waving hand next to him.

"Joel!" World Man said.

Deciding to trust the voice, Joel turned on his side and with more great effort managed to move his bound hands towards the bulwark, towards the extended hand. World Man's hands felt the rope and grasped it.

"Not that knot," Omer said. "Higher, higher! It's that rope. Move it and pull it."

All of World Man's strength seemed to flow into the palm of his hand, concentrating on the pointing finger and the thumb, tightening around the rope like a vice. He managed to undo one of the knots, but was forced at that moment to stop and withdraw his hand. The engine of the tug-boat slowed and the momentum of the vessels decreased.

"What now?" said World Man. A strange note wove into his voice. A foreign note. Omer recognized it.

"Are you afraid?"

"Yes, a little," World Man said. "And more for them than for me. And my wife, and my girls." He looked to the sides. "Do you see anything?"

Darkness surrounded them on all sides, the dolphin whistles cutting through the air. Short pulling motions were felt through the boat. At last, the two vessels collided with one another.

The pilot of the tug-boat appeared clad in a black diving suit, his fair face peeking wet from it, a small flashlight between his teeth. It shone its beam of light across their boat. Without a word, he went about his business, stepping aboard the second boat, marching to the platform serving as World Man's bed. Omer stood back as the tug pilot examined the monitor of a small device attached near World Man's foot. The pilot pressed a button and marched back to the bow. He released the tug rope with practiced hands and tossed it to the aft of his own boat before returning to the tug and shoving the two vessels apart. When the pilot reached the tiny wheelhouse, the tugboat engine growled again, at first with muffled slowness, then with a whiny roar. The engine beat up foam, deafened ears and receded.

"Released the rope and left," World Man said.

"Where did we get to?" Joel said.

World Man turned to Omer. "Can you see anything?"

Omer stood up. Now that the boat stopped advancing, it swayed heavily from side to side. Omer looked out into the distance at first, full perimeter. A large ring of dolphins surrounded their boat: not swimming or leaping in the air, but seated in the water, elongated faces peeking out. They tweeted to each other in conversation.

"There's nothing?" World Man said.

Omer shrugged. "Nothing."

"Not even the shadow of a ship?"

"Not even that."

"We've reached nowhere," World Man said. "But he activated some homing or GPS device here, so we'll probably be picked up by another ship, or by chopper."

Omer approached, bent down, and examined the device: small, square, waterproofed. An unlit screen displayed digits: 00:02:08.

"It's counting down," Omer said. "two-oh-six, oh-five, oh-four."

World Man's voice choked with astonishment and terror. "He booby-trapped me... booby-trapped us! It's a time bomb!"

"I see the charges!" Joel said. "Three of them! They're connected to the platform you're lying on."

"They towed us out to sea to blow us up," Professor Peretz said.

"Can you disconnect the wires?" World Man said to Omer.

"No. There are no wires."

"How much time left?"

"A minute fifty-five, fifty-four," Omer said.

"Another minute and fifty seconds," World Man said. "Quick, help me get the last one out." He turned to Joel. "Listen carefully, you two have to push the platform with your feet and shove it into the water."

With Omer's help, World Man drew out the last transparency. World Man clenched his fist around it, closed his eyes, and held it for a moment to his forehead.

"I dedicate you to my three women," he whispered in pain. His jaw muscles moved underneath his facial skin. He opened his eyes and fixed them on Omer's lost gaze. "And it's dedicated to you as well, Town Man, for saving me for death."

His hand shot out over the bulwark. The sound of the transparency falling echoed clearly through the din of the waves.

"Now they're all with the fishes," he said

All? Where's the fourth? Saved him for death.

"How much time left?" World Man said. His voice seemed to have steadied, turned almost calm.

"One minute thirty-two, thirty-one," Omer said.

"Hey, can you hear me? There's a minute and a half left. Try to push me with the board into the water."

Professor Peretz's sudden cry astounded everyone. "Absolutely not!"

Professor Peretz's eyes were closed and drenched in tears.

World Man's voice softened. "There's no other option, Professor Peretz. I'm done for anyway." His tone changed again, became clear and incisive. "Joel, try to push the board. You have to try to save both of you."

A moment passed, a long, tense moment. At last, Joel's shoe soles pushed against the wooden board. World Man took a deep breath and closed his eyes.

"On my count," he said with lucid slowness. "Three, two, one, now!"

Despite the effort in Joel's face, the wooden board didn't move.

"It's held with straps to the boat," Omer said. "There are like snaps on both sides."

"The board is held with snaps," World Man said to Joel. "I'll open the one here. Try to open on the other side."

Joel rolled sideways over Professor Peretz to the bulwark and spotted the snaps, but couldn't reach them with his bound hand. He tried to reach with his mouth and pull the snap with his teeth, but couldn't.

On the other side, World Man stretched his hand towards the strap. Omer shouted. "Further down!"

World Man's fingers felt around and found the spring plate, instantly opening the snap. "Mine is open. Hurry!"

Joel gave up trying to bring his mouth closer, and instead struggled with all his might to free his hand from the rope.

"How much time?" World Man said, worried.

"Fifty-one seconds!" Omer said.

Joel freed his hand partially from the rope, up to the elbow. With a super-human effort he managed to pull himself to the edge of the bulwark and grab the edge of the snap.

"Open!" he said.

"Now push!" World Man said.

Joel's legs squeezed against the board, and then heard and felt the placing of another pair of feet. World Man's gaze sought Omer. A calm shone in his eyes, a sort of sudden serenity, almost joyous.

"If you see them again," he said, "Tell them I said 'thank you.' And ask Professor Peretz to forgive me. I don't have the courage. And thank you too."

"We're pushing," Joel said. His voice sounded different, thickened by a sort of awkward softness.

"Hurry!" World Man said, and Joel counted,

"Three, two—"

"Michael!" Professor Peretz called out. And said no more.

A fragment of a smile appeared on World Man's face: a tear-drenched grin, but he wasted no more time. He closed his eyes and shouted. "Now! Right now! Quick!"

The wooden board rose on one side of the boat, still secured to the bulwark, and then toppled over at once and fell into the water. World Man disappeared under the board. Only the three charges jutted out of the surf for a fleeting moment.

The explosion was massive. The flash blinded Joel's eyes, the sound deafened him. The shock-wave hurled wood splinters at the boat and raised a plume of water high into the air, falling in huge, salty drops, washing away Professor Peretz's tears and the blood from Joel's face.

Omer saw none of this, only the remnants of a bright stain.

* * *

He opened his eyes and lifted his head from the bench. He stared at the fountain and rose slowly to his feet. A woman passed by, bemused. He began to walk. The wave-like motion still flowed underneath him. He stopped and sat down right away, awaiting something he knew would come. He closed his eyes, and at that very moment saw the blinding flash of the blast, heard the sound, and felt the shock wave throughout his body.

Utterly shocked, only after several moments did he manage to get up. A slow, thoughtless heaviness filled his step. An illusive image rose within him and vanished: the remnants of a bright stain, a mysterious stain. Something about the stain was yet to be revealed to him. His body ached, shivers ran through his limbs. He was already at the doorstep of his home, and almost instantly he found himself on the floor in his room.

He gazed at the ceiling, drained. The stain re-appeared, fainter, as though projected onto the ceiling. He tried to focus on it. The stain faded away, but something in it seemed to float to the foreground and stand out, clarifying: an extremely thin line of light, a trail of light following a tiny, dark dot, glowing in invisible light.

His snowflake.

The stain faded and vanished, and with it the trail of light and the dot of invisible light, but they were already etched in his mind.

His snowflake.

The ceiling vanished, following the stain, evaporating in a morning fog pierced by a huge ball of sun. Omer shielded his eyes with his hand. His nostrils caught a scent-line of vegetation decay. He sat up, rubbing his hands with slow fingers, ridding them of sand and a reddish dust. At the sight of the low-rising flora, a thrill of anticipation overcame him. He leapt up and ran towards a distant baobab tree.

The tapping of the walking cane stopped him. Qualia was nowhere to be seen, but knew the tapping turned towards him. He kept advancing, nearly floating. She appeared by the huge trunk, with her back to him, treading in place with tiny steps, sticking her walking cane in the sandy ground every moment. Its tapping sounded like iron hitting rock.

He stood there in silence, waiting.

A long time had passed before he saw her face. The shuffling motions of her feet carried her in circles, like a compass, around the walking cane. Only when she came around to stand almost directly in front of him did she speak, her eyes closed. "What have you seen, Town Man?"

"His snowflake," Omer said.

Essence!

"I saw... an essence?" he whispered, amazement in his voice.

"The refuse allows us to see the essence in things," Qualia said.

Wait, so what am I...? I'm... a transparencies viewer? Like, officially!

"The refuse is the spinal cord of the Great Spirit," Qualia said.

Fragments of unimportant memories. Omer went down to the riverbed.

"It's deeper than the river," she said.

A small cloud of dust was snatched up from between her feet by a quick gust of wind. Omer followed the receding dust with his eyes, and by the baobab noticed an almost-familiar figure: a skinny boy next to the giant stump. But the boy, with a cunning deft motion, hid behind the tree, only his hand still showing.

The breeze carried a sound, a sort of continuous whine.

"Don't stop hearing the sound," Qualia said. "What did he say?"

Who? Oh, him.

"He said that someone was waiting for him," Omer said, "that this someone was himself. Himself but different."

A foreboding sense struck Omer. He no longer wanted to be there. Wanted to wake up. Wanted to get out.

Qualia didn't stop tapping the sand with the tip of the walking cane. For the first time, her eyes opened, and she fixed him with a clouded gaze.

"That is the danger of too much knowledge, Town Man. As long as you are floating in the Great Spirit, the refuse is expanses of knowledge. Outside the Great Spirit, the refuse is knowing too much."

Someone waiting for him. Himself but different.

"We did not succeed in removing all the refuse from you."

From you.

"I was afraid this would happen."

Afraid?

A wave of burning rage washed over him. "You knew! You knew you couldn't remove all the refuse from me!"

"I was afraid," Qualia said, "but we had to take the transparencies from him."

The words stabbed him like dagger blades. Weakness shook his knees. He wanted to drop to the ground.

"I don't want to go mad," he said. "I don't want to die!"

The figure stood by the tree again. It was himself. His hands on his hips and his face defiant, mocking. A wild flame burned in his eyes. The figure tilted its head and burst into an awful laugh, like that of a hyena— threatening, crazed, deafening.

The tapping of Qualia's cane was sharp and clear. "Go back to the sound!"

Omer found it hard to listen to the faint sound.

"Focus on the sound!" Qualia said. "Listen to it hard!"

With supreme effort Omer managed to distance himself from the mad laughter. The sound became richer, clear, deep, full, to the point where Omer felt himself floating in a stream, in poetry. Dozens of voices, softly singing long words, drew long, lyrical, uniform growls from the vocal depths.

"These are others in the Great Spirit. They hear my call," Qualia said. "Don't stop listening to them. They are gathering for you. Focus on the singing. Get caught in it. Hold on to it like a rope. We will try..."

Shaking, and the sharp clang of iron on iron, forced Omer to open his eyes. A swift motion carried him backwards, flat on his back. He looked at the ceiling and the receding walls, at the red flashes of light coming from all sides. He saw his mother hurrying after him and didn't even try to call her.

The swift motion carried him out of the house. Trembling on the flagstones in front of the building, his mother stopped. While the stretcher was loaded onto the ambulance he felt another turbulence, and heard metallic clicks. A man in a green uniform spoke to him without uttering a sound. His mother entered the vehicle. The doors shut behind him.

Chapter 40

A muffled voice reached him. Broken sentences from a faraway PA system. And a faint waft of a recognized scent. He was looking from an unfamiliar spot, close to the floor, into a room. The legs of a hospital bed occupied his field of vision. Gray rubber wheels. Metal siding. Bed sheet. Everything was a sort of panoramic twist.

I'm a drop on the wall.

He felt himself dripping, not down the wall but rather upwards, gliding upon a thick coat of paint. Two monitors were mounted to the bed. Next to them his mother, seated, inclined forward, her cheeks pale, held in her hands.

In the bed he saw himself. Lonely. His eyes closed, his face expressionless, strange, of indeterminate shade. A clear hose was inserted in his nose. Colored wires dangled from the blanket that covered him.

It was as though the drop slid further up the wall, taking him away from the things he saw.

I'm saying goodbye to myself. Diamond to the bottom of the sea. Shall be gathered.

The thought neither saddened nor frightened him. Only the image of his mother sent grief through him. His drop slid further up the wall, until it met a crack in the paint and was absorbed in the concrete.

Transparency surrounded him, that of a heavy liquid solution on the verge of coagulation. Minute clinks of crystallization echoed from all over. He was moving at high speed, being pulled and sucked toward something, like a meteor to a star's gravity. This gravitational field was an endless sequence of tiny shock waves, as a sound of a jet taking off far away. When he finally saw something, it stole his breath.

The vein!

An immense storm front rose before him: foggy, distant, so elongated, from somewhere down below to somewhere up above. The rapid motion kept carrying him: not directly at the storm column, but as a satellite on a spiral crash course.

Like the lines around the symbol.

The speed seemed to edge him along an invisible smooth wall, tightening and condensing him. A growing, distorting pressure flattened him.

The pressure stopped and the velocity vanished. He remained motionless in the dark.

Where am I? In another dimension. Always the same place but a different dimension.

An abyss yawned underneath him. A conical chasm, like a giant funnel, like a dormant volcano the bottom of which he could not see, hidden in the darkness.

Above and around him, the darkness seemed clear for miles, like a desert night, without the stars, slowly being colored by the heavy blue of dawn.

Far in its wide expanse he noticed gray lines, wide and long, and so large—they seemed to him as galaxies in the universe. He felt—he knew—that they were radiating darkness.

Veins...

He passed between dimensions. And once again he looked out upon empty spaces of transparency. But they were different... he was astonished to understand there was movement in them: countless forms passed by him, above him, underneath him, like a clear school of scary, transparent fish. He neither saw nor felt them, but he knew they were there.

And then he remembered, and his fright condensed into a deep terror.

The things! The things from the borderline dimension. I'm in the borderline dimension.

The memory of the blows came to him, as did their force. He would be torn to pieces. But to his surprise, the forms floated past him and onward. Something, not far away from him, held their curiosity. His mind exerted itself in tracking their motions. They circled something, a sort of elongated, wide, unseen pipe. They advanced and kept trying to squeeze into the pipe, but were buffeted again and again by loud knocking noises heard every now and again, as if sliding along the clear pipe like protective rings. Curiosity got the best of Omer as well. He advanced in between knocks, touched the pipe and was sucked into it.

He was thrown into a powerful stream. It gushed around him, carrying him with a wild force. Then he spread his arms and floated, against the current, as though in a wind tunnel.

He screamed in joy, and laughed.

And listened. The current was a flow of sounds. Fragments of sounds. For a short while it sounded to him like the whistle of a strong draft wind. But careful listening unveiled more voices, dozens of voices, some of them almost familiar.

Singing... gathering for me...

Vague words in spherical ritual rhythms. Singing without beginning or end, voices united but separate, responding to the tapping of a walking cane on earth, of metal on stone.

She's directing them. Towards me. Focus on the singing. Get caught in it. Hold on to it like a rope.

He reached forward and felt the voices—tried to hold on to them as onto many silken ropes. But the powerful hum of the vein was everywhere, not allowing him to concentrate, to focus on the singing. It turned the singing into the froth of sound fragments, turned silken rope to dust lines, crumbling at his seeking touch. A wave of sorrow washed over him, a feeling he missed something, like a man left behind.

Pity.

Last gestures of a drowning man.

His thoughts abandoned him. Peace descended upon him. The sadness dimmed. His movements became slow.

Drowning in froth.

Until his fingers felt a clear continuous line and tightened around it with the indifference of a vine. A fine but clear line in the spray of sound, a flow of warmth. He felt it as a focused beam of light, coming from afar, and began sliding along it, allowing his outstretched hands to lead him.

Once he began moving he heard the tapping once again—distant and twisted, but seeking him, and once finding him becoming clear: the continuous tapping of a walking cane.

Between one tap and another he heard the singing. Words emerging from dozens of singing mouths, singing directed towards him. The unified song of separate voices, accompanying him and carrying him far, far away.

He looked into the room from above, in a sort of panoramic distortion, as though from within a drop. He saw a bed through a haze, the monitors, and next to them, a red-haired head. A long band-aid was stuck to the head, white against short red stubble. She stood there erect, slim, strong.

His eyes were covered with a slowly descending soap bubble. Passing by her face. He saw her pale lips from so close up, slightly parted, the edges of her teeth. Saw her hand extended to the bed.

She was the source of the heat line, of the flow of warmth that gave him strength and led him away: it was her touch. At the edge of the blanket, Noa's fingers clasped his immobile hand.

"You'll be okay," he thought he heard her say. "So are Joel and the professor. They're back. Like you."

His vision blurred. Everything around him was swallowed, along with himself, into an opaque darkness.

Then, he knew he could breathe again. He knew he could think again, hear, feel. And at that short, amazing moment, his fingers tightened around hers.

Chapter 41

Hadassa closed the book and sat for a minute. Two years had passed since the last case of the Body Cooling Phenomenon. It was all history now, the final chapter, a disease that killed and sickened so many. No one knew where BCP came from, nobody knew why it disappeared so suddenly and so thoroughly without a trace—no virus, no bacteria, no DNA sequence, no environmental hazard to look out for in the future.

A miracle, many called it, but Hadassa hadn't used that word.

"A blessing," she said here in the reading room, though that blessing had been too late for her Ari.

The investigation reached World Sales Corporation, yet produced more questions than answers. Key managers of the corporation were not interrogated—of them, one deceased prior to the investigation due to an unknown reason, and three others, CEO Lampston on top, disappeared without a trace. The intelligence services' assessment, given the resources invested in the manhunt, is that they are no longer living.

Intensive interrogation of other managers and employees revealed that the company was preparing for a media crisis—the cause, reasons unknown. Two tunnels—referred to as 'Sites' by employees—were discovered abandoned and empty of any equipment. Sites managers disappeared. It was claimed that some material was removed from the tunnels, taken in containers to the company's studios. The containers were not recovered, nor the material detected. This thread in the investigation remains open.

Hadassa felt the walls closing in, suffocating her like a coffin. She glanced at her wrist to see if it was night or day, but they'd taken her watch. She slid her chair away from the desk and away from the notebook.

Hadassa hobbled on unused legs to the buzzer, longing to see the sun and sky, *or is it moon or stars already? And trees and people and animals.*

The slow pace of the checkout procedure was maddening. Each item she came in with was identified and signed for.

But then Hadassa was out on the street, breathing great gasps of air, luxuriating in the chill of the evening.

The secret service's sedan awaited her. But Hadassa lingered—she wanted to enjoy the world, the real world, for just another moment.

A giant billboard shed its light on the street below. It illuminated buildings, cars and pedestrians with its blinding, colorful light. The Minister of health glanced at it for a moment, distracted. Finally, she entered the car and shut the door behind her.

Made in the USA
Middletown, DE
10 February 2016